Willow looked at Buffy and shook her head. "I can't say for sure. It feels like a really strong vampire has been here, but if it's Kakistos, I can't figure out how he got back. I can still feel his final moments ingrained in the spell."

"Well, we might as well have a look around while we're here." Buffy stepped away from her friends, conscious of the creaking in the floor beneath them. "If somebody's doing a Kakistos imperson- ation, could be they've been here." Buffy moved up the steel stairs leading to the second floor offices.

She opened the steel door between the offices and the main area below, her senses waiting for any sign that the rooms beyond the threshold might be occupied. That was when Kakistos charged.

She had enough time to see his scarred face, his left hand where the fingers had fused into a cloven hoof, and then she stepped back, pushing the door toward his face. Buffy managed to get the door halfway closed before she was knocked from the mezzanine platform down to the area where her friends were still standing. . . .

Buffy the Vampire Slayer™

Available from SIMON PULSE

Chaos Bleeds

James Moore

An original novel based on the hit television series
by Joss Whedon

SIMON PULSE

NEW YORK LONDON TORONTO SYDNEY SINGAPORE

Historian's Note: This story takes place in the
sixth season of Buffy

First Simon Pulse edition August 2003

™ and © 2003 Twentieth Century Fox Film Corporation.
All rights reserved.

SIMON PULSE
An imprint of Simon & Schuster
Children's Publishing Division
1230 Avenue of the Americas
New York, NY 10020

The text of this book was set in Times.
Printed in the United States of America
2 4 6 8 10 9 7 5 3 1
Library of Congress Control Number 2002115627
ISBN 0-7434-2767-X

Acknowledgments

No book is created in complete isolation and *Chaos Bleeds* is most decidedly not an exception. The author would like to thank: Christopher Golden and Tom Sniegoski. These two fine gentlemen actually came up with the story for the computer game, and I am merely fortunate enough to be entrusted with telling the novelization. Without their works, this novel would not exist. Thank you both. Thanks also to Ro Moore, my sister, Stuart Burton, Heather Dutton and Stephen Pagel, for the numerous "Buffy" discussions. We may not always agree, but the talk is fun. Lastly, thanks to Lisa Clancy and Lisa Gribbin, for their guidance, patience, and generosity.

As always, this one is for my wife, Bonnie, without whom . . .

Then

The voice of her husband was strong and deep as ever, but worried.

"Cassandra, it is time."

She rose from her kneeling position and winced slightly at the discomfort the motion caused. For the last fortnight she had spent most of her time in preparation for the task she'd been given. It was not a quest she looked forward to, but one that she knew was her destiny. The Powers That Be had called upon her to do a sacred task, and she would either serve them as they requested or die in the attempt, just as her father had died before her. Some duties needed doing, even if they required generations to accomplish them.

The Enemy was not one that had ever been defeated,

neither by Cassandra nor by the long line of her prede-
cessors, both those who were linked to her by blood and
those linked only by their common goal. Generations
had passed without success and she had spent a trifling
few days fasting and preparing physically and spiritually
for her attempt. The mild pain was nothing. It was her
spirit she had cleansed, and that was what mattered.

Cassandra picked up the object she held as nearly
sacred and set it apart from the whetstone she'd used to
finish it. Once the blade was wrapped in its silken protection she let herself relax just the smallest amount.
She stretched briefly, smiling at her husband's worried
face. He had every reason to be worried about her. She
was his wife, after all, and both of them knew that if
she failed in her task, she would not be coming back.

"I am ready." She reached out a hand and touched
his rough face, the deep lines as familiar to her as the
taste of well water. "Don't fret so, Lars. I will come
back to you."

"That is my only prayer, Cassandra. Come back to
me, whole and well."

"I have you to think of, and the children we shall
have together. I won't fail."

Her father had spoken the same words to her
mother before his turn came. She held tight to the hope
that the next few hours would not make her a liar.

They walked together in silence. They had said all
they needed to each other, and as far as Cassandra was
concerned, if she spoke to him further, she might lose
her calm demeanor and run from what lay ahead. Lars
had been chosen for her long ago, before she could

even walk, but he was the one man in the world she both trusted and admired as an equal. It was not arrogance that made her feel that way. She was a skilled warrior and as strong as most men. She had proven herself in combat and learned the ways of her family as well as any man before her. She'd had no choice; she'd been chosen for this task.

They stopped before the chamber where the ritual would be performed. Lars could not enter the room; it would only be Cassandra. Everything had been prepared, and anyone who walked with her would be taken when the Bleeding Gate was opened. One last kiss and she stepped forward to meet her fate, whatever it might be.

Save for the heavy clothes she would wear and the black well of the Bleeding Gate, there was nothing in the room. Cassandra set down the small bundle she'd been preparing for the last twenty days and dressed herself in the heavy furs and linens. Her right hand remained uncovered; her eyes could be seen. Otherwise there was little to let anyone know that beyond the thick layers was a person, let alone a young woman who was terrified. The final step for preparing herself was the rope, thick and skillfully woven and tested again and again to ensure its strength. Without the rope, her failure or success would not matter. Where she was going there was no way to return without a guideline. There would be no way to find a path back, for there was no path.

When she had donned the clothes the wisest of the elders said would protect her, Cassandra removed the blade from the soft silk cocoon. She had forged the weapon herself, following the rituals laid down by her forefathers, first smelting the ore and then pounding the metal and then all the steps that followed. Fully a year of her life had been dedicated to crafting the blade and the hilt that would hold it if all went well.

It was an admirable accomplishment. The blade was long and lean and sharp enough to shave the hair from a young lad's face without touching his skin. And it was pleasing to the eye as well, with the simple lines, the high sheen, and the single crystal that lay imbedded in the very center of the blade itself. The crystal alone was worth the lives of a hundred men, but the value meant nothing to Cassandra. The only concern it held for her was that it could capture what they most desperately needed to hold and bring back.

It held the possibility of finally defeating the enemy.

Her hands trembled. She told herself it was merely hunger that left her weak, not fear. With her blade held in her right hand Cassandra looked down into the pit below her and made her move. Cassandra Rayne stepped into the darkness.

The darkness was complete. There was no light here. There never had been. But that did not mean that nothing existed. Quite the contrary: Cassandra stepped into the Bleeding Gate and passed not merely through space but through time, to the very beginning, before the stars were born and before the Lord commanded their birth.

She could breathe, though the air felt very thin. She could feel the caress of a bitterly cold wind wherever she was not properly covered, and felt the fine blond hairs on her right hand freeze along with her eyelashes and the moisture from her eyes.

Cassandra waited, uncertain how long she had been there. Aside from the wind there was nothing, no way for her to measure the moments. She counted her heartbeats and waited. She looked around her for several lifetimes and saw nothing.

And then she felt it, the presence. Though her skin felt chilled beneath her cloaks and layers of furs, she felt the change when it happened with her very soul, not merely with her body. The presence slipped closer to her, and she knew it for what it was. This was, after all, the home of the Enemy.

The darkness within this vile thing was far, far worse than the darkness she currently endured, and she knew that the mere touch of the thing could break a man's mind. Had it not ruined her father? Had he not come back from the Bleeding Gate a ruined shell? His face when they pulled him from the room had been frozen in a scream of horror, the lips apart and the eyes wide and staring. He did not breathe, he did not eat, and he did not even know her when she touched his hand. He merely looked at what he had seen in the darkness, his gaze toward the wall of the main hall, but his sight in this place of endless night.

Cassandra smiled. Well, not *endless*.

Just as she had sensed the Enemy approaching, she sensed before she actually saw the blindingly pure presence of Salvation. The moment she had longed for, labored for, and been prepared for came.

And Cassandra was ready.

Chapter One

Xander Harris looked at the two massive stone statues dubiously. For their part, they simply stared into space, just slightly over his head, the broad carved demonic faces leering darkly. Just over his head suited him fine. The idea of them actually looking back at him was Grade-A wiggins material.

"So, who invited the big stone bat things to the party?" The smile on his face was a blend of sardonic good humor with a twist of exasperation. The Magic Box was not exactly a place for finding mundane statuary—thus the name—but even for his fiancée's establishment, the gargoyles were pushing the boundaries a bit. Also, they were huge.

Willow looked up from her schoolbooks and smiled

brightly. "Aren't they nifty? There's a new nightclub opening up in a few weeks and they special ordered those two for the entranceway."

Buffy Summers smiled and tossed her head slightly as she looked from Xander to Willow to the statues and back to Xander. As always, he was struck by how beautiful she was. If he weren't so crazy about Anya, he might have been thinking about reestablishing his high school crush on Buffy. She was one of his best friends and he was glad on many levels that he hadn't managed to ruin that with his adolescent romps through infatuation with her, but still, she was pretty enough that sometimes he almost wished things had worked out differently.

Of course, she was also strong enough to break every bone in his body if they were to ever get serious and then have a lover's quarrel—not that she would and not that they would—and that was a sobering thought at the best of times. Buffy was the Chosen One, the Vampire Slayer, and her petite frame had enough strength to take out the average pro football team inside of ten seconds or so.

He shook the thoughts away as Buffy spoke up. "Anya ordered them a week ago, after getting a down payment of course. She told me the mark up is enough to pay the rent here for a century or so. That little lady of yours is quite the business person."

He remembered something about Anya ordering statues, but he hadn't really thought much about it. His job on the construction site kept him busy, when he wasn't helping Buffy and the rest of the gang off a few monsters. And much as he loved Anya, sometimes she tended to talk about work a bit too much for him to absorb everything.

"Well, I'm sure they'll make perfectly wonderful accessories . . . for the Hellmouth Bar and Grill." He walked past the gargantuan things and moved the rest of the way into the Magic Box. "In the meantime, I brought donuts and coffee."

Buffy smiled and moved in his direction. "Ohhh . . . My hero!"

"Aww . . . You say that to all the guys who bring you jelly-filled donuts."

"True, but you do it better than anyone else."

Xander set down the donuts and the small carrier of coffee cups, barely dodging as Buffy all but lunged for the confections.

"Hey, where's the rest of the gang?" He looked around, not seeing Anya or Tara in any of the places he might have expected around the shop.

"Downstairs," Willow answered. "Anya's still sorting through the latest shipment and Tara's helping." She cracked a quick smile. "This way we get first pick at any really cool stuff."

Xander nodded as the local vampiric mascot of the Magic Box, William the Bloody, better known to his friends and enemies alike as Spike, came up into the main store from the basement. His sharp-featured face was set in a carefully neutral expression. Spike was a vicious murderer and supernaturally strong. That he was also a vampire didn't even begin to make his presence easier to accept. His only saving grace was that he was now a "neutered" vampire. Not all that long ago, a group called the Initiative had caught the bloodsucker and put a chip in his skull that made it almost impossible for Spike to actually attack a living person. All he had to do was take a violent action toward any human being and he would get a nice, crippling migraine. Xander Harris had been on the receiving end of a few Spike attacks in his day, and he had also dealt with the people he cared for being kidnapped and grievously inured by the blond-haired, punked-out creep. While he, personally, would have just as soon seen the vampire who'd killed two previous Slayers dusted, he had to admit there was a certain amount of pleasure to be had every time Spike forgot himself. Spike forgot himself a lot.

Spike carried a box under each arm, moving what had to be a couple of hundred pounds worth of marble and crystal arcana with ease. Spike ignored Xander completely. That was just dandy in Xander's eyes.

Just because he knew the vampire felt about the same toward him as he did toward the vampire, Xander spoke cheerfully when he addressed him. "Hey, Spike. I was just telling Willow and Buffy how much I like the new look around here. I'm for putting up Beware of Demon signs to keep the potential statue thieves to a minimum. What's your take on the subject?"

Xander watched Buffy smirk as she wiped a thin coating of powdered sugar from her lips with the back of her hand. He'd forgotten to grab napkins again.

"Well, I don't know how many actual demons are running around, aside from the usual vampires, but

Xander brings up a good point. There has been a lot of vampire activity just of late, and neither me nor Giles have found anything that leads to a conclusive reason as yet," Willow said, looking at the assortment of donuts and reaching for a Boston cream.

"Maybe they just decided it was time to get their groove on," Buffy said as she reached for her coffee. "Does there have to be a bigger threat behind it every time vamps get together to party?"

Spike shrugged his shoulders. "Not really, but at least the guessing keeps you on your toes."

The door leading into the shop from the street opened, and Xander turned.

He immediately wished he hadn't. Sometimes it was best not to know.

There was a small army of vampires coming through the door, filing in like kids being admitted to the Bronze on a Friday night. Of course, most kids didn't sport fright-faces and fangs, but why be nitpicky?

Xander started to call out a warning, but he needn't have bothered. Buffy was right there beside him, almost faster than he could have tracked. Several of the vamps hissed like snakes, a tendency that still gave Xander the wiggins whenever he heard it.

Buffy tossed a stake to him underhand and he caught it. It was good to be prepared. Xander liked to be ready anyway, just in case a little backup from the Slayerettes was necessary.

Buffy looked at the group spilling into the room and lifted one eyebrow. "A surprise party? For me? Gee, thanks!"

Several of the vampires moved forward, adding in a fine compliment of menacing noises and threatening gestures to go along with their poor sense of fashion. The first two charged, moving with all the finesse of a gazelle with broken legs and a serious concussion. Xander dodged under a wild swing from a kid he was pretty sure was actually even geekier than he had been as a freshman, and rammed the stake in his hand deep into the zit-faced vampire's chest. The thing bucked and screamed as it exploded in a fine layer of ash.

Buffy did a spinning roundhouse kick across the jaw of the one coming toward her, and then lifted him off the ground as she impaled him.

"Don't look at me!" Xander shook his head, mock-frowning. "I wanted Anya to jump out of a cake. Wait, that was for *my* birthday."

Xander might have continued the banter, but the next second a dozen or so of the fanged, pasty-faced crowd surged forward, pushing him and Buffy both backward, past the gargoyles on either side of the door and into the Magic Box proper.

Spike's arrogant features split into a feral grin, and a second later he was sporting his own face from a fright flick as he stepped up next to Xander. Without saying a word, he hauled off and decked the closest vampire—who, obligingly, went stumbling back and bowled over a few of her companions in the process.

Willow called out as she dodged Turner Wilson, a jock they'd both known in high school. He'd never been the brightest of jocks, to say nothing of people, and Xander wasn't sad to see him go when Willow cried

"Incendere!" and gestured at the second-string football player. One second Turner was a has-been vampire jock, the next he was a screaming ball of burning ash.

Willow blinked, looking pleased, confused, and worried all at once. "Um, guys, not to extinguish the levity, but there are an awful lot of these vampires!"

Spike broke a chair over the head of one of the invading force of undead, shaking his head. "Too right. Haven't seen this many other bloodsuckers since the blood orgy Dru and I had in Bolivia this one time—"

Buffy grunted, staggered by a savage right hook that caught her off guard. There were too many of them, and Xander took two glancing blows at the same time. Xander lowered his head and charged like a bull, knocking one of the vamps backward and almost knocking himself on his butt simultaneously. Buffy rammed the wooden stake into the one who'd just clocked her on the jaw and was moving to grab one of the two feral things attacking Xander even as she responded, "And much as we'd love to hear that story—"

Willow cut her off, her voice alarmed. "Buffy, where's Tara? She was helping Anya with the inventory. This place is getting vamp infested fast. You don't think—"

"I don't *want* to think. Damn it!" Concern for his own girlfriend made Xander turn away, and he used his own momentum to heave the closest vampire through the air. The female monster let out a screech as she landed on the stake Buffy placed in just the right spot to help break her fall. "Anya! Ahn!" he called, but there was no answer.

Buffy moved behind him, covering his retreat, her banter making light of the life-and-death struggle. Every one of her friends knew the score the same as she did. It wasn't a game, but now and then a few bad jokes seemed to smooth out the rougher edges of the fear as they fought. "Sorry, boys, I don't have time to be gentle." Xander didn't see what she did, but he heard the sounds of someone's bones being broken and knew from the loud scream of agony that it wasn't Buffy. "We have to finish them fast, guys! Xander, you take the training room. Spike, head down to the basement. Call if you need help. Willow and I'll keep them busy in here."

Willow blinked. "We will? Well, yeah, of course we will." Willow backed away as three of the vampires that had slipped past Buffy moved toward her. "Just, y'know, open to suggestions. You're the *Slayer*. But, hello, just *Willow* here." Willow beat a hasty retreat from the trio heading her way. Her eyes cast around for something to use as a weapon. While she was thinking about her options, Spike reached out to the one closest to her, wrapping an arm around the thick neck of a man who looked like he probably ate cars for breakfast and spit out motorcycles when he was done. The brutal figure let out a decidedly mousy squeak and fell backward as the smaller Spike broke his neck. The downed vampire snapped and snarled, not dead but incapacitated. The smile on the blond vampire's face was pure, sadistic pleasure. Willow's skin crawled as he started waling on one of the others who'd been pressing toward her, knocking the other vampire backward with a graceful but powerful spinning kick that broke the jaw of the new vampire he was fighting.

Willow was seriously thinking about how nice it would be if she and Tara could, say, move to a less insane town, when Buffy interjected. "Will, you're a witch. *And we're in a magic shop.* Find something useful."

Willow smiled, her face lighting up with excitement. "Ooooh. Good idea. Something with a lotta bang for my buck. Now that you mention it, Giles just got a first edition of *Kraus's Compendium of Magickal Combat.* If I can find it, maybe I can—"

Xander turned away as she started talking, his mind on Anya and Tara. They might need help, and he had to find them.

"Less talking! More doing! Everyone get going!" Buffy flipped the table near the front of the store forward and onto its side, then kicked it hard. The wooden barrier rammed four vampires backward into the continuing wave that was trying to get in. A walking slab of beef in a black leather jacket and pegged jeans bulldozed his way through the rest of them, heading for Buffy with a murderous glint in his eye.

Buffy stepped forward, ready to knock down King Kong's slightly shorter cousin. He was big, but she'd had to take on bigger. He was also aggressive. She barely had a chance to blink before he was throwing her through the air. He was strong, and definitely stronger than the average blood-sucking corpse. Buffy cleared twelve feet of air before she landed on the glass counter next to the cash register and shattered the top.

She shook her head, dazed by the unexpected

strength of her opponent, and shook it again as he walked right past her, saying, "Nothing personal, Slayer, but I've got business with someone else." The wide, feral face grinned at her. "I'll come back and kill you in a few minutes. Scout's honor."

Before she could come up with a properly snide retort, he was past her and moving through the store. She might have taken the time to, say, kill him a few times, if it hadn't been for the dozen or so vampires coming her way. None of them seemed quite so eager to dismiss the Slayer. They seemed more interested in playing.

While Buffy was learning how to fly, Xander moved toward the training room. Willow was already halfway up the loft and Spike was moving down the stairs into the basement.

The biker vampire of Sunnydale followed after Spike, his hands balling into ham hock-sized fists as he stomped across the Magic Box's floor. Xander had just enough time to notice that before he passed through the threshold into the exercise room.

He entered the area just as the back door flew open, bringing along a chunk of the wooden frame that held the lock. The two vampires that came through the door looked like they were trying to relive the disco era. Xander looked around for a weapon or twenty and spotted two. The battle axe was closer than the crossbow, so he grabbed it.

"Come on, guys, haven't you ever heard of knocking?" His voice didn't sound *completely* like he was going through puberty again.

The Saturday Night Fever Gang didn't think much of his sense of humor, and that was fair. He didn't think much of their sense of fashion. The first one didn't so much run at him as leap across the room. Xander was hardly a master of the axe—a situation he promised to remedy some day soon, assuming there was a some day soon in his future—but he took a swing anyway and managed to hack deep into the arm of the vampire. Tacky leisure suit and left forearm went one way, while the afflicted undead bloodsucker went the other, screaming bloody murder.

Before he could celebrate that particular scream-fest, the other vampire tried hard to knock his face clean off his skull with a savage backhand. He did a pretty good job too, which meant that Xander staggered back with his eyes closed and an explosive field of lights sparkling behind his closed lids.

He opened his eyes just in time to see the two leaning over him, teeth bared in a matched pair of nightmarish grins. "Oh," he said. "Monkey poop."

Willow scrambled up the ladder with a small pack of vampires on her tail. She managed not to scream, but it was an effort. She'd seen and fought more vampires than she ever wanted to think about, but still, after all this time, they made her want to hide under the covers until the daylight made her safe again.

A middle-aged man with roughly forty extra pounds around his stomach moved after her, hitting the stairs with hands and feet alike, like a dog bounding up the flight. Almost instinctively, she held out her hand

and cast a spell. "Hecate, grant me your blessings! Cast the unclean away from your servant!" Her reward was watching the fangy businessman blasted backward into the two Goth girls behind him. All three fell backward in a pile of arms, legs, and hair. The two Goths managed to keep their hair on their heads. The businessman lost half of his as his toupee fell off. It looked sort of like a hairy spider, the way it landed. Willow didn't much care for that notion. Her head was ringing already, feeling like someone had struck a very large bell between her ears. She figured she wouldn't be able to do too much more before she needed to rest, and there just wasn't any place where she could sit and recover, especially since Tara was somewhere down below her and possibly in real danger.

"Giles always puts the books with real power up here. Heeere book, book, book." Willow looked over the shelves, scanning quickly, looking for the new tomes that stood out a bit more. "And don't I hope it doesn't answer back?" Nothing. She knew every book on the shelves, had read at least a portion of all of them. She sighed. "I'd better search the rest of the shop."

The new book hadn't been filed in that area. She turned around to see the trio of vampires now rising from their mutual pileup. One of the two girls must have set her hand in the wrong place. The portly older vampire hissed at her and swiped at her head with his meaty hand. The slap was resounding, and the sound of her retaliation made the first strike sound like a firecracker when compared to a hand grenade. While Willow was trying to figure the best way around the trio, they opened a path for her by starting their own private war. She was quick to use the clearing before it fell apart again.

Willow had survived high school and its many trials in the tried and true methods of the socially unacceptable: She had learned not to be noticed. While she was a different woman than the girl she'd been, that particular talent still came in handy from time to time. She wove past Buffy and the growing wave of vampires, slipping through areas where most people would have certainly been caught. A stranger might have thought she was being a coward, but Willow was simply being smart. In hand-to-hand combat she knew she'd only last a minute, maybe even a few seconds. Vampires were stronger, faster, and had big sharp teeth.

What Willow had was her magick, and she intended to use it to the best advantage she could manage. She had to trust to Buffy to be okay until she could come back and help her in a big way. That didn't mean she had to like it very much. Or even at all.

Though it seemed to take forever, Willow managed to get behind the counter. A pair of legs as thick as tree trunks blocked her way, and she looked up in time to avoid a size fourteen boot that was aimed at her skull.

She backed up quickly, looking for something, anything she could use as a weapon. "Listen, I'm really, really busy right now. Could you maybe come back later and try to kill me?"

The vampire attached to the legs as thick as her waist looked down at her, his face mostly hidden by a cowboy hat. "Not really what I had in mind." He shrugged. "I'm gonna have to be rude and say no."

Willow nodded and tried to think of something witty to say. Nothing came to mind, so she grabbed a box from under the counter and threw it at the vampire. He caught it easily and actually took the time to look at the picture on the cover. She'd thrown so fast that she hadn't paid any real attention, but if it kept him distracted, she was all for it.

Willow turned tail and ran, moving as fast as she could for the stacks where she hoped she'd find the book. If only she could remember the spell she'd looked at earlier. She heard Buffy call out to her, and looked to her left just in time to see a vampire explode into a cloud of dust. Willow nodded a thanks and then slid hard to the right, ducking under another of the vampires. This one wasn't attacking, but instead was reacting to Buffy's foot trying to punt him out of the building. She worried almost constantly about her best friend and whether or not she would survive her calling as the Slayer. Now and then she was reminded that Buffy was beyond merely good at her job; she was phenomenal. Still, all it would take would be one slip up, and her being here, where Buffy was distracted enough to watch her back was almost enough of a distraction to get Buffy killed.

Buffy Summers must have had the same notion. She took the offensive and moved toward the front door of the shop, battering vampires along the way. "This is my life. Don't try this at home." The words were maybe not meant to be heard, but hearing Buffy say them seemed to ease a little of the dread Willow was feeling. Buffy had that knack. Before Willow could fully grasp what was going on, the Slayer had pushed and shoved and staked her way through the exit. Outside she had more room to maneuver and could really cut loose on her enemies without fretting overly much about the property damage and the risks to Willow.

The vampires saw Buffy on the move and turned almost as one unit to follow her.

Willow managed to get to the stacks without any further encounters, and she located the book a few seconds later. It was locked in a glass case. And where was the key? Why, that was over where it belonged, safely behind the counter where the cowboy was still standing, looking around as if he could wait all night for her to come back. The other vampires might have left, but he was still there and looking at her, his feral grin spreading wider still on his lantern-jawed face.

"Your move, little darlin'."

Spike slid down the stairs with the natural grace of a predator. Somewhere down below there was every reason to believe that Tara and Anya were struggling against a few of his own kind. There was a time, and it hadn't been that long ago, when he would have been among the ones trying to drain them of blood.

Then some blood bags in military garb had put a chip in his head and ruined all of his fun. He was nothing if not a survivor. He learned to make do with what he could get. Right now, what he could get was a little brutal satisfaction beating all the crap out of a few other vampires.

He heard the two girls down below, their heartbeats and their rapid breathing. Either they were struggling against something without a heartbeat—like, for instance, a few other vampires—or Tara was teaching Anya a thing or two about the fairer sex. That put a grin on his face. He could just see Harris's stupid expression if he heard about *that* sort of business. The notion sent a pleasant chill through his cold flesh. Most thoughts of making Xander Harris miserable did that to him.

Anya let out a scream of protest and something broke. Sadly, it seemed he'd only have a few monsters to kill. No dice on ruining Harris's life.

He made it to the concrete floor just as a pale vampiric girl in a Sunnydale High cheerleader's outfit—who reminded him far too much of Harmony for his own tastes—finished hog-tying Tara's wrists together. Tara had a look on her face that was pure unadulterated panic. Under different circumstances, Spike would have been perfectly glad to savor that expression. He held to the belief that a good fright made the blood taste sweeter. These days, he considered Tara, if not a friend, then at least not as a viable food source. He wondered if he was going soft.

Anya was on the ground trying to fight off two other vampires. She might have given up if they were female, but both of them were male and enjoying her discomfort. Spike knew that wasn't very wise. The girl had spent centuries as a vengeance demon in the service of D'Hoffryn. Her specialty had been making men suffer for what they did to women. Even if she no longer had the power to alter reality, she still had a dangerous imagination when it came to making men feel pain. The evidence of that fact was the other two vampires on the ground. One of them was just a pile of rapidly disappearing ashes. The other was trying to deal with what she had done to his anatomy with a wooden stake. It wasn't fatal, but the odds were he was wishing it was.

Spike let his vampiric nature take full hold, his face reshaping itself along the way to show the demon that hid inside his flesh. He didn't bother with introductions, he just moved in for the kill. There were some fates he wouldn't wish on any man. Out of respect for the suffering involved, he took out the screaming Mimi on the ground with an improvised broom handle stake. Anya looked disappointed. *Maybe I'm getting soft in my old age. That, or hanging around with so many sodding humans is messing with my sense of priorities.*

The remaining vampires turned to look at Spike with animalistic anger on their faces. They were having a party and he'd gone and ruined it. *Well, if they want to make me pay for that, they'll have to get started.* Without missing a stride, he swung the broom in a wide arc and broke it over the face of the closest bloke. The broom made a nice crunchy sound as it snapped in half. The vampire's face was even more satisfying. Spike liked it so much that he followed through with a head butt that sent his opponent stumbling backward.

The other lad who was still standing—and who

looked like he should have been dating the cheerleader if his letterman's jacket was any indication—let loose with a roar and charged at Spike. He was fast too. And stronger than your average buck. The tackle sent both of them through the air and into the wall. Spike hit hard enough that if he'd had a breath in his body, it would have been forcibly knocked loose. The broom handle stayed back where Spike had been a second before and fell to the ground with a loud clatter.

Spike clubbed the kid in the head and may as well have been knitting a sweater for all the good it did him. The jock bulldozed into him again, crushing him against the wall and hit him in the stomach with a fist that was at least two sizes too big. The kid was strong, no doubt about it, but he lacked finesse. Spike had finesse to spare and decided to give some to his opponent. He brought both of his hands forward, swinging them up between the bruiser's broad shoulders, and caught the boy in his jaw. As his opponent's head snapped back, Spike pushed himself up from his crouch against the wall and kneed the youngster in the groin. As the jock tried to recover, Spike pushed him back enough to allow for a little leg room and delivered a roundhouse kick that would have made Bruce Lee jealous. The boy hit the ground with his head facing the wrong way. *One broken neck, easy as you please.* It wasn't fatal, but it certainly took him out of the action for a moment.

That was when the cheerleader came for him, screaming bloody murder and holding the broken broom handle like a sword. Spike smiled and waited, and as she brought the makeshift stake down in an over-head swing, he rammed the wooden stake he'd been carrying in his pocket right through the heart-shaped pendant she wore. The metallic heart and the fleshy one both got torn apart. He stepped through the ashes of her falling body and caught the broom handle as he went. Was he cocky? Certainly, but he'd earned that right a long time ago. It wasn't every vampire that had bagged a Slayer, and he'd scored two so far in his life. He nailed the crippled football player to the ground and watched him crumble into little more than ash.

Anya started standing up, her chin swelling slightly from where one of her would-be abductors had scored a hit. Spike started toward Tara. He reached down for the bindings on her wrists and stopped only when he heard Anya call out a warning.

Spike felt something grab the back of his head and squeeze hard enough to make him yelp.

"You disgusting freak!" The voice was deep and really, really angry. Even without seeing the face that went with that rumbling tone, he could imagine a look of anger that was passionate and sincere. Of course, the pain from having his head in a vise grip was making the image a little easier to picture. He dropped to his knees and leaned forward, managing to get away from the hand that was trying to make an omelet of his brains.

"Right, what's crawled up your backdoor then, mate? Just looking for a good reason to get yourself dusted?" The words were pure bravado, his head was still reeling, but Spike had definitely been through far worse, and recently at that.

"You're a traitor!" The vampire was big, dressed like a longtime fan of Elvis in leather, and looked ready to chew through a few feet of concrete if it meant he could tear into Spike. All in all, not the most comforting notion. "You sold us out to hang with the Slayer!"

Spike spat on the greaser's shoe and sneered. "Can't sell out who I don't know, now can I? What's your name? I'll write it in your ashes."

The giant stomped in closer and Spike stepped back warily. The rebel without a clue was trying to psych him out, and he wasn't going to play that game. Every step and gesture the larger vampire made was deliberately telegraphed to make Spike think his opponent was slow and ponderous. Spike knew better. The stranger had snuck up on him and that wasn't an easy task. Just because he looked like he should be clumsy didn't make it the truth.

The brute feigned an attack and Spike blocked the blow. He thought he'd had the giant's number, but he was wrong. While he was deflecting the fist almost as big as his head, the other vampire shot a knee up into his stomach. Spike was lifted off the ground, the pain from the impact traveling all the way from his stomach to his shoulders, and that was when the other fist hit him.

Spike crashed into the basement floor, dazed, and looked up as he tried to gather his thoughts. The black, steel-toed boot that hit his face seemed more like a Mack truck. He slid across the ground, all the way to where Tara was still bound, and tried to remember his name as a hundred stars went supernova behind his closed eyes.

"William the Bloody! Terror of Europe and half of Asia! I looked up to you, man! I heard stories about how you were going to kill a third Slayer, and all I could do was hope to be half as tough as you!" He kicked again, catching Spike in the ribs, and Spike used that to his advantage. He took the blow and rolled with it, letting the momentum of the attack roll him across the floor in a manner that looked purely accidental. It hurt, but that was okay. The pain was worth it if it got him to his goal. His fingers touched the broken broom handle and rested on it, still loose and unmoving.

"I spent years dreaming of meeting you, a legend among vampires! I wanted to work with you, man. I wanted to learn from the best! Instead, all I get is the chance to rip your head off and spit on your dust pile!"

The man brought his foot up and aimed at Spike's head. That foot would surely come down like a pile driver if it connected, but Spike had listened to enough and was ready. When that thick, powerful leg was at the highest point before coming down, Spike kicked out and slammed the heel of his boot into the other leg, shattering the kneecap of his would-be killer. The brute was as big as a tree, and he dropped like one too. Spike swung his body around and held the broken broom handle up as the giant fell. A second later he was covered in the fine dust that was all that remained.

Anya stared at him, slack jawed for a moment. Tara's eyes were wide. Spike looked at the ashes that fell to the ground as he stood up and dusted himself off. "I hate fan boys. Right then, ladies, let's get you upstairs." He'd won. He should have felt great about it.

Somehow, it just wasn't the same when he knew he couldn't live up to the expectations of his peers.

Xander rolled out of the way just in time to avoid being made into construction worker sushi by the two disco-challenged vampires. He scrambled hard, hindered by the axe in his hand, to reach for the crossbow and maybe just a little breathing room. Axes weren't exactly on his list of weapons he'd learned to do anything with, but he'd had a little time to play around with the crossbow from time to time. Still, in a pinch the axe would have to do. The one-armed vampire reached for Xander again, and this time he managed to catch hold of one calf. Xander kicked with his free leg, hitting the man in the elbow and getting a few choice profanities for his trouble. What he didn't get was free from the claw that was pulling him back across the floor.

He kept kicking, and when that didn't work, he took another swipe with the axe. The blow should have hit, probably would have too, if the other vampire hadn't interfered. The thin arm of a man who'd probably been a little bit on the anorexic side when he was alive caught the axe just below the blade and came close to tearing the muscles in Xander's arms as it stopped his swing.

The axe was pulled from his hands and the skinny geek in the leisure suit flipped it effortlessly, offering the weapon to his one-armed friend. The vampire gave up his grip on Xander's leg and took the offered weapon. "I might let you live, boy. But believe me, I'm going to take a few limbs even if I do. . . ."

Xander pushed himself back away from the two vampires, his hands and feet moving in an almost constant blur. He wasn't thinking about what he should be doing; he was thinking about how hard it would be to work if he had, say, two legs and an arm missing.

"Okay, I can see we're not agreeing on this the way I wanted to. Maybe we should try a different tactic."

The vampire who still had two arms, jumped over his friend, clearing the crouching axe man with ease, and landed with one leg on either side of Xander's body. "What did you have in mind? Me? I'm thinking we could settle it over a nice bite to eat."

Xander reached out with his hands, pushing past a few of Buffy's workout supplies as he propelled himself across the concrete floor on his butt. There were several pads to protect whoever got stuck as her sparring partner, over to the side was a wooden thing that he knew must be used for something but he couldn't have guessed what, and halfway under that thingamajig, a cross. He thanked God for Buffy being a little sloppy from time to time and grabbed the crucifix in his hand.

"You know what? I'm thinking I don't like your ideas any more than I like your clothes." Xander lifted the cross and promptly shoved it against the standing vampire's chest. The polyester suit and the shirt and flesh beneath it started smoking instantly, and a second later the vampire was backing away, hissing and trying to hide from the crucifix. "See? Now I think we can come to an understanding."

The one with the axe didn't agree. He threw the weapon through the air and straight at Xander's chest.

Xander didn't have time to think and that was probably what saved him. He put his hand up in front of his chest and blocked the blow. The wooden cross caught the edge of the blade and sent the axe on a different trajectory. Working on purely automatic, he grabbed the axe before it could go far and swung it like a baseball bat.

Xander Harris cleaved the head off the vampire that had thrown the axe. Ol' One-Arm staggered back and crumbled into a pile of ash before he could actually hit the ground. It would have been a flawless maneuver, but he didn't compensate for the strength of the swing and wound up sprawled across the floor again, the axe a few feet from his hand as he dropped it to catch himself.

The good news was that he was finally in range of the crossbow he'd been trying to reach. The bad news was that the other disco vampire was right beside him. "You killed Barry!" he hissed, eyes narrowed with hatred, teeth bared in an angry snarl.

"It was a mercy killing! Disco's dead!"

"Not half as dead as you're about to be!" The two of them struggled, Xander using one hand to push the vampire's face away from his neck and the other to reach for the crossbow. It was rough; Xander was forced to revert to slapping madly because he couldn't get any real leverage for a proper punch at the monster's face, but at least the slaps kept the vampire distracted.

Said undead Saturday Night Fever reject was working hard on the Bite-Xander-in-the-Throat game and doing a fine job of barely missing. Xander wanted desperately to keep it that way. When Mister Fangs got a little too eager for the slapfest to stop him any longer, Xander hauled back with his steel-toed boot-clad foot and kicked as hard as he could into the polyester vamp. The vampire managed to hold on for the first impact, and the second as well, but try number three finally knocked him away, rolling and snarling.

The vampire came off the ground like a rabid jack-in-the-box, roaring his frustration and ready to kill. Xander found the crossbow first. He managed to put a bolt through the heart of his enemy. He watched with satisfaction as the vampire stumbled back and collapsed into a foul-smelling cloud of fine powder. There were times when he worried about whether or not he could hold his own, even after several years of hanging with the Slayer. Now was not one of those situations. After a few seconds to catch his breath, Xander gathered the axe and crossbow and a smaller axe and several stakes in one of Buffy's little black bags. He even grabbed up an extra cross. He was relieved to be alive, but Anya was still missing. His stomach did roller coaster drops when he thought about her being hurt.

"And look at that. Vampires, zilch. Xander Harris . . . still alive." He looked around the room and loaded the crossbow. There might be more coming along any second, and besides, it was best to act like a Boy Scout and be prepared.

"But no Anya and no Tara in here. Which means the basement. Which means it's up to Spike." With loaded crossbow in his right hand and a good hefty axe in his left, Xander looked like he was ready for some serious action. It wasn't a look he really meant to convey. He'd rather look like a guy who was relaxing with his honey and watching a few cheesy kung fu movies. "Spike. Wonderful."

That was when the next wave poured into the work-out room, pushing through the ruined back door. This time there were a lot more. He took aim and fired without even really thinking about it. Over the years he'd learned what a crossbow was for. The axe might still elude him, but ranged weapons were a different story.

Xander Harris put the first bolt directly through the chest of the vampire closest to him and retreated back into the main store. There was nothing for him to do here. Right now he needed to get to Buffy and he needed to find Anya and Tara. As the vampires approached, he slammed the door shut and ran. They'd be coming through in a minute or two, but right now Buffy was without any serious weapons.

The undead cowboy moved fast, leaping over the ruined glass counter with all the ease of a kid jumping rope, and started toward Willow. He stopped moving forward when she began walking in his direction.

She had something to do, and there was only one obstacle between Willow and her task. Willow Rosenberg was not an intimidating figure under most circumstances. Back in high school she'd often considered herself to be "most likely to be walked on like a cheap carpet" on her more morose days. If it hadn't been for Xander and Buffy and, later, Oz, she would likely have kept that attitude. Now and then, when she least expected it, those feelings came creeping back to claw at her, true enough, but there were also times when she remembered that she was pretty good at casting a spell when she had to. This was one of those times.

While the redneck vampire was looking at her a little dubiously, wondering what had just changed about her, Willow was busy thinking about her friends and about Tara, who was somewhere in the Magic Box and likely in mortal danger. She reached out with her magick and wrapped her power around a part of the frame that usually held the glass in place on the counter.

By the time the vampire had decided she was bluffing, that, in fact, her sudden change in attitude was all a ruse, the makeshift javelin was ripping through the back of his clothing and piercing his heart.

Just as quickly as she'd let the building power inside of her loose for a second, she pulled it back inside. Willow seemed more herself when she grabbed the key for the locked case and then started back toward the loft.

Two minutes later she'd found the spell she was looking for, and five minutes after that she was gathering the ingredients she needed to cast it. It's just possible that part of her was scared about how easily the spells worked for her on most days. If so, she hid it well. Even from herself.

"Okay guys, this is just getting stupid!" Buffy lashed out with a brutal spinning kick that sent a short, muscular, and very tattooed vampire flying through the air. The illustrated goon stopped himself from going too far by using three of his peers as a cushion. All four of them landed in a mass of cursing, spitting undead flesh. Normally that would have been enough to let Buffy catch a breather, but there were just too many of them coming her way. There might have been a few times when she'd faced more vampires at once, but she couldn't actually think of any right then. "Why don't you just line up nicely, take a number, and I'll kill you just as fast as I can. Promise."

They weren't going for it. In fact they seemed to think it was a pretty good idea to send a dozen vampires at her all at the same time. The Slayer did her best to kill them fast anyway. The first one died in mid-leap. The second one hit her like a freight train and sent Buffy down to the ground under a wave of fangs and clawing hands. Buffy squinted her eyes almost closed and started stabbing, the stake in her right hand punching through clothing and bone to decimate hearts at a terrifying speed. Teeth gnashed the air a half inch from her face, and she thrust the heel of her left hand into a brunette vampire's jaw. The monster pulled back with a sharp cry of pain, her tongue impaled on her own fangs. Before she could do much more than pull her tongue back, Buffy staked her.

But they just kept coming. For every vampire she took down, it seemed like three more were waiting to get her. Sooner or later she'd make a mistake, and if that happened, she wouldn't be slaying vampires any more, she would be so much snack food.

Thoughts like that got her motivated in a big way. Buffy rolled backward, kicking out with her feet as she did a backward handspring. Two more of her least-favorite vermin got a taste of her shoe leather and she got a chance to stand up again.

From a good distance away, she heard the leader of this little party calling out orders in a harsh voice. He was dressed in camouflage fatigues and sporting a buzz cut. Somebody had gotten their teeth into a military man, and he was good at telling his subordinates what to do.

He looked her way and grinned. She saw it in his eyes. He wanted her for himself, but he also wanted her worn down a bit before he got to her. One of the vampires closest to her got off a lucky kick, and Buffy felt her arm go numb from the wrist to the elbow. In addition to losing the feeling in her arm, she lost the stake she'd been holding.

Buffy watched the wooden weapon spin through the air, her eyes tracking it with dismay as it sailed almost lazily across the street and clattered on the asphalt. The vampires around her watched too, practically stunned by the thought that she'd been disarmed. The vamp that had kicked her arm looked at the stake then back to Buffy with an almost apologetic look on its demonic face.

For one second there was complete silence. Then the creep in the fatigues called out, "Get her!" at the top of his lungs and ruined everything.

The air was filled with the roar of the vampires as they surged forward, a wave of bloodlust. Buffy was "feeling the burn," as her aerobics instructor used to say back in L.A., but that wasn't enough to make her give up the fight. Not when she had a little sister to watch over, and not when all of the people who mattered most in her life were just beyond the door she was standing near.

The first vampire that came toward her fell to the ground with a broken neck. Buffy leaped over the next three, who were trying to break the laws of physics and occupy the same space as her, and came down with one foot planted hard in the stomach of yet another vampire. She couldn't get an exact count, but there were roughly enough vampires to fill the Bronze on a Saturday night. One of them grabbed her ponytail and yanked hard enough to stagger the Slayer. "*Not* the hair!" She pushed back hard and slammed her elbow into the flesh behind her. Something in Mister Grabby's ribcage broke with a satisfying crunch. But she didn't even have time to really enjoy the sound before a hot pain raked across her stomach. One of the undead in front of her had scored a swipe, and four long lines of blood ran across her midriff.

Buffy let out a yelp of pain and tried to step back to get more room, because there were just too many of them. Her heel caught on the one she'd already incapacitated, and even as she tried to regain her balance, the group of vampires moved in again.

And just as quickly they moved back, covering their faces and screaming in pain as a grapefruit-sized ball of brilliance caressed their flesh and left bubbling sores wherever it touched.

Somehow the sun had risen in the early hours of the evening, only it had gotten very, very small. Buffy decided to question it later, like after she'd finished dusting the whole gang of bloodsuckers. Buffy kicked hard into the knee of one of the vamps backing away from her and followed through with a second kick that dropped him like a tree. Before he could rise, the small sun swooped down and ran the length of his body. The vampire screamed as his flesh burned away. In less than two seconds there was nothing left but smoke and ash as evidence that he'd ever existed.

From the direction of the shop, Buffy heard Willow's voice chanting softly and spared half a second to look. Willow stood in the doorway with her eyes squinted and her face strained; where her eyes moved, the burning sphere of light followed, and it moved through the crowd of vampires, burning them as it touched, incinerating creatures that would never die of old age, but only from violence.

The vampires broke apart, no longer a solid mass, but rather islands of death and destruction. They learned quickly and did their best to avoid the miniature sun, shielding their bodies with their clothing and even trying to hide behind each other. That was just fine in Buffy's eyes. The more they were confused and frightened, the easier they would be to drop.

"Buffy!" She turned as her name was called and saw Xander holding an axe in his hand. He stood just outside the open door to the Magic Box and offered her hefty blade. She nodded, he threw, and a second after that she had a weapon again. Buffy started swinging, and the vampires that were already halfway to panic went the rest of the way there.

They left like they'd arrived: en masse, and moving

fast. Buffy moved back into the Magic Box, her eyes wide and alert, her body speaking volumes about how willing she was to hack her way through ten times as many vampires as she already had in order to keep her friends safe. Xander and Willow backed in with her, their feet shuffling and pushing back debris.

She crossed the threshold and sighed with relief. Willow and Xander were both there and still alive. Xander was looking a little slapped around, but she'd seen him looking worse after an argument with Anya.

She looked to Willow. "Thanks for the save, Willow. You okay?"

Willow smiled and nodded her head once, for emphasis. "Yep. I managed. Well, me and Mr. Kraus and this really bad habit vampires have of never wearing sunscreen."

Buffy frowned as she dabbed at her stomach. "This many vamps in one place . . . they're following somebody's orders. Just wish I knew whose. Did any of them say anything to you?"

"You mean besides Grr . . . arrghh? Not a whole lot."

Xander nodded too, licking his lip where the vampires had split it for him. "Saw the new trick, Will. You definitely need to bottle that one and sell it." He winced around the small grin on his face. "And look! Goodies! Goodies with which Buffy can make the vampires into lots of pieces."

Buffy looked around, her nerves still jumpy. It was almost too easy and she never trusted too easy. "No sign of Anya and Tara?"

Xander got completely serious again. Buffy was

sometimes amazed by how quickly his facial expressions could change. "Nope. I'm headed for the basement to back Spike up. Or to dust him. Haven't decided yet. Depends on if he's rescued them."

Buffy nodded and took the crossbow from him as well. "Thanks for the save."

"Hey. It's nothing. I prefer delivering donuts, but, you know, whatever is needed." He called the words over his shoulder as he moved toward the basement, cross in one hand and small axe in the other.

Before Buffy could come up with a proper response, the vampires came back. They came spilling from the exercise room and from the front door at the same time. Better armed than before, Buffy started swinging, and Willow moved behind the counter again, her whispered chant starting as her pet solar flare moved into action.

The vampire she'd seen in fatigues before came right at her and dodged the first swing from the axe in her hand with ease. "Not this time, Slayer. I'm ready for you!"

Buffy let her own momentum swing her in a full circle and whacked the vampire across the side of his head with the flat of the axe. She'd meant to actually chop instead of only slap, but the grip slid a bit in her hand. Captain Fang let out a grunt and staggered back. The name on his fatigue blouse read MACKIE, and she took note of it. "Well, Mackie, a lot of guys have said that to me over the years, and still I leave a trail of broken hearts. . . ."

Mackie snorted in anger and shook the blow off

like a boxer who'd just been popped by the champ. He hit like a boxer too, as Buffy learned a few seconds later when his meaty right hook connected with the side of her face. *No.* She had to correct that thought as she crashed into one of the stone gargoyles that now adorned the Magic Box. *He hits like a wrecking ball.*

Willow moved her vampire burning sunlamp through the air, and Mackie was driven back for a second, but he recovered almost as quickly as Buffy and the fight began again, even as another vampire combusted when the spell Willow used touched its undead flesh.

Buffy used the gargoyle closest to her to push off with her hands and planted both of her feet in Mackie's broad chest. She stayed in the air for a moment and then dropped. As she hit the ground her hand caught the handle of her axe where it now lay at the statue's base and she came back up swinging. Mackie wasn't where he had been. He'd grabbed another of his cohorts who was trying to avoid the burning spell and held the screaming demon up as a shield. Buffy cleaved his new toy in half, leaving Mackie holding nothing but ashes.

Mackie roared, a full-throttled bellow that half-deafened the Slayer, and came at her with all the finesse of a runaway buzz saw. Buffy dodged just in time to realize she'd been set up. While she nimbly danced away from his hands, Mackie's boot swept her off her feet. The Slayer was strong, but not exactly very heavy. She spun and angled her body to take the impact as best she could, but before she could do much about being in the air, he followed through with a savage double fist into her side.

The part that bothered her was that she almost enjoyed it. Buffy fought vampires so often that she sometimes seemed to slay them on autopilot. Mackie was making her work for her victory. She could have done without the ribcage that was threatening to break, but it was unsettlingly pleasant to have a decent sparring partner. No matter how short his unlife span might be. Mackie was trying for another brutal double-fisted hammer strike—this one to her face—when she blocked the attack with the axe blade. This time the blade was dead on, and Mackie let loose with another shriek as his left hand was hacked in half. He gnashed his teeth a hair's breadth from her face, and as she instinctively pulled back, brought his elbow around to slam into her chest.

It's fun to get a challenge now and then, but this is getting ridiculous. Buffy rolled back away from the skilled fighter and kicked him in the face as she moved. He barely even seemed to notice. His head twitched a bit, but other than that he maintained his course, determined to kill her at any cost. That was only fair, as she was pretty much planning the same thing for him.

"I was just gonna kill you, girl, but now I'm gonna make it hurt!" His fist broke the wall next to her. Buffy blinked the plaster dust from her eyes as she hopped back again.

"Blah, blah, blah! Get a new line, Mackie!" She feinted with the axe, and as he slipped under it, the heel of her other hand shattered his nose. Mackie staggered back, disoriented, and suddenly looking a little less like he had a chance of winning.

In true bad guy style, Mackie used his own cronies to promote his escape. He physically threw a teenaged girl at Buffy. The girl screamed like a banshee, but she started clawing in the Slayer's general direction as she went. Buffy crouched low and came up with a stake just for her new friend. She was on the move before the dust settled, but Mackie had already shoved another vampire in her direction by that time. When she'd carved through the newest distraction, the vampire soldier was at the exit to the store.

Mackie shook his whole fist at her, snarling. "That's it! I'm outta here. But this ain't over by a long shot, girly-girl."

Buffy scowled. "Girly-girl? Who you calling girly?" She shoved another would-be shield out of the way and stormed after him, back into the night. "Come back here, Mr. Macho. I'm gonna drive a Malibu Barbie right through your heart."

Mackie turned and swung at her, his fangs bared and his eyes narrowed to angry slits under his military crewcut. "You want me? Come and get me. Enjoy your little victory, Slayer. While you can. Soon Kakistos will destroy you and yours, once and for all. Kakistos will have you, and he'll make you wish I'd been the one to take you out!"

"What're you smoking, Spanky? Kakistos is dead. And so, by the way, are you!"

Buffy shut him up by removing his head. She frowned, barely breathing hard and scarcely even noticing the pain in her ribcage. "Kakistos? Did I hear him right? Kakistos is dead. Faith killed him." She spoke to the air around her, which chose not to answer her.

Kakistos had been brutal, a vampire almost as old as the Master, his body physically marred by centuries of hosting the demonic presence that had changed him from a living human being into a vampire. He had been vile enough that whatever he actually did to Faith's watcher back in Boston had left the other Slayer scarred and jaded enough to kill without remorse, or at least helped her down that path. Faith had not been as lucky as Buffy in many ways, but Kakistos had been pivotal in the girl going rogue. In the end Faith had killed Kakistos, but the damage had been done.

Faith and Buffy had gone toe-to-toe in a vicious fight that left Faith in a coma for several months. When she'd come to, Faith had initially planned on killing Buffy, and for a while it looked like she might succeed. The situation only got worse when the rogue Slayer had actually switched bodies with Buffy for a time. In the long run, after fleeing to Los Angeles, Faith had finally recovered enough of herself to turn herself in for the murder she'd committed. These days she was sitting behind bars, doing penance for her crimes. That suited Buffy just fine. There was far too much bad blood between the two Slayers. Intellectually she understood that Faith had been dealt a bad hand. Emotionally she felt more hatred for Faith than she did for most of the demons she'd encountered. The demons had an excuse: They were monsters, after all.

Behind her the vampires in the Magic Box screamed and burned, victims of Willow's magick. In a few minutes it was all over. Those remaining vampires with a well-developed sense of self-preservation took off again, and this time without any plans for returning.

"What was that about?" Willow's voice came unexpectedly, but it was welcome. "It's like those stories you read about Japanese soldiers lost on some island for decades, not realizing World War II ever ended." She flipped her hair bangs back from her forehead absentmindedly. "I mean, Kakistos *is* dead, isn't he?"

Buffy nodded emphatically. "Really most sincerely dead. Saw Faith kill 'im myself."

Spike, Xander, Anya, and Tara moved out of the basement. Anya looked bruised, and Tara looked more nervous than usual—it was really just a look she had. Tara was really amazingly brave, all things considered, but she tended to look a little terrified most of the time.

Spike looked around the room and shook his head. "Well, it's all nice and cozy quiet up here, innit? Glad I don't have to clean up this mess." He kicked lightly at the broken glass, ruined pottery, and thick layer of ash that was all that remained of a sizable army of vampires. "'Night all. Next time you're having a party like this one, leave me off the invite list, yeah?"

He didn't wait for any replies, but merely walked into the darkness beyond the Magic Box. Buffy barely noticed. She was busy focusing on other things. It was amazing how much power a single name could have . . . Kakistos. She shivered slightly in the warm air.

Willow darted across the room, moving to Tara. "Oh, baby, are you all right?"

Tara joined Willow in a hug, kissing her face softly. "I am now. All the things the vampires said they were going to do to you . . . but you're okay. So I'm just fine, honey. Right as rain."

Xander hugged Anya against his side with one arm, and she leaned her head against his shoulder, closing her eyes for a moment and savoring the contact. "A few cuts and bruises, but it looks like we're *all* okay." Xander frowned a bit as he continued. "Now we just have to figure out where they all *came* from. We don't usually get a wave of vampire immigration that size without Buffy getting wind of it first."

Willow turned her attention from Tara to the others. She took the time to look at every person in the room. "The last one Buffy killed mentioned Kakistos."

"Kakistos?" The voice belonged to Rupert Giles, who entered the Magic Box with a hangdog expression on his handsome face. Most times he did a remarkable job of hiding his feelings. Just at the moment he was failing. The devastation was substantial, and Buffy bit her lower lip as she watched the older man nudge a few broken trinkets with his foot and step on others as he moved closer. Giles was Buffy's Watcher and an all-around good guy. He hid an amazing level of cool under his often-stuffy British exterior. As far as everyone in the room was concerned, the man could just about do no wrong.

"Giles. We're . . . we're all so sorry. We tried to keep the wreckage to a minimum." The statement wouldn't have held water in a court of law and she knew it.

Giles looked at her as he managed to resettle his face into a semblance of his normal calm. "Oh, well done then. Hate to see what would've happened without your gallant efforts." He took his glasses off and rubbed at the spotless lenses with a handkerchief he pulled from his jacket pocket. "Now what's this about Kakistos? He cannot possibly be behind this, but perhaps there's another vampire masquerading as Kakistos to trade on his reputation?" He put his glasses back on. Anyone who didn't know the man would have thought he was actually calm. Buffy knew better. He was most decidedly not happy. She couldn't blame him in the least. "Well, whatever the case, I've just had a phone call from Wesley that confuses matters even further. Apparently, Faith is no longer in her prison cell."

Xander lowered his eyes for a second and shook his head. "Why don't I like the sound of that?"

"Kakistos was the only thing Faith was ever afraid of. I can't *not* think there's a connection here."

Giles slipped around the counter, automatically starting the long process of cleaning up the mess that had once been product for sale. "The authorities are saying that she broke out on her own, but Angel believes that something may have broken in to abduct her." The Watcher looked around almost desperately, no doubt seeking a dustpan. "He and his team will continue the investigation in L.A."

Willow nodded her head once. "And we'll look into it from this end."

Tara moved toward the utility closet, almost on autopilot. She came back out a moment later with a broom and a dustpan. Even as Giles smiled his thanks, Tara looked like she was afraid someone would yell at her when she spoke. "Willow and I could perform a spell to confirm that Kakistos is really dead. But w-we'd need to do it in the same place where he was supposedly killed."

"The factory." Buffy spoke softly, her mind still trying to absorb the information about Faith. "I can take you there."

Giles started sweeping. When he spoke, it was as proper and seemingly casual as ever. He looked up, his eyes catching Buffy's, but he never stopped sweeping. "I'll remain in touch with Wesley. Meanwhile, however, this place is a shambles. If I want to be open for business tomorrow—"

Anya interrupted him, her expression saying there would be no arguments. "'If?' What do you mean 'if'? Tomorrow's a Saturday! Lots of people bring us their money on Saturday. We *have* to be open!"

Giles nodded. "Well then, Anya, I'm sure you'll be equally enthusiastic about helping restore a bit of order around here."

Before she could respond, Xander was up at bat and speaking fast. "You have fun doing that, sweetie!

Me, I'm going along to the factory. Buffy may need me. And there's gonna be magickal rituals!"

Anya gave a very small scowl of exasperation. "You're only going because you're hoping it will be a ritual that involves nudity."

"All the best ones do." Xander smiled, a playful teasing grin.

Chapter Two

The night had become early morning before the group got to the warehouse. There had been a time when the place had been used for something meaningful, but like so many places in Sunnydale, the building was abandoned, left to rot slowly over the decades. It was taking its time, but the old building had definitely seen better days.

Buffy, Willow, Tara, and Xander entered the massive old structure with caution. It was just the sensible thing to do. The structure was dark and had no power to make it lighter. Xander, on the other hand, had flashlights. The big ones that seemed, in Buffy's eyes, to almost go hand in hand with construction workers. The beams cut through the darkness and left little doubt about what was hidden in the shadows wherever they touched.

"Well, it *looks* empty at least." Willow spoke in a whisper, almost as if she had entered a church or a library. It was an instinctive thing, a simple cautious note that made sense. Vampires weren't really known for offering tea and cookies to the people who entered their lairs.

"Yeah," agreed Xander. "It looks nice and deserted. 'Course, any vamps running around and calling this place home would probably be out now and trying to score some fresh dinner."

"That's what I've always liked best about you, Xander. Your ability to look on the bright side of any situation." Buffy nudged him with her elbow and allowed a small, sardonic grin.

"Life gives you lemons, you gotta make a key lime pie . . . or something like that."

Willow stopped, her head tilted at an odd angle, as if she were listening to something. "I think this is a good spot."

Willow and Tara worked quickly but carefully, tracing lines on the floor with simple white chalk. To Buffy the scrawls looked like a right-handed child had been trying to figure out ancient Sanskrit and copy it all down with a crayon placed between the toes of the left foot. She knew they were supposed to mean something, but she had no idea at all exactly what the scrawls represented. She didn't have to know. Will and Tara were the ones who needed to understand. While she and Xander kept their eyes on their surroundings, the two witches placed several candles, a few powders, and a long, sun-bleached bone within the markings they'd made.

"So, Faith might be coming back to town. . . ." Xander looked into a dark corner as he spoke, trying his best to sound casual. Buffy knew better.

"Not on your top ten good times list?" Buffy returned the favor, trying to pretend that the idea of facing the other Slayer didn't bother her.

"Gonna have to call that a big no, Buff. But hey, not really keen on juggling chainsaws while blind-folded either."

"Well, maybe she won't show up here." Buffy's voice got a little wistful. "Maybe she just got trans-ferred to a different prison and no one noticed in all the daily paperwork."

"Well, sure, that could happen. Hey, have you heard the one about the fat man who comes down chimneys on Christmas Eve?"

Willow paused for a second, looking up with a glint in her eye. "No, but I heard about Chanukah Joe when I was a kid."

"You're kidding, right?"

"That Santa Claus plays favorites with the little Christian children is not my fault. Chanukah Joe just picks up his slack."

Xander got a look on his face that said he was thinking about debating the finer points of Christmas again. Then he just smiled. "Still, no Snoopy Dance from Chanukah Joe."

"That's why I always had you, Xander." Willow

smiled brightly and Xander mirrored the smile.

Tara cleared her throat nervously. "I think th-that's all of it. We can start now."

Xander and Buffy stepped back a bit to let the witches do their work. The words meant as little as the things they'd written on the ground, but Buffy knew that whatever they were doing was calling forth power. She could feel it in the air. Or maybe that was just the power the two of them had together. Willow was a strong witch, but with Tara as a connection, a second source of energy to tap into, she sometimes seemed almost limitless. Anyone other than Will would have had Buffy worried when that sort of power came into play.

"Do you hear something?" Xander's voice sounded doubtful. His face said he wasn't certain if he'd heard anything over the chanting or not.

Buffy listened, and she felt something more than heard it. A low vibration, not constant, but there. She frowned, trying to concentrate. "Something . . . I just don't know what. Keep sharp. There might be a few of the local residents trying to sneak up on us."

Xander nodded but kept quiet as Willow and Tara finished their chant. If something happened, it didn't produce any flashing light shows. The air was suddenly filled with a loud, sighing wind that started above a smoking incense bowl placed between Willow and Tara. Aside from that, nothing at all seemed to happen.

Xander looked around as if he was expecting something more. "Well, that was bracing."

Buffy looked at Tara and then at Willow. "Not to criticize my favorite witches, but was there supposed to be something besides stinky incense?"

Tara looked puzzled. "I don't get it. We followed the ritual exactly."

Willow nodded. "We were definitely looking for more than stinkiness. Either the spell just failed or it's being blocked somehow."

Xander shrugged. "Maybe it's just confused."

Willow looked at Xander, her eyes acknowledging the jest. "Hmm. You tease, but there might be something to that." Will looked at Buffy and shook her head, looking extremely disappointed. "I can't say for sure. It feels like a really strong vampire has been here, but if it's Kakistos, I can't figure out how he got back. I can still feel his final moments ingrained in the spell."

Xander flashed that little grin of his again. "Maybe a Magic 8 Ball would help? They give you answers like 'Ask again later' too, but you don't have to write anything down."

"Well, sometimes magick isn't all that easy. It's not like computers, Xander. Sometimes even if you say all the right things it doesn't like to work out." She got that pouty-defiant look on her face that Buffy always found endearing.

Xander held out his hands in mock surrender. "Relax, Will. You know I'm only joking."

"Well, we might as well have a look around while we're here." Buffy stepped away from her friends, conscious of the creaking in the floor beneath them. "If somebody's doing a Kakistos impersonation, could be they've been here." Buffy moved up the steel stairs leading to the second floor offices. Most anyone else treading on the steps would have made a noise like a small tank bouncing off walls. Her footfalls made a faint whispering scratch, that was all.

She opened the steel door between the offices and the main area below, her senses waiting for any sign that the rooms beyond the threshold might be occupied. That was when Kakistos charged. She had enough time to see his scarred face, his left hand where the fingers had fused into a cloven hoof, and then she stepped back, pushing the door toward his face. Buffy managed to get the door halfway closed before she was knocked from the mezzanine platform of the second level, down to the area where her friends were still standing.

Buffy Summers was many things: agile, graceful, tougher than anyone would ever guess by looking at her, and fast. Very fast.

She was also as embarrassed as she was angry about the sudden attack. She cursed herself for getting sloppy as she twisted in the air. Kakistos's blow had left her disoriented, would have, in fact, probably lead to major bone breakage in someone who was not the Slayer. As it was, she managed to land on the ground below, but not as well as she might have hoped.

She didn't actually break anything when she landed, but it was close. Buffy's left foot buckled outward even as her right foot was hitting and she went down in a sprawl of limbs, her impact lessened slightly when Xander tried to catch her. It was good for her, but Xander took the brunt of the fall and wound up on the receiving end of a vicious punch in his head from the floor when he fell.

Before she could even check to see if Xander was all right, it started raining vampires. Kakistos must have been a very busy little monster, because despite the carnage she'd heaped on his forces earlier, there were a lot of bloodsuckers falling from the mezzanine above.

The first of them landed with even less style and grace than Buffy had managed. He was a businessman once. Now he was a business vampire and he grunted as he hit the cement floor and slipped, the slick heels of his loafers finding no grip. Even staggered and off-balance, Buffy staked him before he could recover.

"What? Did he hire these guys at a temp agency?" The next three to hit the ground were scarcely in better shape. Not a one of them seemed like they'd been a vampire for very long, and while she knew looks could be deceiving, the whole batch of them was made up of men and women who'd last had exercise sometime back in the eighties.

Xander shook his head and swung a hard fist into a soft undead gut. "No way. I use temps sometimes. These guys don't have enough calluses on their hands to be temps. Kakistos is using full-timers."

"I'll take your word for it." She might have kept talking, but that was when the world tilted under her. One second she was planting her left foot across the jaw of a portly woman in a lime green business suit, and the next she was falling backward, away from where she'd meant to follow through with a stake to the chest.

"Buffy! The floor!"

Xander's warning came too late. The groaning vibration they'd heard earlier revealed its source as the ground beneath her crumbled away. Buffy reached for the disintegrating ledge, but instead only grabbed a fist's worth of lime skirt. The junior executive to the vampire in charge of mayhem took the spill with her as she fell into a subbasement amid a shower of water-damaged concrete and rusted steel.

Buffy landed hard. The vampire made it worse by using the slayer as a cushion. Dead or not, she was a heavy woman. The manicured nails tore at Buffy's scalp, yanking her head back as she tried to recover from the fall. Buffy brought her elbow back and shattered bone on the pudgy vampire's face. The undead woman hissed and snarled, but did not let go. She pushed forward with inhuman strength and tried to ram Buffy's head into the ground. It took two more elbow strikes before the creature finally let go.

Buffy made a note not to underestimate the middle management among the undead. Just because they weren't fashionable didn't mean they weren't dangerous.

It took her a second to regain her composure. That was about all the spare time she was allowed. While she was catching her breath, the vampires spilled down into the hole around her. There were disadvantages to the situation, to be sure. For one thing, she was vastly outnumbered and in a rough terrain. For another, it was dark in the hole. The only source of light came from above, and that was weak at best. But there were some good points too. The biggest one was that without her friends right next to her, Buffy could cut loose properly. She was always worried about catching an innocent in the crossfire when she started fighting, and the idea that she might accidentally hurt one of her friends was enough to leave her feeling slightly hindered most of the time. She had learned to work around that problem for the most part, to keep a tighter reign on her attacks, but times like this were the ones where she didn't have to hold back at all. There was a reason she was the Slayer. The vampires around her learned that lesson quickly.

Dangerous or not, it became obvious to her long before she was done with the vampires in the pit with her that they had never been fighters in life and hadn't learned anything new about martial combat since they'd been embraced. Buffy cut loose and attacked with everything she had. It was almost embarrassingly easy.

So naturally, she knew something had to be up. As she was dusting a gaunt vampire in a gray pinstriped suit, she saw the next wave coming toward her from the darkness. This group moved with the grace of stalking panthers, crouched low and darting forward in small, fast movements. Buffy braced for the fight as they stormed into the light from above, their vampire faces showing and their fangs bared in snarls of hatred and hunger.

Above her, she heard Willow cry out and Tara scream. Both of them said one word: "Xander!"

Buffy took a blow to the back of her head that had her on her knees in an instant. The vampire who'd struck her took both of her heels in his chest as he tried to pounce on her. Buffy used her momentum to handstand into a kick and then used the force of the kick to roll into a somersault. A moment later she was on her feet again.

Being able to let herself go was wonderful, exhilarating even, but it was only useful as long as she had a chance against the numbers approaching her. As it stood, there were more vampires than she could easily handle in the tight quarters. Claws and fists struck her body for each blow she managed to deliver. Worse, the vampires were closing in so tightly that she could barely manage to put any real strength into her blows.

She hadn't quite reached the panic stage, but she was getting close when the tides changed abruptly. The vampire directly behind her let out a screech before suddenly collapsing into dust. Almost immediately, the female on his left dropped down, clutching at the back of her leg where a thick red slash of cold blood started spilling from her hamstring. Several of the vampires turned away from Buffy as something short and fast moved through their ranks. One or two of them let out squeals of fright and indignation; the others let out yelps of pain.

Buffy didn't take the time to see what was helping her. She just took advantage of the fact that something was there. The small reprieve was all she really needed. With the vampires distracted, she moved at speeds no normal person could hope to achieve and began cutting through her enemies.

There was no time for thought, no time for planning. All of the training Giles had forced her to endure over the last few years, all the combat she had already been through, came into play as Buffy Summers earned her title again. She was the Chosen One, the Slayer, and as far as the vampires were concerned, she became the Grim Reaper. Several of the vampires escaped her, but most fell quickly.

Before all was finished in the darkened subbasement, Buffy was sore from the beating she'd taken and bloodied in several places. Her hair, still in a ponytail, was half spilled from the hair tie she'd used, and the silence around her was almost complete. She could feel eyes looking at her, but could not tell where they came from. Even straining to hear any slight sound failed to do her any good. Whatever was down there with her was not breathing. Something short, dark, and unbreathing had just saved her butt from extinction. The thought didn't comfort her as much as she might have hoped.

"Whoever you are, thanks." Buffy looked at the hole in the ceiling above her and crouched low before leaping up high enough to grab the edge of it. The weakened floor threatened to give out under her, but held.

Willow fought as best she could, with Tara and Xander beside her. Xander didn't stay beside her for long, however, before he was pushed aside by several more vampires raining down from the balcony.

"Just how big is that room?" His voice sounded strained and Willow could understand that. She felt Tara's fingers sliding between her own and the resulting wave of energies that came whenever they performed magick together. There was little need for words; the two of them together seemed to form a powerful symmetry. Though their minds were still separate, it seemed they could understand exactly what the other was feeling and thinking. Despite the danger and the overwhelming numbers, Willow felt secure and strong when Tara was with her.

Willow looked at a vampire charging toward her with a murderous leer on his brutal face. A second later, that same face switched to an expression of fear and pain as the heat within his chest bloomed into a full-blown conflagration. Tara's mind reached out and another vampire let loose a roar of pain as the flames devoured it. Sometimes it seemed the magick just kept getting easier. Now and then that worried Willow, but with Tara there she didn't really feel she had much to fear. Tara kept her anchored and stopped her from letting the heady feelings become too much. That was one of the things she loved about Tara.

The vampires reacted the way vampires normally did to the idea of sudden flaming death: They started to scatter. The roaring voice of Kakistos above them all made them change their minds. "Your deaths will be slow if you try to run!" From what little she knew of Kakistos, the vampire was legendary for his abilities at torture. The rest of the vampires seemed to know that little rumor too. They came back and fought, despite the threat of burning to death.

Xander was overwhelmed and Willow looked his way as he was buried under a wave of vampire flesh. *"Will!"* His voice cracked hoarsely as he went down.

Willow chanted quickly, her hands breaking away from Tara. The only way she could hope to get to Xander at this point was to use the spell she'd learned earlier and that would require both of her hands. Tara cast a spell at the same time, igniting one of the vampires that came too close to Willow for her comfort. In the distance, above the spot where Xander had gone down, a globe of light formed, brightly illuminating the area. The vampires Kakistos used as his army might have been intimidated by him, but instinct alone drove them away from Xander as the magickal sunlight caressed their cold, dead flesh with searing heat. Several of them began to burn, their clothes smoldering and their skin blistering instantly.

Xander was not where she expected to see him. As the crowd broke apart, all she saw was dirty concrete where she'd fully expected to see her best friend for as long as she could remember.

"Xander? Xander! Where are you?" She looked around frantically, searching in vain through the crowd of retreating vampires. Kakistos was not there to control them; he too ran from the deadly rays of the sun, but that didn't mean they were eager to give over their prize.

As her concentration wavered, so too the globe of solar energy that bobbed about at her command. The light was still brilliant, but it dimmed slightly. Willow felt her chest tighten in apprehension. She would never forgive herself if Xander got himself killed because she was too slow.

She forced herself to concentrate, and the powerful spell grew brighter for a moment. Then it faltered and faded as she felt the impact from behind her. She never saw the face of the vampire that hit her. She felt the long feminine fingers gripping her wrists, and she felt the powerful, lean body that tackled her, driving her to the ground, but she never saw the face.

She never took the time to look. She might have, but that was also when Tara cried out in pain and Willow let herself get distracted. That was also when the vampire behind her hit her in the back of the head and made her vision go all fuzzy. Before she could recover, the vampire beating on the back of her head was thrown across the room, a victim of Tara's power. Willow crawled up to her hands and knees just in time to see Tara grabbed and lifted by a vampire who moved like an athlete. The blow was brutal and Tara had the wind knocked out of her by the attack. The last Willow saw of her was her beautiful eyes imploring her silently before the light disappeared.

Dazed and disoriented, Willow tried to summon enough of her thoughts together to form a spell, but nothing happened.

In the near-darkness, she felt her eyes start to sting, felt the threat of tears forming, and tried to force them back. Tara gone and Xander with her. It couldn't possibly get any worse. Except maybe for the very irate vampires moving her way, ready to get a little payback for the burns they were now suffering.

A teenaged vampire turned her way, the girl's pretty face burned on one side and half her hair scorched away. "Look what you did to my face! I'll kill you!" She stomped angrily toward Willow with a sneer on her face. "My brother Todd went to school with you. He said you were weird, but he didn't know the half of it!"

Willow looked away from the ruined face. Todd

Williams had been one of the many kids she'd worked with in computer science, and though she wasn't really sure the girl sneering at her was Todd's sister, they looked enough alike to make her think they were related. Just another insult to add to the injuries. She'd thought Todd was a nice kid, if a little nerdy.

Her eyes caught movement, and she focused on the hole in the ground just in time to see Buffy climbing out of it.

Behind the Slayer, she thought she saw Tara and Xander struggling against the vampires who held them. In all the fighting and chaos she'd lost them and thought them gone, but they were simply in a different part of the room. "Buffy! Over here!"

Buffy almost seemed to flow across the ground as she rose from the hole and moved toward Willow. Her face was set in a look of concentration, her pretty features almost petulant as she carved a path through the vampires between where she was and where Willow was.

Willow finally managed to regain her feet as Buffy reached her side. "Will, where's Xander?"

"They've got Tara and Xander over that way." She pointed. The ringing in her ears was lessening and she could almost focus again. "I don't even know if they're still alive!"

"They'd better be." Buffy backhanded a vampire who got too close and sent the foolhardy bloodsucker down the pit she'd climbed out of herself. "You hear me? My friends better be alive and unvamped!"

"They are for now." The voice came from behind Willow, and she turned to see Kakistos looking at her.

The elder vampire shoved her aside casually, his scarred face bared in an angry snarl. The same hooved hand that had brushed Willow aside hit Buffy Summers in the jaw hard enough to lift her off the ground and send her sailing. Buffy landed on her feet, narrowly missing a second trip into the subbasement. "They are until I decide otherwise, Slayer. If you want your friends alive, you'd do well to give yourself to me."

"Yeah, I see that happening in the near future." Buffy came back at Kakistos and planted her heel in the side of his head. Willow just barely managed not to get caught by the vampire's flailing arm as he fell back, shaking his head and stunned by the violent blow. "That'd be right after I'm done kicking your ass!"

The blow might have broken another vampire's neck, but it barely fazed the ancient. He came back in a savage charge and slammed his full body into the Slayer, lifting her fully from the ground and carrying her with him as he kept moving. His massive arms wrapped around Buffy's narrow waist as her hands slammed into his thick neck, chopping hard, but not hard enough apparently. Before Willow could do anything at all to help her friend, Kakistos had slammed Buffy into the cinderblock wall and cracked the cement with the force of the impact. Buffy grunted and wrapped her legs around Kakistos's thick torso, scissoring them together and squeezing with all of her strength. Even from a dozen feet away Willow heard the sound of bones cracking. Kakistos let out a roar and slammed his fist into Buffy's side.

"I have had enough of your interference, Slayer.

You defile my sanctuary and kill my servants! This time there will be no escape." The words were harsh, but his voice was a little weaker than before. Cracked ribs apparently didn't make vampires feel too energetic either. Buffy ignored his comment and brought her elbow across the bridge of his nose. He let out a second grunt of pain and staggered back, freeing her from where she'd been pinned to the wall.

And not ten feet off to the left, Xander was taken through a doorway that led who-knew-where. Tara was being dragged in the same direction.

"Tara!" Willow whispered under her breath and gestured with her hands. The vampire that had Tara in his grip caught fire, his back rapidly burning. As he let go of Tara, trying to beat out the flames, Willow pushed him with her magick, sending him staggering before he collapsed in a flaming heap.

Willow moved as fast as she could, heading toward Tara, ready to join with her again and fight back the tide of undead around them. Before she reached her soul mate, the vampires moved in again. Tara let out a whimper and shook her head before she vanished through the same door where they'd taken Xander. Willow felt hands on her back, pushing hard, and barely had time to brace herself with her arms before she met the door face first. Even with her arms taking the brunt of the blow, she had the wind knocked out of her. The room she fell into was darker than where she'd been, but there was still enough light to let her see Tara where she was held down by two vampires. That was the last sight she managed to take in before the fist hit her in the face. As she staggered away from the offending fist, a heavy hissing noise filled the air behind her. She looked around just in time to see the bay door roll into place, sealing her off from Buffy and any hope of salvation.

"Willow!" Tara struggled against the vampires that held her, bared fangs poised close to her neck. Willow didn't even bother to think, she just dusted them. Had anyone told Willow Rosenberg in high school that she would even be powerful enough to cast flames from her hands without concentrating, she'd have scoffed at the idea. Now she managed with ease, even though she was almost exhausted.

Willow's knees felt like someone had carefully removed all of the bones and replaced them with Jell-O imitations. The vampires were gone and she was glad of it. "That was a close one."

Tara moved to her side and held her. Even exhausted, the touch made her feel better. "We're t-trapped in here."

"Tara? Where's Xander? I saw him go through this door." She heard the tide of panic start rising in her voice but couldn't stop it from rising higher.

"I don't know, I didn't see him. But they can't have taken him far." Tara looked at her and put a hand on the side of her face. "We'll find him. I think I heard Kakistos say we'd be safe for now, and we'll find him."

Willow nodded and rested her forehead against Tara's, breathing in the scent of her lover. She looked around the room again. It was small and it was dark and there was barely even a hint of light from where the door should have been. The bay doors did not belong, they'd been added later, probably by Kakistos as a fail-safe against the sun. "We might even be safer in here than out there with Buffy." She swallowed, the sounds of violence from the other side of the door were muffled, but obvious. "Oooh. Buffy."

Willow and Tara worked their way over to the bay doors and began hitting them, making noise in the hopes that Buffy would notice. Both of them called out together, unconsciously in perfect sync with each other. "Buffy! In here! This way!"

He's dead! I saw him killed! I saw him go all ashes to ashes and now he's here and doing a swell job of beating me black and blue. If she thought about it too much, she was pretty sure she'd just go a little crazy. Vamps were supposed to stay dead when they were killed, especially by a Slayer.

Buffy lost track of Willow and Tara, but she couldn't do anything to help them until she managed to get away from Kakistos. And getting away from the elder vampire was going to be a lot easier if she didn't have to contend with the rest of his flunkies at the same time.

She dodged under a swing of his cloven hand and swatted his elbow with her own fist at the same time. Kakistos blinked, maybe for the first time catching on that she wasn't just another pretty face. He swung again and she ducked without thinking, which left her open for the kick he'd been planning all along. Buffy felt the blow strike her mid-thigh, and after a brilliant second of pain felt her leg go numb.

Buffy hopped back on her good leg and then dove for the bag she'd brought in with her in the first place. The stake she'd been using earlier was gone—dusted with a vampire it got stuck in—and she needed a new one. *Also, an axe or two would be useful.*

Kakistos kept up with her, moving to stop her from reaching her tools of the trade. He tried to grab her bag in his misshapen hands, clutching too eagerly for his own good as Buffy swept her leg low and caught him just above the ankles.

Kakistos's hands fell forward into the leather bag, amid several stakes and short-bladed weapons, and among half a dozen crosses and glass containers. One of the small bottles shattered against his left hand, and the elder vampire threw himself back away from the bag as the holy water spilled across the thick nails on his cloven hand.

Buffy was glad to take his place, her hands searching through the contents and finding two stakes and a short double-edged axe. The first vampire to come too close lost an arm and then got his heart pierced for his troubles. Even with her new weapons, there were a lot of vampires to deal with, and Buffy reached back to pull out a heavy crucifix. The effect was immediate: Most of the vampires recoiled as if they'd seen the sun, and as they did so, Buffy took advantage and started wading through them, the cross pushing them back and letting her take out a few at a time.

It was a good plan, and one that worked for all of ten seconds before one of the vampires got cocky and knocked the cross aside while she was impaling another one. The hands that grabbed the cross burned as the vampire grabbed and pulled. The bestial face twisted into an even uglier mask of pain, and then the vampire was staggering back from the broken remains of the crucifix, both hands seared by the contact. Buffy took his mind off the pain by planting her stake in his chest. She left the stake behind and grabbed the other one from the back pocket where she'd set it. The first stake was replaced and so was the crucifix. Two more vampires ran at her, both of them looking like rejects from a movie about Valley girls, give or take the fangs, and both dropped quickly.

Kakistos was on the move, running from her, several of his flunkies between where he was and where Buffy stood. He snarled as he retreated. "This isn't over, Slayer! Your friends are trapped. You can follow me or save them." He turned and moved away from her, a small gathering of rather nervous-looking vampires closing ranks behind their master. From off to her left she heard the sound of Willow and Tara calling frantically. There was nothing to see, nothing but a large metal divider that closed the room off from whatever lay beyond it.

"Dammit!" There was really no choice. She could go after Kakistos later, after she'd saved her friends. The room echoed with her footsteps as she moved into the darkness, seeking the source of the voices she heard. There was a short corridor and at the end of it a rolling steel bay door. The door was down and it was not budging. Buffy tried lifting it several times, calling out to Willow. "Will? I'm right here. Hang on, I'm trying to get this stupid door up."

"Buffy, thank God." Her voice was muffled, but still intelligible. "Xander's missing and something's going on in this place. Something's inhibiting our magick in here. Can you break through this gate?"

Buffy blinked, feeling that dread that had haunted her so many times in the past. *What if I screwed up and something got Xander? Really got him?* She forced herself to focus on what was before her, instead of what might be going on somewhere else. "I'm trying, but I don't think so." She strained, lifting with her legs and back, but something was blocking her efforts. "Why can't anyone ever come up with a nice, simple door that I can kick in half?" She didn't get an answer, but she hadn't really expected one either. "There's gotta be a mechanism to unlock this thing. Lemme see what I can find."

She searched the edges of the door along the floor and along the sides without any luck.

"No go. This place is like the funhouse from Hell. Without the fun."

Tara's voice carried through from the other side. "Maybe you can get in from the second floor?"

"I can try. . . ."

Even after she climbed to the second floor, it took almost five minutes, but finally she found a bar across the top of the door that was spring-loaded. It was too heavy for the average person to lift. Buffy had no real difficulties. As soon as the bar was lifted away, the door rolled up a few inches. Before Buffy could get back down to the lower level, Willow and Tara had rolled the door back up into its slot in the ceiling.

Willow smiled wanly, her face pale. Tara held her girlfriend up with an arm around her waist. "That's a relief. I didn't think we'd ever get out of here."

Buffy got down to business. "Well, I'm not exactly out of here yet. You two head back to the Magic Box and tell Giles what's going on. That was Kakistos all right, in all his glory. I hate it when the bad guys don't stay dead." Her voice was calm, but inside she was wound tightly. When she first got to Sunnydale she'd had a little problem with an ancient vampire who called himself the "Master." Well, okay, it was sort of a big problem that wound up with her being dead until Xander came along and revived her. Though she'd killed him in the long run, he still held a special place in her nightmares. And there had been an attempt to resurrect the Master as well, one that she had stopped. If Kakistos could be brought back, was it possible the Master could make another appearance? Of all the vampires she'd ever faced, he was the most powerful, and she wasn't certain that she'd ever faced him when he was at his full power. *Not an idea that works for making with the happy thoughts.*

Willow nodded and looked around the darkened building. "Especially the really ugly ones."

Buffy followed suit, her eyes drinking in the details of the warehouse. "Kakistos and his crew weren't using the front door. That means there's gotta be a secret entrance somewhere in this maze." She gently ushered her friends toward the entrance of the building. "If I can find that, maybe I can find Xander."

Willow looked like she was getting some of her

strength back. Maybe it was being with Tara. Buffy had long ago noticed that Willow seemed almost more complete when she was with Tara. Willow glanced back at her as they reached the door. "We'll get Giles working on it."

Tara stared at Buffy, her face serious and almost sad. It was a look Tara wore a lot. "And if you can't find Xander . . . maybe *we* can."

Willow mimicked the expression of Tara's face unconsciously. "For all the luck we're having with our magic fingers tonight."

"With the conjuring, she means." Tara shook her head. Apparently she wasn't very happy with their success rate. Buffy couldn't have agreed less. Without Willow's help at the Magic Box and here, she wasn't all that sure things would have gone as smoothly.

"Right. The conjuring . . . of images that should *not* be in my head." She pointed to the door. "Go. I've got a scarface vampire to kill and a lost Xander to find."

Willow nodded, her face clearly showing her thoughts were on Buffy and Xander far more than they were on her weakened state. "Gone." She didn't wish Buffy good luck. She didn't have to. Buffy knew how Willow felt.

It took precious time she didn't have to discover the secret of how Kakistos had vanished. She went back into the room where Tara and Willow had been trapped and after a bit of searching and toying discovered a chain in a hidden recess in the west wall. The chain looked like it belonged on a ship, as the links holding an anchor. After a few experimental tugs she discovered that pulling would cause the room to move up or down. The room was actually a lift, but one that, again, no ordinary human could hope to operate without heavy duty tools. There was no way Willow and Tara could have made the lift work without their magick, which, coincidentally, didn't work in the lift, though Buffy had no idea what might have caused that.

Even with her own strength, it was a difficult task to get the room in motion. Pulling on the chain, she managed after a few minutes to get the lift down to a lower level. Kakistos had been busy when he was around the first time, and who knew how long he'd been around again. Whatever the case, she'd managed to find out how he disappeared. Now all she had to do was figure out where he'd gone.

The area where the lift came to rest was a crudely carved cave that branched off in half a dozen different directions. The darkness was close to complete in Morloch Central, but Buffy felt she could see well enough.

Certainly she could see well enough to recognize the ventriloquist's dummy that stood not ten feet away from her. She'd met him before, back in her first year at Sunnydale high school. His glassy eyes were focused on her and his head slowly went from side to side.

"Sid?" Even she could hear the doubt in her voice.

"One and the same, kid." His thick dark eyebrows went up as his eyes moved slowly over her body. "Gotta say, give or take the dirt and bruises, you're looking even better than before, Buffy." The dummy moved closer, and Buffy blinked, her eyes seeing but her mind having trouble absorbing. *Just how many dead people are going to pull a* Sixth Sense *on me today?* "Long time no see, Slayer. How's tricks?"

"Sid?" She knew she was in trouble—she was repeating herself.

"The one and only. I know, I know, you haven't been the same since I left. That's what they all say." One small hand reached up and rapped three times sharply on his forehead. He made an appropriately hollow sound. "The ladies love the wood."

Buffy rolled her eyes and smiled for an instant, surprised at how happy she was to see the demon hunter. A long time ago he'd been in the same line of business until he got himself cursed. "Lovely. You're still a class act." She resisted the urge to reach down and give the dummy a hug. He would probably take it the wrong way and she didn't have the time. "What are you doing here, Sid? I thought when your demon hunting days were over, your soul had left that dummy body behind, moved on to the old proverbial better place."

Wooden shoulders shrugged in a way that should have been impossible. "Been there, done that, babe. And now I'm back." It was impossible to read much from the wooden face or the glassy eyes.

"You're not the only one." Buffy pulled her eyes away from the animated dummy and cast her glance down the myriad dark tunnels.

"I know. Kakistos."

"How—"

"No time for punch lines, sweetheart. The vamps aren't the ones who took your friend. That's a whole 'nother ballgame. Don't know which way they went, but if you're looking to go after Kakistos, he went that-away!" His right hand jerked out and pointed to a tunnel almost behind him.

"But, Xander—"

"Ain't gettin' any younger, I know. But I can't help you with that. Just this. You better hurry if you wanna catch Kakistos." And again she had that problem. She was good at reading human faces, and even some demons were pretty much open books. Dummies, on the other hand, were the masters of the deadpan expression.

"Fine. But we're gonna have a talk later, you and me." It was driving her crazy, the questions she could have asked him, but she didn't have the time.

"Wouldn't miss it for the world, babe. A magnum o' cheap champagne, you in a corset, and Tommy Dorsey on the Victrola." The face barely changed, but Sid's voice had taken on a leering quality that worked at least as well as a smirk would have. "Rrrowrr." The articulated eyebrows rose and fell several times rapidly.

Buffy sighed and shook her head. "I may just have to let Kakistos rip my throat out."

Sid started down the tunnel, moving quickly. Buffy did her best to follow, but from time to time the tunnel narrowed with unexpected spills of fresh dirt that had fallen from the ceiling. It looked like Kakistos or one his followers had tried to cause a cave-in to slow her down, and they'd been only partially successful. It was really only inconvenient, but the fresh mounds of earth meant she had to crawl through in order to get where she was going. Sid was short enough that he could basically run through without ever even crouching.

"Sid, slow down!"

When his voice came back, it was farther away than she would have expected. "No can do, Slayer. Got places to go and people to see. You're on the right path for Kakistos, just keep going and stay to the right." For a second he was silent, and then she heard him grunt. "Catch you on the flip side, toots."

Buffy called his name again, but he was either not in the mood to talk or he had left the area.

It took her almost fifteen minutes to finally get to the end of the tunnel, and during that time she was forced to slither like a snake through several narrow points in the cave. She promised herself that she would personally stake the vampire responsible for the cave-ins. The mud might do wonders for her complexion, but it was wreaking havoc on her hair. It wasn't much of a joke, but it was the best she could do. Being stuck in the tunnels where they narrowed was a little too much like one of her personal favorite phobias: being buried alive and unable to get free. *Been there . . .*

That feeling was made even more intense when she finally climbed out of the tunnel and into a cemetery. The territory was familiar. All of the graveyards in Sunnydale were familiar. They were her usual hunting grounds when it came to bagging her limit on newly risen bloodsuckers. This particular cemetery was close to home and where Spike had set up his residence. His mausoleum was off to her left, and home was only a few blocks away. It boggled her mind to realize how far she'd traveled under the ground. "One of these days I'm mapping these things. I mean it this time."

No one answered her half-joking words, but she heard someone speaking just the same. The voice was deep, but made faint with distance. She recognized it. Kakistos was speaking, the words unintelligible from where she stood. Buffy moved in his general direction, keeping low and constantly looking for unwanted interference. She had no idea how many more of his flunkies might be ahead.

She stayed luckier than she expected. There were only three vampires that she encountered on her way to pay Kakistos a visit. Each and every one of them obliged her by being easy to stake and quiet about dissolving into dust.

One of them was near her mother's grave. She paused for a minute after staking him, trying to remember how to breathe. Her mom was dead, and that was a pain that was still far too fresh. She was doing all right taking care of Dawn, and she kept telling herself she was handling her mom's unexpected death as well as could be expected, but damn, it hurt to think about never seeing Joyce Summers again. It hurt a lot, and thinking about it for too long made her want to curl up and die.

Buffy made sure none of the vampire's ashes touched her mother's plot. The grass was just taking root and she didn't want her mom's final resting place tainted by the vampiric remains.

Buffy shook off the grief as best she could and concentrated on work. The longer Kakistos was around, the greater the chances that someone else she loved would die sooner rather than later, and she needed to find Xander too.

Kakistos stood in the middle of a field of graves, most of them in perfect rows, even if the markers failed to match. The ancient vampire stood alone, his mouth moving softly, speaking deep guttural words that meant nothing at all to the Slayer, but filled her with a sense of unease.

Or maybe the gemstone floating in front of him had something to do with that.

The crystal was crudely shaped in the form of a crouching horned demon with a leering face. She guessed it at around seven inches in height, and actually had to squint her eyes to look directly at it. The red gem let off a brilliant crimson glow that bathed Kakistos and made him look like he'd been wading in a river of blood. His misshapen hands were held out before him, and the gemstone floated a few inches above the thick hooves where fingers should have been.

Suddenly the vampire stopped chanting and turned his head to look at her. Sometimes she forgot how acute the sense of some vampires were; though she was walking softly, he'd heard her approach. His eyes glittered and flared with the crimson light from the gem. "You're not easy to kill, are you Slayer?" His voice sounded almost amused, which left Buffy feeling more than a little dubious about what that floating thingamabob of his might do.

That better not be Red Kryptonite for Slayers, she thought. *I don't want to end up as a giant pink gorilla, or worse.* She looked at the gem and then back to Kakistos. *And I have been spending* way *too much time hanging with Xander. Seriously.*

Buffy shrugged her shoulders, letting the motion swing her hands to the small of her back and the stake and axe she had tucked into the back of her jeans. "I could say the same thing about you."

Kakistos lowered his arms and flexed his hands, rolling his shoulders like a boxer getting ready for a fight. His voice when he spoke was filled with a tone of dismissal, as if fighting the Slayer was almost more of an inconvenience than a real threat. "Oh, I'll have my turn at you eventually. But there's another I've got my eye on. You're just the appetizer."

His thick hooved fingers touched the gem in front of them briefly and a slight, cruel smile spread over his bestial lips. When his hands moved away, the light within the gem flared until even he was forced to look away and glowing ropy tendrils of energy lashed out with almost explosive violence. Buffy was prepared to jump out of the way of the lightning streamers, but they never came to strike out at her. Instead they lanced into the ground, dancing across the lawn and scorching the grass. Almost as quickly as it had started, the pyrotechnics were finished.

Buffy frowned, puzzled. *Did he make a mistake with the spell casting? Pretty red lights that burn the grass are normally saved for falling fireworks on the Fourth of July.*

She had her answer a moment later when the ground began to shake, softly, but with growing force. California has a reputation for earthquakes and the Slayer had seen her fair share. This didn't feel at all the same. Even as she thought about the quality of the vibrations, the ground in front of her bulged, knocking over a headstone. Hands broke through the lawn, followed almost instantly by a body. Buffy had a brief second when she thought it was a vampire rising. She knew better when she saw the rotted flesh falling from the gaunt form. What crawled quickly from the ruptured turf had been a human being once, now it was a shell. The thing looked at her and gnashed its teeth together in a near frenzy.

Buffy looked quickly at the surrounding graves. The same thing was happening everywhere the lightning strikes had touched. "Guy's like a Vegas bookie. He keeps changing the odds."

Kakistos laughed, a sound not unlike a bear roaring, and moved away, confident that the Slayer would be unable to follow. She might have proven him wrong if it hadn't been for the zombie that grabbed her from behind, jagged yellowed teeth snapping together right next to her face. Rancid, cold air blasted forth from long dead lungs, and Buffy fought back the need to gag. She also grabbed the greasy cold flesh around the zombie's neck and leaned forward at the hips, flipping the corpse through the air. Her hands kept their grip on the dead thing's neck, and when the body went forward, the head stayed behind in her hands.

"Eeuuww! That's just sick!" She danced back, her hands shaking as the head rolled to the ground. Vampires were savage and murderous, but at least they normally managed not to leave gobbets of themselves all over her.

She dropped down to her knees and grabbed up her

axe and stake from where she'd dropped them to flip the now headless corpse. "I have *sooo* got to take a shower. . . . Ewww . . . Ewwww . . ."

Three more corpses forced themselves from the ground, each in a different stage of decomposition. The first was little more than a skeleton in the remains of a white dress. It had no eyes but seemed perfectly capable of seeing just the same. When it tried to gnash its teeth together, several of them fell from the sockets in the jaw. That was okay, there seemed to be maggots aplenty ready to fill in the gaps. The second was a young man who seemed almost like a statistical freak in Sunnydale: He'd actually died because he was stupid enough to drive his father's SUV into a wall while blitzed on spiced rum and beer. His eyes were a little filmy, and there was a deep indent in his skull from where it had met the steering wheel the night he died—the wax that had filled the dent flapped like a loose scab—but otherwise, he was unsettlingly fresh. His teeth were perfect, right down to the braces, and they clacked like castanets as his clouded eyes stared at Buffy. The third had been grossly overweight, and big chunks of wet, moldy flab sloughed off as it rose.

Buffy fought off the urge to vomit explosively as she waded into the flesh. The nearly skeletal one fell apart with a single blow. The fat one—she couldn't actually guess what sex it had been—took three chops from the axe and a roundhouse kick before it collapsed on the ground and lay still. The high school kid took a stake through his chest that pinned him to the marble angel behind him, and while what was left of his brain tried to figure out how to get free, Buffy used the axe—slicked handle and all—to take off his head.

"Zombies should be old and dusty . . . definitely needs to be a rule. Zombies should be old and dusty." Buffy kept talking, if only to hear a sound other than the chattering of teeth. She tried not to think about what she wiped from her hand and the axe onto her jeans. It made her stomach want to move to another state without her. By the time she'd finished with that simple gesture, there were almost a dozen more zombies crawling, shambling, and staggering in her direction.

Kakistos looked back at her, the gem flaring brightly in the air near his left hand. He had a grin on his face that was pure malice, and Buffy made a silent promise to carve that expression off his skull just as soon as she could get to him. He'd moved a good distance away. She followed, cutting through the zombies at an almost savage pace. Where she went, the animated corpses went as well. At least they weren't trying to eat the brains of all the people in Sunnydale. They were after her, apparently, and that made the work a little easier, if no cleaner.

Spike ignored the sounds for as long as he could before he finally rose from his crypt. He might have even kept right on ignoring them—including the distinctive sound of the Slayer getting knocked about a bit—if the coffin off to his right hadn't decided it was time to evict the current resident. He opened one eye and looked up as the mortal remains of his neighbor slid out of the casket and looked at him.

"What's this then? Somebody have insomnia?"

The zombie opened its mouth and began gnashing its rotted teeth. Aside from a grunt, it made no other sound, but it came straight at him, and he was forced to get up and defend himself or become snack food for a dead thing. The only dead thing he wanted snacking was himself.

"Gettin' so a fella can't get any rest in this town." Several other bodies were trying to get out of their final resting places, but the reason he'd chosen the crypt was because he liked the heavy stone sarcophagi that could be used as furniture in a pinch. Most of the local residents didn't have enough muscles left to actually lift the lids and were having a little trouble with the whole self-excavation angle.

He paid a little more attention to the noises outside and decided it was time to investigate. Before leaving, he drove his fist through the head of his restless neighbor. The ponce had made a mess of his crypt, and he'd been trying to keep it neat.

"Let's see what this is all about, then. I could use a little extra carnage." Sometimes it bothered him that he'd started talking to himself. Not often, mind you, but now and then. It was either that or start having meaningful conversations with the likes of Xander Harris, and that was not a notion that sat well on the best of nights.

Spike opened his door and looked out into a scene from a bad zombie movie, only with pretty bloody good special effects and a charnel house smell instead of the scent of buttered popcorn. Several graves in front of his comfy little home had been opened, and there were corpses either crawling from them or moving around the holes where their fellow stiffs had already vacated the premises.

"Well, this is a bit of a twist, isn't it?" Spike took the time to light a cigarette. "Not every night we get a block party in this neighborhood." Most of the walking dead ignored the vampire, heading toward something just west of his home. One of them, however, looked right at him, and he thought he saw some dim spark of intelligence behind the ruined, deflated eyes.

Spike smiled tightly when the zombie came his way. "I remember you, darlin'." He nodded and stepped back the two paces it took to reach into his crypt and grab the axe he kept near the door for unexpected visitors. Some of the local demons had taken it personally, his hanging with the Slayer, and now and again one of them came down to try to pulp his skull for him. It was always best to have a little security in case they got through the door.

The corpse wasn't the fastest zombie he'd ever seen, but it was definitely determined and it wanted his head as an ornament. *That's fair enough,* he supposed. *Kill a tasty young meal on legs, and now and then you have to expect it might want to return the favor.* This one had been among the first sweet girls he'd found in Sunnydale. He had no idea which funeral home had taken care of her mortal remains, but they needed to be commended. Almost three years since her death and she was still recognizable. He was impressed.

"Come to see about another dance, luv?" The girl's

corpse hissed cold, wet gasses from its mouth. "That's all right, then. The Big Bad is always glad to oblige a lady, even if she's seen better days. Besides, how many times do I get to kill a girl twice?"

For all her desire for revenge, if in fact that was what motivated the thing, it failed to get very far. Spike took the head from the shambling wreck in one swipe and watched the body fall to the ground. "All that fuss for nothing." Spike spat on the ground next to the corpse. "Hardly seems like you picked a good night to get out of bed."

Spike looked at the corpses moving past and blinked with surprise. He knew more of them than he might have realized. It was nice to get a few reminders of what his existence had been like before the government boys had put a chip in his skull. "Hello, mates. Thanks for the memories." He shifted the axe in his grip and moved into the growing tide. Whatever they were all after had to be at least a nice diversion, and with any luck he could find a way to put them back where they belonged. If not, he'd be stuck a week or so cleaning up the mess before he could feel comfortable in his own home. It wasn't the idea of corpses so much as the stench of them that was the problem. Not exactly an easy smell to wash out of his clothes, and he'd just stolen the jacket a few days ago.

Because he could use the exercise—or translated into non-Spike, because he was bored—the vampire started hacking his way through the zombies. The first few obliged him by falling like so much dead foliage into a wood chipper. Then they took notice of him and started trying to return the favor.

That little darling he'd had as a snack so long ago had been dead for a while and it showed in her reflexes, even if she'd been fairly well preserved. Some of the fresher ones—normally dripping embalming fluid and a few body parts—were faster and stronger. More than one of them managed to get a grip on his clothes and on his flesh, trying to tear through both with the same ferocity.

There are advantages to being a vampire. He threw zombies through the air, hurling them like sacks of garbage. Most got back up, but it bought him time to deal with the rest.

It hadn't been all that long ago that he could have torn through an army of living, breathing humans in much the same way, give or take interference from the Slayer. These days, as Harris kept saying, Spike had been "neutered." Somehow it wasn't quite as fun terrorizing the humans when he couldn't actually do anything more fearsome than saying boo without feeling like his head would explode. That didn't mean he didn't still have the urges. So he did what he could to get in a little satisfaction, despite his unfortunate limitations. In this case, he took out his frustrations on the dead things that walked among him and were trying to chew his skull open. He also played back a few pleasant memories as he moved, filling in the sound of his past victims' screams in substitution for the chattering sound of a few dozen zombies gnashing their teeth in his general direction.

And if almost all of the zombies he fought bore the superimposed faces of the people he most often found himself associating with, well, that was his little secret. He drove a fist completely through the skull of a zombie he pretended was Xander Harris, a feral grin on his face as he did it. He broke the neck of Rupert Giles in his mind and reveled in the wet popping noises. The next four were almost too fast for him to really imagine properly, but that was all right. After a little while he just thrilled at the carnage.

As he fought, the zombies did their damage to him as well. Dead hands clawed at flesh and took their pound a few scratches at a time. Rotting teeth clamped down and chewed ferociously even as he broke the jaws that held them in place. The pain was nothing, a mere whisper next to what the blokes from the Initiative had done to his noggin, and for every scrape he took an unlife. Spike waded through his newest enemies and felt truly complete again.

When the few that had attacked him were finally done away with, he followed the rest, striking from behind most of the time, and feeling not the least bit of guilt about the sneak attacks. Not far away he could hear the sounds of a living, breathing person grunting with effort, and he could smell the sweet tang of blood in the air. Fresh blood, not the rotted filth the walking stiffs spilled with their embalming fluid. It made his mouth water.

Then he spotted the lone human among the sea of corpses and shook his head. "Right. Why am I not surprised?" One of the zombies turned and hissed gasses in his direction, then caught him a solid blow across his jaw. Spike fell down and came right back up again, his hands slamming into the sides of the dead thing's skull and crushing the bones until a thick, black syrup spilled over his clenching fists. "Girl brings a party with her wherever she goes."

The twice-dead corpse hit the ground and his feet as he watched Buffy dance with her new partners. She was bloodied and bruised, her skin sweating heavily even past the ichor that covered her. She looked lovely, and he hated that he worried for her safety. Hated it so much that he angrily forced the feelings down below the surface, doing his best to pretend he didn't love her. He didn't *want* to call it love. The very idea was ludicrous. Angelus might be stupid enough to fall for a human girl, and suicidal enough to fall for the Slayer, but Spike wanted no part of it. *Just a damned shame my heart won't listen to reason . . .*

He let himself get distracted, and that was when the zombies hit him from all sides. Just when he'd figured he had their number, the little sods had to pull a fast one and start working together. It didn't take a genius to catch on that they were being directed, and even as Spike fell under the sudden assault, he saw a monstrous brute of a vampire moving around a tree to leer at Buffy Summers. He'd never met Kakistos, but the ancient vampire's reputation preceded him.

One of the deaders clawed its bony fingers into his hair and into his scalp, yanked his head back savagely, and another bit into his throat as the ancient vampire moved closer to her.

Buffy was aching all over. She'd reached the point where she was no longer certain where the blood from her wounds ended and the gore from the zombies began. And despite her best hopes, she couldn't get over the foul stench of the dead things. Her hair fell in a wild spill, obscuring her vision to the point where she was almost constantly flicking her head to get the strands out of her eyes.

She flipped backward over a flesh chomper trying to eat the back of her thigh and brought her axe down on the crown of what had once been someone's grandmother. Balanced on her left foot, she planted her right heel in another one's neck and felt the head separate from the body. That was when she saw Kakistos as he slid around from behind a tree to watch the show, his red gem flaring like a lightning storm next to him.

"Slayer. How nice to see you again." His dark eyes looked at her, amused by her dilemma.

"It's good to be popular." Buffy panted as she spoke, but she reached into the back of her jeans and pulled free the stake she had planted there. "This is all just some sick game of Twister for you, isn't it?"

"There's more truth to that than you'd think." Kakistos rested both of his hands on the closest headstone, looking down at the writing there. "This has been fun, Slayer, but I think it's time for me to be going."

The zombies stopped for a moment as Kakistos focused on her. Buffy took in a few deep breaths, her eyes on the vampire. "You can keep running, but you know I'm going to dust your ugly carcass eventually."

Kakistos nodded, patting the headstone affectionately. "I'll be running along. And you, Slayer, can decide what's more important." Smiling, he looked down at the stone, and then back at her, his hooflike fingers marking the marble, digging faint gouges into the nearly glassy surface. "Catching me, or stopping the spell before it resurrects *all* of the dead in this boneyard." His other hand snatched the gem from the air and it did another impersonation of a sun going nova, lighting the entire area in a brilliance that left her seeing spots before her eyes.

Kakistos laughed, a deep roaring laugh of pure, sadistic delight. "Your choice, Slayer, but I'd be careful which way I chose to walk right now. The price of stopping me is higher than you think."

Kakistos turned and ran, his thick, powerful legs devouring distance faster than a human being could ever hope to manage on foot. Apparently he'd forgotten that Buffy wasn't exactly a normal girl. She shook her head. "Oh, no. Not this time."

Buffy moved toward him, determined not to let him get away, even as the gem unleashed another volley of crimson lightning strikes across the ground and into the graves around her. Buffy made another seven steps before the ground began bulging again, violent, earth-shaking tremors that stopped her as she tried to keep her balance. She almost made it, almost kept her footing, until she caught the name on the headstone Kakistos had been toying with. On the marble the name Joyce Summers showed clearly in the fading corona. That was pretty much all it took to make Buffy stumble and then fall. Kakistos, little more than a distant shape and already almost out of reach, was forgotten completely.

The headstone shifted marginally, and from behind her, Buffy felt a dead, emaciated hand clutch at her jeans. The turf bulged in front of her, and despite her combat instincts, Buffy ignored the clawing hand that tried to grab her thigh and tear through the denim to the flesh beneath. Something frozen bloomed inside her stomach, an arctic despair that started low inside her and spread rapidly up to her heart.

"Oh, my God, no . . ."

Buffy shook her head, denying what she saw, what was happening to the grave where she'd laid the most important woman in her life to rest. Her feet kicked at the lawn, pushing her back away from the grave.

"Mom . . . No . . ."

Chapter Three

There had been a time in his mortal life when Spike had been a bit . . . softer than he was in his modern existence. Well, okay, he'd written some of the worst poetry ever penned and he'd doted on a woman who couldn't have cared less about his even being alive. He had, in fact, repulsed her with his ability to be wishy-washy and his talent for mixing metaphors with a heavy dollop of treacle.

You could say he'd been something of a sentimentalist. When the woman had broken his heart, he'd been prepared to die and had, that very night, been taken by Drusilla. His unlife had started and his world had changed for the better as far as he was concerned. Until very recently he'd lived his life by his own rules and wreaked havoc wherever he chose to go. It had been a life-altering experience, and in a positive way.

The damned chip in his head had changed his life as well, and not really for the better. The alteration was just as drastic, though possibly not as dramatic. Forget the flashy stuff, most of the change was internal. No one could understand how completely his life had been turned around, because no one else had gone through it.

Buffy Summers, the Slayer, had been through a few of those kind of changes in her short life. Spike knew that. He understood that when she became the Chosen One it had altered her life in ways she had never been prepared for. Oh, surely there had been other moments that were as profound or came close: losing her innocence to that ponce Angel and then having him lose his soul; that had been a dark time for her, and for Spike as well, though for entirely different reasons. That was probably close.

Losing her mother? That was up there too. Though he'd been fighting against his feelings for her then, Spike had still been by her side as best he could manage when her mom had shed the old mortal coil. He'd seen how hard it was for her to face the days and nights. He'd seen her struggles to be a proper guardian and big sister to little Dawn, the other Summers woman he cared about. The Slayer was stronger than she normally gave herself credit for, and she gave herself a fair deal of credit.

But that particular wound was still fresh, and he had his doubts that she would recover if her mother came out of the grave in front of her and started trying to chew her face off. Bloody hell, he was a vampire and he'd have probably had a few problems with that notion under similar circumstances.

Joyce Summers had been a strong woman too. Though she sometimes seemed fragile, she held her family together through rough times, learned painful and difficult truths about her extraordinary daughters, and endured all the horrors of having a part of her brain cut out. She'd gone through more than a lot of people could have and she'd done it with style and grace. Spike had genuinely come to like and admire the woman once he got over the fact that she was the Slayer's mom. She'd proven to be intelligent and she'd earned his respect. She, like her daughters, had treated him with a level of decency he really hadn't been prepared for. Treated him like a man, not a monster. He could have seen himself becoming friends with her. None of that really mattered much, of course, because situations were simply what they were, nothing more and nothing less. Still, he'd been fond of her. Just as he was more than fond of her daughter.

So when he saw the ground bucking and humping upward, and when he saw Buffy Summers, a girl he knew could face almost endless horrors without breaking, kick away from that one particular grave, he knew what the score was.

There was one glowing red gem, a few hundred zombies, one very attractive Slayer on the edge of a complete mental meltdown, and one grave starting to open. A year earlier, even a few months earlier, he'd have watched the show and chuckled through it. Then he'd have done many nasty things to the Slayer before killing her. The Big Bad liked a bit of torture before eating, like adding just the right spice to a perfect meal.

Funny how life changes.

Spike shoved past two zombies doing their best to make him into their next meal and ran up the front of another that was shambling his way. His left foot hit a slightly squishy thigh, his right foot followed through with a bounce off the head of the zombie, and then he was airborne. Had he allowed himself time to think about it, even he would have been impressed—well, more impressed than he usually was with himself. Spike's left foot hit the top of a headstone and he jumped again, like an aquaphobic crossing stepping stones over a rough river. In a few more strides he was within three feet of Buffy Summers and the ground that was starting to push past the new sod over her mother's grave. He leaped hard, his legs scissoring in an imitation of a fast run through the air, and grabbed the fiery glowing stone that was above Buffy's head.

The gem flared brightly, and his hand pushed it into the tree another two feet away. It was a good, solid oak tree, and the force of his hand's impact ran all the way up to his shoulder and neck, leaving his arm numb. His hand survived the crushing blow. The tree withstood the force, which, frankly, would have bent steel with minimal effort. The gem did not make it. The gem exploded, sending lightning blasts through his arm and the tree alike as it shattered into so much crimson dust.

The pain was like an inferno in the palm of his

hand. Spike stood perfectly still, his eyes clenched tightly shut and his teeth bared in a rictus. It took all of his effort not to scream, but he didn't want to show that much of himself at the moment. No sign of weakness, no flaw that would show how much he had just done for the Slayer. It wasn't that he didn't like to brag, because he most certainly did enjoy talking about himself when the fancy struck him. But even William the Bloody knew that there was a time and a place for that sort of thing.

Behind him, he could hear the Slayer's rapid, shallow breaths, could hear the delicious pounding of her heart and smell the ambrosial scent of her freshly spilled blood. He could smell the pure, undiluted terror on her flesh that he'd never quite managed to produce in her when they were fighting on opposite sides, even when it was life or death for the both of them.

From the corner of his eye he could see the zombies falling to the ground, once again merely dead instead of walking dead. Their souls, like his, had long since gone away. Their bodies were just a little slower to catch on, was all.

His arm trembled and it felt like he had burns on the bone and deep tissues, even though there was no visible damage aside from a few bite marks left by the now inactive corpses. Slowly, in the utter silence of the cemetery, he heard the Slayer's breaths calm down. She let out a faint whispery gasp, and for a second he was sure she would start screaming herself, the pressure of the moment overwhelming her.

She held it in. She was strong like that. He gave

her a few more seconds to regain her self control and her composure before he turned to look at her. He made his face shift back to a human countenance. Not long ago, even if he'd helped her, he might have cut her deep with a remark or two, taken advantage of the situation provided to hurt her for the sheer pleasure of it. Part of him still wanted to because, really, every time he saw her was both pleasure and exquisite pain. Unrequited love always is. That was what the poet he'd been had understood better than most, even if he'd never been able to express it very well.

"Well then, Buffy. What's this about? Couldn't fancy the idea of not seeing me before the night was over? Come by for a kiss goodnight?" He kept the right level of scorn in his voice. Enough to hide that he understood what she'd just gone through and enough to work like a light slap on her face, more to snap her out of her distress than to actually hurt. The thing about being an expert at torture is one learns a trick or two about keeping the victim's psyche uncrushed. They're never as much fun when they've been completely broken, after all.

And was that gratitude he heard in her voice when she spoke again? Not blatant, but more like an undercurrent? He chose to think not. "Spike, I'd rather kiss a slime demon."

That was good then. He wasn't actually looking for her gratitude at the moment. Just looking to keep her whole. "Obviously, you never kissed a slime demon."

Buffy got up and dusted off her fanny. She looked

at him with an odd smile and nodded her head. "Right you are. That's Drusilla's specialty."

"Watch it, Slayer. That's dangerously close to below the belt." They started walking and she shrugged.

"Only in your dreams."

The inside of the Magic Box was starting to look like a place of business again, though, frankly, not one that would be favored by anyone with a savory background. Rupert Giles was tired, but at least he was keeping busy. Most of the glass had been swept away, the ruined stock had been disposed of, and the glass-top counter had become a board-top counter. It was a start.

He did not jump when the phone rang, but he almost wanted to. He absolutely hated waiting to find out if Buffy was all right. "Magic Box."

"Giles, it's me." Buffy's voice. He let himself breathe again. She sounded more tense than usual, but it had been that sort of night so far. "Listen, no time for a whole recap. Willow told you about Kakistos?"

"Yes, but where are you now?"

"Ran into him again. It was a whole thing with zombies." She tried to make it sound casual, but he knew better. He resisted the urge to ask if she was all right. She'd have told him if her injuries were serious. "Cemetery jamboree. Also, I saw Sid. The dummy?"

"The ventriloquist's dummy? I remember him."

"Well, looks like Kakistos isn't the only dead guy up and walking around. And Kakistos is being all cryptic—no pun intended—but he keeps making comments that make me think there's more going on here. That this is all bigger than just him."

Giles nodded, fully aware that she couldn't see the gesture through the headset. "That makes sense. He *was* dead, after all. Whether it really is him or some sort of doppelganger, this is sorcery on a level we're ill-prepared to deal with. I've got a few theories, but they require more research." He hesitated for a moment and asked the question he dreaded. One of these days he knew the answer that came back would break his heart, be it Buffy or one of her friends that he'd grown so very fond of. "Any luck finding Xander?"

"No. Sid seemed to know something about it, but he was all mysterious too. I hate that in a wooden puppet."

Giles smiled, shaking his head softly. "Yes, we all do. Fortunately, Willow and Tara performed a locator spell that they hope will lead them to Xander. They're out trying to track him now."

"How's Anya?"

"She wanted to go along, but she was too hysterical about Xander being in danger to be of much actual help. She's trying to straighten up the mess in the basement."

"All right. Spike's with me now. We're headed back to the factory to see if Kakistos returned to the scene of the crime again. I'll be back at the Magic Box as soon as possible."

"Be careful."

Buffy's voice tried for light and joking but came out more along the lines of furious. "It's my middle name. When I'm not as pissed off as I am right now."

Buffy hung up and Giles slowly set the phone down. It never seemed to get any easier, the worrying. He stepped back from the counter and looked around the Magic Box. After a moment of surveying the remaining damage, he grabbed a broom and started sweeping the floor that was already clean. It kept him busy. Sometimes that was enough.

Chapter Four

The warehouse looked the same, but as they approached, she felt a slight shift in the atmospheric pressure. There and then gone, like breaking through a soap bubble. Spike tilted his head and sniffed the air.

Buffy frowned when she saw the expression on his face—a blend of curious and hungry that was decidedly unsettling. "What's wrong?" She told herself it was only concern for what might lay ahead, not worry that his little mind chip might have suddenly gone on the fritz, that made her voice sound that way.

"Nothing you could smell, Slayer, but there's enough blood in the air to paint the whole town pink, and it just showed up out of nowhere."

She thought of Xander and felt her stomach try to

wrap around itself. If he'd been hurt there would be a lot more dead vampires in Sunnydale come morning. There'd also be no end to the guilt she felt for dragging him into her world. She dealt with the idea of her friends dying regularly and knew they would be there even if she tried to push them away—just as they had in the past when she tried—but that didn't make it any easier to face the solid possibility. "Xander . . ." The name slipped out of her mouth before she could stop it.

"No, I don't think so. Or not him alone. I mean a *lot* of blood, Buffy." If his words were meant to comfort, they failed. But one look at Spike's face told her he wasn't thinking much about how she was feeling. He was focused on the blood. Much as she didn't like to think about it, she knew the scent had to be enough to make him ravenous. These days his regular diet was chilled black market human blood or pig and cow blood from the local butcher shops. She also knew that was about as satisfying for a vampire as a BLT hold the bacon. She wasn't shocked when his fang face showed itself, but she wondered if he even knew he'd changed.

"And it's coming from inside the warehouse?"

"Oh, yeah." He licked his lips. Then he shifted back to his human visage.

"Let's go." She moved ahead, hefting the bag of Slayer goodies she'd grabbed at her house in her left hand. She hadn't had time for a shower, but a few extra weapons were never a bad idea and she took care of it. Dawn wasn't home, and for a moment she'd been terrified. Then she remembered that her little sister was staying with her friend Janice. It was a risk having

Dawn away from home, but on this night that wasn't exactly a bad thing either. Her sister needed protecting, and better that she be with a regular family for the night than be at home alone when Kakistos was out and roaming the streets.

Buffy moved up to the main doors of the warehouse, and by the time she reached them, even she could smell the blood. Slaughterhouse didn't begin to cover it. She made a gesture, a tilt of her head, asking silently if Spike was ready. Though she half expected him to be too distracted by the scent of what had to be a gourmet feast as far as he was concerned, he nodded.

He took the door on the left, and she the one on the right. The warehouse was as empty as ever, but the scent of blood was overpowering. Another step forward and that odd pressure was back, pressing down on her, and then it was gone again.

Buffy blinked her eyes, and when she opened them, the warehouse had been transformed. The dingy walls and barren floors had vanished, replaced by a complex line of conveyor belts and tubes, the likes of which made the average milking machines look small and tame. The darkness was gone, driven back by bright lights that showed every detail of the massive room in vivid Technicolor. The conveyors ran the length of the room, along all four sides and down the center as well, where several vampires were gathered and talking. They worked as they chatted, placing lids on bottles and sealing them. Each of the bottles was clear glass and filled just to the very edge with a dark red fluid. She traced the conveyors back from that spot with her eyes, frowning in concentration. A long stretch of metal pipes ran through where the wall that divided the offices from the main structure should have been, and that was what lead to the final destination. Though she couldn't actually see what was going on where the executive part of the building was, she could most definitely hear the sounds of screams emanating from the distant area of the building. Screams, and a wet, thick trickle like a river of milk. But only if the milk was dark, dark red. Heavy machinery ran up there, where before she'd had only a glimpse of desks and carpeting.

From that location on the second floor, there were still more conveyor belts rumbling and rolling. It was on these belts that she first saw the product being moved for what it was: people. The figures she could clearly see were all stripped down to their birthday suits, but there was nothing remotely provocative about their nudity. They were bloodied and obviously unconscious, or wishing to be. Gaping wounds showed on torsos, bellies, and legs, thick, deep wounds that looked to have taken out three-inch-wide chunks of flesh. Universally, the people there were pale and shaky, most often in shock and close to death.

She barely had time to acknowledge the rest of the place, from the spot where the vampires gathered—dead ahead, roughly seventy-five feet away—to the first station on the victims' way to the grape presses for pulping their bodies down to so much blood and meal. Buffy's mind was already working on how best to destroy the slaughterhouse that hadn't even existed a few minutes before.

"What . . . what is this place?" She couldn't keep the disgust out of her voice, but she kept it down to a soft whisper. *Not really thinking I should call attention to myself just yet. I feel like the only cat stuck in an overcrowded dog pound.*

"Looks like Heaven to me." Spike could not keep the desire out of his own words, though he really didn't try very hard. "The Devil's own little blood factory."

"I was just here. It didn't look anything like this."

Spike sniffed the air, his face changing into its bestial visage. "Cue that old *Twilight Zone* music." He looked around carefully, true, but not as carefully as Buffy would have liked. He didn't seem nearly as worried about getting spotted as she was. Then again, he was a vampire, so he was already doing pretty well in the camouflage department. "What did you have in mind then, Slayer? We just gonna waltz on up and ask them if they have all the proper licenses?"

"There are prisoners up there. Get to them, Spike. Get them out of here. I'll handle the factory workers."

"Right, because, really, this is such a horrible idea. Wouldn't want to have a steady source of real food." Despite his words, he moved off, stalking toward the room where the processing apparently started. In half a second he was lost to Buffy. She was distracted by the vampires gathered near her, who had finally decided to notice her.

She'd already had the sort of night she didn't like to think about. Her muscles were sore and she was tired, which when one is the Slayer, is a rather challenging situation to get into. Still, midnight hadn't even come around yet, and she had a lot to get finished before she could even consider hitting the sack.

First up: slaying time. There was no time for thought, only for action. Buffy got a running start and moved into the mass of undead monsters like a vengeful god. She reached into her bag of treats and came out with one stake and one cross. The crucifix went through the air and toward the vampires, who backed away from the icon, spitting and cursing. She dipped back into her satchel and came out with a hand-held axe. The first one was staked before the majority of the vamps ran into her.

Spike shook his head, angry with himself for helping the Slayer again. "Would someone please tell me why it is I can't just have a nice, ordinary life as a vampire?" He climbed the stairs to the mezzanine, reaching into the folds of his duster for the axe he'd used earlier. Buffy carried axes too, and he wondered if he was following her lead or she his. It didn't matter. The thing about a good axe was it could be used to cleave or just to beat someone down to size. As far as he was concerned, a good axe was better than having a dozen mates at your side and ready to fight for you. You couldn't stake an axe and have it bloody disappear on you. A good weapon was better than boy scouts and a few soldiers besides.

As he topped the stairs he saw the first of the local vampires. Weird thing about this one: He looked just like the little nancy boy twit the Slayer ran into from time to time: Jonathan, that was his name. The kid looked at him, a puzzled expression on his pouty face. "You know why I like axes so much?" he asked the boy.

Jonathan stared at him and shook his head.

"I like 'em because they're great for weeding out the sloppy sots. They keep everything running like a classic Bentley." He swung the blade in a short, savage arc, and watched Jonathan's surprised face rise into the air along with the rest of his head. The body was ashes when he walked through. "You get a lot of chaff with the wheat, mate. Nice to keep the two separated."

The smell of blood in the air was thick and ripe and sweet. Spike licked his lips without any conscious thought and moved deeper into the area. Below him, he could hear the sounds of Buffy fighting, and a part of him worried about whether or not she was all right. That was so wrong he wouldn't let himself dwell on it. But it was one of those things. He thought about copious flows of blood and he thought about the Slayer at the same time. Just a side effect of having done in a couple of the little tarts over the years.

A conveyor belt rumbled off to his right, drowning out the sounds of conflict from below. He looked over and saw the struggling forms of blood bags trying to get away. Oh, he didn't speak of humans as blood bags around Buffy very often, but most of them were little more than walking meals as far as he was concerned. The problem was that these days he was on a forced diet of bloods that just didn't taste as good as what he smelled. His stomach rumbled, or at least he imagined it did. A girl, who was doing her best to escape her bonds, looked over at him, pleading with her eyes. She might have done some begging if it hadn't been for the gag covering her mouth. Her clothes were rumpled and dirty as if she'd been held for several nights before they decided to bleed her. *What sort of operation have they got then? How can they get this many people and no one catches on?* He shook his head, amazed. *Wonder what it costs to get a game like this up and running.*

He walked along the length of the conveyor belt, almost intoxicated by the smell of fresh human blood. "'S'like being on canned food when there's a buffet spread all set up." He lowered his head as he moved into the room at the far end of the mezzanine. And once there he saw the set up that other vampires had concocted for their food supplies. He was right with what he'd said to the Slayer. It *was* like a little slice of hell on earth, and most of him responded to that notion very favorably indeed. There were hundreds, literally hundreds of people locked in pens, like fresh veal calves ready for filleting. Most of them were looking a little underfed, but that didn't matter much. As far as Spike was concerned, it wasn't diet but emotional state that made the difference in the taste of the blood. There wasn't a one of the whole bloody lot of humans in the cells that wasn't terrified.

The other vampires in the room were seeing to that. Some of the makeshift cells for holding the humans had special tables and torture devices that would have made a Grand Inquisitor green with envy. He had to admire the restraint some of his peers seemed to show. Most of the tables where they strapped down their favorite pets had almost no blood on them. *Waste not, want not.*

The scent of fresh blood was beyond distracting. It was almost painful. But he couldn't give in to the temptation, not if he wanted to stay relatively sane. He had to avoid getting himself rehooked on the notion of human blood if he wanted to survive the damned electrical thing stuck in his skull. Not really a good idea to get fond of what one can't have. He'd already gone the whole cold shakes and migraines route once. Also, though he still didn't like to admit it to himself, he didn't want Buffy's disapproval.

He was still thinking about his little problem with being stupid enough to fall for the Slayer when he caught the sound of footsteps behind him.

A deep voice called out softly, "Who are you?"

Spike turned around and took in the beefy vampire staring at him, bestial visage showing and fangs bared in a sneer of contempt. This one was too cocky. Spike answered him with a foot to the side of his head and followed through with his trusty axe.

"That's the problem with most of your vampire leaders. No sense when it comes to recruiting good help." He turned back the way he'd been going, and made it a whole four steps before the two vampires hiding in the rafters landed on his back. He made a noise that was one part pain and two parts anger at himself for getting sloppy. One of the lads who was using him as a rug had on steel-toed combat boots. They left a deep tread on his right shoulder.

Spike took a few blows to the ribs before he managed to regain his feet. They hurt like hell, but nothing he couldn't handle. The two who faced him looked familiar, but he couldn't place them easily. What bothered him about them was that he was pretty sure he'd killed at least one of them before. Of course, after a few decades of the whole kill 'em and eat 'em routine, a lot of the faces started to get a little fuzzy in the memories. He dodged a blow from the smaller one, noticing the brass knuckles as they shot past his face. Spike brought the axe handle around and clocked Shorty in the face. The larger of the vampires moved in, ready to break a few bones, and Spike blocked the first blow with the blade of his axe, cutting the vampire's hand nearly in half. The burly vampire hauled his hand back, screaming in agony. Spike grinned. He spun his whole body around in the swing he took and caught the bellowing vampire in the chest, chopping through flesh and bone and meat until the edge of his axe carved through the heart. The sodding clown wouldn't take that as a hint to stay down. He pushed back to his feet and tried to attack again. Spike decided to lighten his load and used the weapon to remove the stubborn vampire's head.

He kicked the remaining vampire in his short chest and sent him over the edge of the mezzanine walkway. The vampire let out a yelp as he went over, and Spike started running. There was no more time for dawdling over what his life had become. The little welcoming party had taken care of that. The doors in front of him were closed, and he'd fully expected that. What he was after would be the sort of thing that was well guarded under the most casual of circumstances. Most of the vampires that lived long enough to actually gather a following tended to want their prized possessions defended from easy access. And would the office for this factory be considered valuable? Oh, yes. At least to the vampires.

Spike went through the door and into the offices behind them like a runaway train. If there were vampires in the room, the screams and fighting had surely alerted them. If he were going to stop them, he'd have to work fast and be brutal.

There were vampires in the room. Every last one of them sitting around a coffee table, and apparently having a business meeting. That was just wrong as far as Spike was concerned. Vampires weren't supposed to have power lunches. They were supposed to wreak havoc and revel in bloodshed. Though they just about had to have heard the fight only a few feet away, they seemed preoccupied with other things. Looked to be five of them, and that was just as right as rain in Spike's eyes. He was in the mood for a little mayhem, especially if he was the one causing it.

"Hello lads. Let's just forget the introductions and concentrate on your death if that's all right."

Every person in the room turned to look at him as he pushed past the broken door and sliced his axe through the first vampire's neck. The vampire obliged him by dying instantly. The next three weren't so accommodating. From their sitting positions in the large office space, they took aim and fired. The bullets from the two pistols hurt. The crossbow bolt that punched through his ribcage a few inches below his heart, on the other hand, that hurt a lot. Spike staggered back, his free hand pulling the thick, short arrow out of his chest. He didn't actually let out a scream so much as a whimper of pain, but his anger stopped him from caring about the sign of weakness. The chair that had been occupied a moment before by a vampire with a splitting headache was now empty save for a thick scattering of gray powder. He hooked the seat with his boot and launched it through the air at the gathering of vampires across the table from him. The two with the guns moved out of the way. The one with the crossbow was too busy trying to put another bolt into the channel and got beaned across the top of his skull. He grunted as he dropped the weapon and clutched at his head. Spike kicked the thin table at the group and watched as they scattered, appalled by how ill prepared they were for a fight. Well, okay, and pleased too. His chest was still on fire from the near miss and the lead-lined holes that ran through him.

The table went over and the vampires went over too, hitting the ground before they threw their meeting place to the side. Spike followed through with a heel to the face of the one who'd almost killed him, and swatted another in the face with the flat of the axe. Both blows broke bones. Neither of them stopped the vampires from continuing to attack.

The one who hadn't actually tried to fight back yet screamed at his cohorts. "Have you lost your mind? We don't have time to deal with this upstart!"

"Upstart?" Spike looked at the fleshy-faced vampire who'd insulted him and threw his axe across the room. The businessman flinched and raised his hands to protect his face. Pity for him that wasn't where Spike aimed. The blow wasn't fatal, but every male in the room imagined the pudgy fellow was wishing it had been. Any way you looked at it, the chap wasn't going to have any fight left in him. "Listen, you sorry lot of wankers, the only upstarts around here are you. Me? I've been doing this for centuries."

The one who'd been using the crossbow got up and charged at Spike, catching him in the midsection, his clawed hands tearing at the red wound where the crossbow bolt had pierced earlier. Spike roared, beating down on the man's back with both of his hands, raining a dozen or more sledgehammer blows into the exposed ribcage. The grabbing hands slipped as the man tried to defend himself and pulled back a bit. Spike drove his knee into the vampire's jaw and shattered it. Bone fragments cut into the flesh of his joint, but he didn't care. The pain was hardly a new thing, and mild next to what his skull kept trying to do to him.

The last two vampires stared at him as he brought the heel of his boot down on the one with the broken face. The heel cut deep into the neck, bruising and tearing as it went. Spike ground down harder as the vampire gurgled beneath his foot. The hands clawed at his leather pants, but he ignored them, his eyes staring at the last two vampires that posed an actual threat. One of them looked ready to rabbit. The other looked ready to try his luck with the Big Bad. Beneath him, the one who'd been trying to fight back suddenly stopped struggling as his neck broke. He wasn't dusted, but he wasn't really capable of doing much until the massive trauma healed.

"Now, anyone else want to make an issue of how I handle things?" The two vampires eyed him, and even Mister Jumpy was apparently thinking that running away might be for the best. "I'm thinking if you leave now, I might be too busy looking around to actually kill you." He shrugged. "Pretty sporting of me if you want to know the truth. Normally I just kill everyone and forget to be pleasant, but I'm on a deadline." He leaned over and picked up his axe. "What's it gonna be then?"

The two vampires vacated the premises in nearly record time. Spike kept his ears attuned to the sounds they made as they left, the better to make sure they didn't come back. The far wall of the room was little more than a curtain and a door. He finished the job on the paralyzed upper-management type he'd been standing on, then took the time to push past the curtain and into the room on the other side.

"That's the jackpot then, isn't it?" The room was filled with control switches and more dials and monitors than he'd seen in all of the Initiative. Spike looked around for all of thirty seconds before he started flipping switches. When that got boring, he took his axe out again and made sure the controls stayed inoperative. Before he was done, the rumbling sound of conveyor belts had ceased. The sound of machinery had faded away. All that remained was the sweet echo of people screaming in agony.

He left the room a minute later and followed the

sounds of pain and suffering. Like as not, that would be where he'd find the humans the Slayer wanted him to save. "Isn't this grand? Bloody vats of fresh, sweet blood, and me without a straw. . . ."

As he moved from the office and out onto the mezzanine, he saw Buffy below, running like all the demons of Hell were about to take a chomp from her bum. She looked up, saw him, and called out. He was about to ask her to repeat herself when he felt the hand close around his entire head, engulfing his skull like a baseball glove.

Buffy was winded, but she seemed to finally be getting close to the end of the vampire assault. These weren't like Kakistos's earlier troops. These vampires seemed more competent. The evidence was in the bruises she felt blooming under her clothes and the cuts that went through those same garments and into her flesh in multiple places. Half of the twisted devices the vampires had been using were already ruined, but the worst of the lot was still ahead. The first stage of the horrors had drained the vital bloods from living, screaming victims. The second stage had taken the same victims and gotten what was left. Buffy had already taken care of the vampires who hoisted the unconscious or nearly comatose humans and drained them by slashing their wrists. This, the final stage of the processing plant, was designed to get every last drop of blood that remained. The wine pressing thing she'd seen earlier was not crushing grapes, it was crushing human remains. She'd already seen four people pulverized by the heavy weights that dropped down from the ceiling and slammed together like a nightmare version of a waffle iron. What came out when it lifted back up was almost completely bloodless and looked like so much hamburger. All she had to do was get past the last small horde of vampires and she could turn it off.

Of course, they weren't feeling much like letting her just walk past, and this group was looking a bit peevish. They were also well armed with a fine selection of wooden clubs, and a few hand guns.

"No fair playing with guns, fellas. I left mine at home." She moved in fast, breaking the arm of a trigger happy housewife who screamed a lot and managed to put three holes in the ceiling above them. The screams stopped when the stake punched through her chest. Buffy blocked a baseball bat to her head and returned a kick that knocked the king of the Louisville Sluggers over the conveyor belt. Seeing that, she got an idea about how to speed things along.

The Slayer took to the high ground, flipping over the head of another baseball enthusiast and landing on the slowly moving device. She ran quickly, dodging the bloodied, comatose people on the track as she made her way toward the pressing device. Even as she neared it, the press slammed down again, this time on a boy who was awake enough to scream as the massive weight landed on him and crushed him flat. Thick blood and fluids spilled from the sides of the press and filled a pan below it, before trickling into the tubes that took the liquid away to be bottled, she supposed. Buffy swore it would be the last person pulped as she jumped over the club aimed at her knees and kicked the vampire swinging it hard enough to snap his neck. She caught the weapon as he dropped it and broke it over the head of a woman who looked like a grandmother gone bad. Then she jumped the next person in line for becoming a vampire's idea of freshly squeezed orange juice and shoved the club into the space between the ceiling and the rising weight of the press. The motors on the thing started grinding as the stout wooden bludgeon caught between the side of the press and where the weight wanted to go. The wood creaked, but did not break. The press groaned but continued to try lifting higher than the club would allow.

Several vampires made rude comments about Buffy, her heritage, and her willingness to sleep around. She took out the one who talked about her mother first. Two girls who looked about twelve years old, with short dark hair, freckles, and matching Britney T-shirts, tried to jump her at the same time. They were twins, and they might have been cute in life. Now they were little bloodsuckers who weren't happy with what she was doing.

One of the twin terrors bit her in the thigh, sinking her fangs in deep and worrying at the wound like a small terrier with an attitude. Buffy cried out and grabbed the girl by the shoulder, yanking her off and losing a bite-sized piece of her leg in the process. The girl licked her lips and screeched furiously. Her sister bit Buffy in the other thigh.

"Geez! If she jumped off a cliff would you copy her too?" She pulled the other one from her and felt more flesh tear away. She wasn't quite used to dealing with the half-sized variety of vampires. The end of the club was sticking out from where it was holding the press in place, and Buffy took advantage. The end of the wooden weapon was blunt, but she managed to force each of the twins onto it just the same. She had to remind herself that they weren't really little girls anymore but monsters.

The power went off and the massive room dropped into complete blackness for a moment before the emergency lights came on. Though the area was darker, the machinery had all stopped working. Several of the vampires looked around, puzzled. Buffy frowned, still thinking about the two little girls who'd been made into demons by another of the creatures she had been chosen to battle.

She was still trying to reconcile that little issue of age when she got hit from behind. Buffy staggered forward and caught herself before she could actually get impaled on her makeshift stake, but it was a close thing. She turned quickly and saw the next one in line. . . .

And froze, dread filling her stomach with ice. The girl who looked at her was dressed in black leather and should have probably been walking the streets for money in that getup. But that just wasn't possible, because Buffy knew Tara. Tara would never, not ever do that.

Naturally there had to be some sort of mistake. "Tara?" She barely recognized her own voice, which had suddenly gotten very weak. The face was Tara's, but the clothes, the demeanor were all wrong. If she'd been made into a vampire, it was the fastest transformation Buffy'd ever heard of. How could she ever explain to Willow? "What-what are you doing here?"

Tara didn't say a word, merely turned on her heel and ran. Buffy ran after her, leaping over another vampire as she gave pursuit. Tara moved too fast, was almost certainly superhuman in her speed. Had she cast a spell on herself? Was she in disguise in an effort to help? No. Because people who are helping you aren't generally the same people who kick you in the back.

"Oh, damn. Oh, Willow . . . I'm so sorry." There was only one thing for her to do, and as much as it pained her, Buffy would do it. Up above her, on the mezzanine level, she saw Spike looking down. "Spike! I just . . . I think I saw Tara here! I'm going after her!" If he made a response she didn't catch it.

She darted down a hallway, Tara just ahead of her, running into the darkness and wishing she'd, just once, thought to pack a flashlight.

As if her wish had been granted, the lights came back on as she spilled into another massive room. If she didn't know better, she'd have sworn the building was actually bigger than it had been before everything went crazy. And everything had definitely gone crazy.

The room was filled with machinery that was once again grinding into life, and as it did so, the human captives in the room began to scream. People were hanging from chains around their wrists, some of them trying to kick and get away, but all of them held still by the vampires who grabbed at their ankles. She had found the true heart of the place, where the fresh "stock" was bled for the first time. Massive machines pumped air through tubes that were slammed into the bodies of the human captives, effectively vacuuming the blood straight out of their bodies at high velocity. The pain must have been overwhelming, because most of the people being siphoned held their mouths open in silent screams of pain. A few seconds later, the lucky ones either passed out or died from the shock of sudden blood loss.

Ahead of her, Tara wove through the long lines of suffering people, her laugh light and airy, barely even taking the time to look back at Buffy. Buffy sped up, determined to find out what had happened to Tara and to stop the insanity around her. *I know what happened. Oh, Will . . . I'll never be able to forgive myself for doing this to you.*

As she passed the first round of people hanging from the ceiling and being bled, the vampires let go of their prizes and turned to follow her. Buffy was fully aware of them, just as she was aware of Kakistos when he stepped forward on a small balcony at the far end of the massive room. Tara was heading for that balcony and Kakistos was looking down, a triumphant grin on his face.

"So glad you could join us, Slayer. Let's finish this, once and for all."

Spike really hadn't been expecting an attack. Oh, it happened now and then that he got caught off guard, so he could live with that—he hoped. It was the size of his attacker that bothered him. Very few vampires could throw him around like he was a rag doll, but the chap that caught him by surprise did it without any trouble at all. He lifted Spike by he head and then caught him in the crotch with his free hand. Spike had just about enough time to realize that he must be dealing with a behemoth before he was thrown into and through the wall.

The solid surface collapsed around him like an overly thick eggshell, and Spike slammed into another wall behind it as well. Before he could turn around, the giant was on him again, and a fist almost as big as Spike's entire torso caught him in the belly and punched him through the second barrier.

He was ready to hit the floor on the other side of what had to be a simple crawlspace between two pieces of chalkboard. He didn't hit the ground on the other side. At least not immediately. Instead he plummeted down an extra fifteen feet onto a dirty Linoleum floor. The room stank like a sewer, and the reason was obvious almost instantly. There were cages above him, where he found still more humans waiting their turn in the blood juicers. These weren't the ones he'd seen earlier in their pens, oh no. These humans were in wire cages and had been there for a little while, being prepped for their final journey to the afterlife. The heavy gauge steel cages were soaked, dripping water from the looks of them, and here and there were vampires with pressure hoses, cleaning the livestock for their trip into the blood letting machinery. The people were wet and scared and miserable. He loved this place more by the second.

He could have done without the giant that came through the wall behind him. There was a loud crunching noise and then the plaster showered in a hailstorm that half covered him in chalky dust. Spike rolled out of the way just before the vampire landed on the ground where he had been a second before. He was almost surprised when the concrete didn't break under the sudden weight.

"What have they been feeding *you*?" He looked up at the vampire, and kept looking up until he thought for sure he would strain his neck. Who'd have guessed that Frankenstein's monster had a bigger brother?

He was, hands down, the biggest vampire Spike had ever seen, and he'd seen a lot of vampires over the years. Sometime in his mortal life, Spike figured the chap had been dragged behind a truck for a few hundred miles. His skin was a mass of scars and deep gouges where the flesh had not grown back in properly. His hair, what little there was of it on the top of his head, was patchy and black, cropped down to a crew cut that revealed every ding, dent, and bump on his oversized cranium. His face was twisted and ruined, and his eyes were as black as pitch, surrounded by coarse, ragged flesh. He was also over seven feet tall, and built like the average Mister Universe contestant.

The vampire smiled at him, revealing teeth that would keep an orthodontist in easy money for a decade. "Mister," it rumbled, its voice as coarse as its face and twice as deep as a philosophy convention. "I don't know who you are, but I'm going to enjoy tearing you in half."

"Oh, bloody hell."

The wrecking ball that passed for Goliath's fist caught Spike in the side of his head. Spike hit the floor, twisting and managing to take most of the force on his left arm and shoulder instead of his skull. "Right then . . . Where's my bloody axe? . . ." He looked around, ignoring the stars in his field of vision, and searched for the axe through the heavy puddles on the floor. King Kong kicked him in the ribs before he could grab it. Spike rolled across the floor, feeling all too much like a soccer ball, and winced as his tender side slapped the cold concrete. The cages above him swung as he brushed past them, and the oversized vampire pushed them out of his way, likely in search of Spike's body to pulp again.

Spike slithered on his back under the cages. The catch here was to get the humans free and avoid having the mountain that walked like a vampire follow through with the promise to rip him in half. It took him a second or two to puzzle out the best way, but it came quickly when he saw that the cages had bottoms that could be dropped out with just a couple of pins. Simple enough, really: A thick band of metal framed the bases—a good five inches thick at each edge, which was just right for stopping the captives from pulling the pins if they decided to have a look-see. But it wasn't that different from an oversized birdcage. Pull the pins and the bottoms fall out for quick and easy cleanup—or, if necessary, removal of the bodies. Spike slid across the ground faster, yanking the pins as he went.

The people dropped from their cages with a variety of noises. It was fun, really, listening to the sudden

yelps as the floors went out, and then hearing the roar
from Frankenstein's vampire as he realized that the
ingredients for the bottled Blood Lite were getting
away. Two birds with one stone, and all he had to do
now was find a weapon to take care of the thing that
wanted to chew him into bite-sized morsels.

Everywhere that his new best friend went, cages
were flung into the air, which might have been useful
for the chap if they didn't tend to fall back down right
afterward. The cages snapped to the end of their chains
and then rattled and clanged in small circles as they
settled back into their normal positions.

And while they danced their crazy jigs, Spike got
some distance covered and found one of the other vampires in the area, most of whom were still trying to figure out exactly what was happening. The fellow had a
cattle prod—the better to torture a few humans—and
Spike wasn't at all afraid to take it from him. While the
pimply-faced vampire was sneering as menacingly as
he could at the humans who were running like jackrab-
bits, Spike slid up behind him and grabbed his chin and
forehead. One quick, brutal twist and the bloke fell to
the ground, neck broken and body paralyzed.

From across the room, a good forty feet away, the
ugly giant let out a noise that shook the chains of the
closest cages and charged in Spike's direction. Spike
snatched up the cattle prod and made sure it was armed
and set for the maximum charge.

The close-set cages between him and the vampire
that wanted him as a new chew toy rocked and swayed
madly while the giant pushed past them. Many still had

humans sitting inside them, but a lot were empty now. That part of the task was at least half done.

Spike ducked down and waited, keeping his eye on the columnar legs coming his way. He caught flashes of the monster's face, saw the eyes squinted down to angry slits and the mouth that panted like a jungle cat's. When his prey was close enough, he jumped forward, triggering the cattle prod even as he tried to shove it through his target's broad chest. A few hundred volts of current sputtered through the vampire's chest, and he jittered in place, his muscles twitching and doing their own little dances before the prod broke skin and pushed into meat and bone.

Spike bared his fangs in a victorious grin.

And then the damned prod broke with a loud snap and a shower of sparks.

And then the giant got very, very angry.

Buffy staggered under another half dozen blows from the vampires all around her. This was not what she'd had planned when she got up that morning. This was nothing at all like her idea of a good time anymore. To make matters worse, Vampire Tara was smiling down on her, while Kakistos almost lovingly ran his misshapen paws over Tara's shoulders. She was acting as different from Tara as possible, and watching her with the ancient vampire was like watching Tara betray Willow. It hurt and it angered Buffy. It also made her want to cry, thinking of how badly she'd failed.

There was a commotion from not far away, clanging noises and screams loud enough to be heard over the sounds of her own combat. She hoped those sounds meant Spike was making progress, because there were still people dying in the room with her and she needed to hear some good news.

It was hard to free the prisoners and not get torn apart by the vampires around her, but she was doing her best. The problem was, trying to do it all at once was getting her slowly beaten to death.

Kakistos and Tara turned away, content to watch her die from a distance if they bothered to watch at all, and Buffy decided she could only handle one mission at a time. She needed the vampires off her before she could help anyone else. And having decided on a course of action, the Slayer executed it.

Buffy grabbed one of the feeding tubes and ripped it from its moorings, whipping it around her head like a chain and cutting loose on the vampires closest to her. The thick, razored tip of the tube slashed into undead flesh and left wounds that made all but the most suicidal back away from her. But that was really just a distraction. It was her feet that started doing the most damage. She slid across the floor unleashing a volley of kicks, each one breaking bones, while she continued to whip the cable around in a frenzy and used her free hand to defend herself from the majority of the blows.

A vampire grabbed her from behind and lifted her into the air. She rolled herself out of his arms and dropped to the ground behind him, driving her knee into his spine hard enough to break several vertebrae. He fell down, still trying to move, and Buffy used him as a stepping stool for better reach when she lashed out at the next one in line. Another threw a knife at her and she caught it, only realizing too late that it was a diversionary tactic. Even as her hand clutched the tip of the blade and she flipped it to catch the weapon by the hilt, she was tackled from behind.

Buffy rolled with the blow and all but bowling pinned another vampire, knocking her feet out from under her. She spun from her half-kneeling position and whipped her leg around in an arc that sent three vampires to the ground, to her level. The tubing in her hand shot out in a straight line and impaled the face of a surly-looking soldier-type. A few of the vampires got smart and started backing away, probably feeling they could get away from her and Kakistos both if they played their cards right.

She finally felt like she was starting to get the upper hand. Buffy climbed to her feet and several more vampires stepped away, yielding before her as she whipped her new weapon around again and planted the dagger deep in the heart of another of their ilk. The dagger didn't cause a proper death, but if the screams were any indication, it hurt a lot.

She never saw the spear coming until it sliced through her side. If she hadn't been in motion, the oversized weapon might well have pinned her to the floor. Buffy grabbed it without thinking, working purely on instinct, and swung it in an arc around her body that knocked several more of the undead away from her. She used the sharpened point to impale the vampire she'd already stabbed in the chest and watched him crumble into dust.

Buffy barely had time to prepare, but she got into a defensive stance just as Kakistos came charging, knocking his own minions out of the way to get to her. Buffy ducked and pistoned out with her left arm while hauling back with her right. The tip of the spear caught the elder vampire across the chest, but he turned his body enough to avoid being impaled. His right hand snapped the spear in two. His left hand punched Buffy in the face hard enough to send her through the air and to leave her seeing fireworks for a moment.

She was regaining her feet when the door exploded not five feet from her, increasing the noise factor a dozenfold as a wet and dusty Spike came sailing past her amid a shower of wood. Something that looked like a hairless Sasquatch came after him, plowing through what remained of the doorway and bellowing like an angry bear.

Spike came up fast, his face bloodied and his expression promising pure murder. Buffy threw half of her broken spear in his direction and called his name. He plucked the makeshift javelin out of the air and charged the mountain of flesh heading toward him with an inarticulate cry of his own.

Spike's stake rammed completely through the giant's chest, and the oversized vampire staggered backward, his body crumbling into dust even as he fell. Buffy spun hard, throwing her own half of the spear at Kakistos, who looked at her with wide eyes, realizing that he couldn't get away before the missile cut him down.

And even as Buffy allowed herself a small smile at the thought of his dying, Kakistos vanished. The room shifted and Buffy felt as if her body was being pulled through thick gelatin for an instant before the darkness came back. She blinked her eyes, looking around at the abandoned warehouse, the dust thick on the floor, the scuffmarks in the layers of dirt on the ground from when she'd been there earlier.

The only other thing in the room that was moving was Spike, who had a look on his face that she was sure mirrored her own puzzled expression—give or take the fang face.

"Whoa." Yep. That pretty much covered her witty repartee at the moment.

Spike looked at her, his bestial eyes gleaming in the almost-darkness. "Now there's something you don't see every day."

Chapter Five

Willow and Tara looked at the remains of Sunnydale High School in the darkness and Willow couldn't help but shudder. The things she'd witnessed at her alma mater were still with her, and sometimes, in the darkness, they chilled her blood.

Directly ahead of them a seething, twisted meteor storm of small red lights moved slowly, leading them deeper into the ruins. Tara's hand touched Willow's and she sighed softly, grateful for the touch, even if Tara didn't realize that the contact meant so much.

"Wow, Willow. I can't believe how well this locator spell is working. This kind of magick is usually so unreliable."

Willow nodded her agreement before realizing

Tara was looking around instead of at her. "Maybe it has something to do with what we're looking for? Half of magick is passion."

Tara squeezed her hand playfully, a curl to her lip, her eyes half-lidded. "You can say that again."

Willow blushed. It wasn't often that Tara made her blush in that way, but it happened now and then. And it was nice. Tara was always surprising her. "I just mean, 'cause, y'know, nothing's more important to me right now than finding Xander. That gives the spell some major juju."

"I know, honey." Tara's hand squeezed more for comfort, a subtle change in their non-verbal communication that said all Willow needed to hear without even a whisper passing Tara's perfect lips.

They moved into the darkened halls, the only light coming from the stars above and the glowing comet trails of the locator spell. There was little wind, and almost no noise from the odd scraps of paper that rustled in the ruined school. Tara's hand tightened slightly again, this time her body language, even the feel of her grip was a warning.

"W-we're not alone."

"I know. I can sense . . . something. Maybe some things."

Tara nodded. "I don't know what they are, I can't see them, but I can feel their presence and I don't like it."

"Okay, we need to set up shop." Willow looked around and led Tara through a door into what had once been the Computer Science classroom. Back when she'd become a teacher for a few months. "Like we discussed, let's see what we can do to keep this neat and clean."

With a simple incantation, they barred the door. It slammed shut solidly and little less than a bulldozer was going to open it until one of them decided it was time.

Something bumped against the door, a sound not unlike a tennis ball bouncing against it. A second later another one struck, and then a volley of what sounded like a hundred impacts, all of them low to the ground and not hard enough to do more than make the wooden barrier shiver slightly.

"What are they, Willow?" Tara's voice was perfectly clear in Willow's head, but Tara never moved, her sweet face stayed calm and peaceful as Sleeping Beauty's. They were getting very good at sharing thoughts, feelings.

"I don't know, but I think one's coming in." To prove her point, the bottom of the door cracked with a sound like a gunshot and something dark and very, very fast darted into the room. It was also very, very small. Like the size of a rat, but running on two legs.

"You have just *got* to be kidding me." Willow shook her head.

Tara opened her eyes and looked at the tiny creature as it charged at them. "Willow! Goddess, what are they?"

For half a second Willow wondered what she meant by "they" but caught on when she saw the others pushing into the room. She groaned. Her heart beat faster at the thought of the tiny teeth and claws on the creatures.

"They're called Bakemono. We dealt with them a couple of years ago. They go from cute and cuddly to vicious faster than a cheerleader. Long story." The creatures' almost-round faces were lightly scaled and they had streaks of fine white hair that ran in lionlike manes around their heads. Their long bony fingers ended in wickedly hooked claws that would have been better suited to a jungle cat, but that Willow knew could cause a world of hurt when they started tearing into flesh. And their mouths were filled with enough teeth to give a shark a bad case of envy.

"I don't think we have time for a long story." The tiny shadowy forms swarmed through the broken door in a frenzy, and Willow stood up.

"Short version then. Nasty little things. Kinda goblin-esque. Where there's one, there's a hundred. Popular wisdom is, don't feed the Bakemono."

Willow cast a quick spell and the creatures flew back from her as if hit by a hurricane. Several of them hit the wall and broke in a dozen places. Others came back snarling.

The ones that sought to attack Tara bounced back, hurled by a gust of wind. "They're going to break through. I . . . I don't think we're up to this, sweetie. Neither of us is powerful enough."

"Not separately. But if the Unity Spell is working the right way—"

"You'll be able to siphon my magick to feed your own. We have to make it work, Willow." The connection that was already there seemed to grow stronger, though Willow would have thought that impossible.

"Are you sure? You'll be somewhat protected in the Fusion Sphere, but not completely. And when we're bonded—"

When Tara spoke again it was in her head, without the need to actually speak.

"It'll be more intimate than anything we've ever done. And you'll be protecting me. So what are you waiting for?"

They worked quickly, in a comfortable silence, as they set out what they needed for the spell they'd been practicing. As much as Willow could have spent every moment of every day simply touching Tara, there were times when it wasn't really appropriate, and this was one of them. If all worked the way they'd planned it, however, they could still be in contact, even from a distance. Even more importantly as far as Willow was concerned, Tara would remain safe throughout the spell.

They chanted, summoning their magickal power to them and feeling it surround them like a warm, comforting blanket.

When they spoke, it was in unison. "By the strength of the emanation of Kantu Yoray and the glory of Hecate, Queen of Night, let that of mine, be that of thine."

Their power, not one or the other, but both together, wrapped around and through them. When the incantation was finished, Willow looked to Tara and saw the glowing, purplish field that surrounded her. She whispered words in her mind, and Tara responded. Even a few feet apart, she felt Tara with her, beside her, and in her. It was wonderful, almost as nice as actually touching, and at the same time a thousand times more intimate than a kiss.

Willow looked at Tara, where she lay within that bubble of energy, and felt her heart swell with joy. "Do you have any idea how much I love you?"

Before Tara could answer, even in Willow's mind, one of the Bakemono landed on Willow's head, the tiny claws tearing frantically. Tara's presence inside her kept her calmer than she would have been otherwise. With an almost casual gesture, she cast a spell that blasted the tiny creature into dust.

"Okay, let's get this show on the road. I have a Xander to find." She looked back over her shoulder, saw Tara where she rested in a lotus position, and saw the fine purplish cord that adjoined them even as she moved to follow the glowing trail of the spell they'd cast to locate her best friend. She gestured and the door opened, spilling a seething mass of the creatures into the room. They hissed like snakes as they spilled over each other, eager to rend and tear at her flesh. Several swarmed past her to leap toward Tara, bouncing off the sphere around her.

Willow allowed herself a small smile, grateful that the protective spell was holding. Several small flashes of pain ran across her lower legs, and she looked down at the Bakemono who were doing their best to whittle her away, one bite at a time. And was it her imagination, or were they actually bigger than before? She couldn't say for sure, but they seemed bigger and that was enough to worry her, because at the size of mice, they were sort of cute and maybe a little dangerous, but any bigger and they would stop being sort of cute and just get lethal. One of the creatures bit deep into her calf and Willow stopped thinking about their looks and started working on getting rid of the creatures. Tara's mind was linked with hers and together they quickly found a simple spell for casting the creatures away in a hurry. With a few simple words and a two handed gesture she forced the tiny monsters back. Then she spoke again and the miniature demons exploded into balls of white-hot flame.

"I wish it was just this little batch, but I don't think they come in less than a zillion or so to a box."

She felt Tara smile, though she could no longer see her. As Willow started down the hallway—a hallway she'd walked a thousand times when the school was intact—she saw more of the small shapes slithering up the cinderblock walls, crawling like spiders, their almost delicate-looking claws punching holes into the cement with ease. Their eyes glittered in the faint light and they chittered, angry at the deaths of their kin and ravenous for the taste of flesh. Willow wanted to run. Even with Tara's presence inside her, she was afraid, there were just so many of the things. But the meteor storm of crimson lights was leading her through them to where she needed to be, to where Xander was.

Willow closed her eyes for a moment and then gestured, Tara's voice in her head matching the chant she uttered. From each fingertip a thin flash of electrical power lanced out to strike a Bakemono. And that same lightning leapt from the first of the demons it struck to caress another's scaly hide with enough power to blacken flesh and boil blood. The power might not have stopped a human-sized target, but it made crispy shells of the demons it struck. The sibilant noises the creatures made became shrieks of agony as they fell, and the ones who managed not to be struck by the spell slid backward warily, eyeing the witch with new respect for her abilities.

"Gonna have to find a new way to fight, fellas. Because I'm just getting started, and I don't think they make little rubber suits in your size." She lashed out with the same spell a second time and almost flinched as a dozen of the beasts fell to the ground, little more than blackened lumps. Tara kept saying that Willow was a powerful witch, but she'd never done anything like this without Tara's help before. She didn't even know for certain if the spell was one she or Tara had learned, or one that they created on the spot. Whatever the case, she knew they'd have to try to remember this one.

Willow stepped further down the hallway, watched as her location spell twisted down toward the remains of the library, where the Hellmouth lay, dormant for the moment. *Please let it be dormant. It needs to stay dormant, because I want this to just be a demon army, not the first wave of a really big demon invasion. Big Hellmouthy things not really on my plans for today. I have classes to study for, and that's just a little too much to handle if I want to get a good grade in Economics.* As she saw the tiny demons scattering before her, Willow allowed herself a small smile. It felt good to have the monsters on the run for a change.

And while she was thinking about how easily she'd gotten the demons on the move, the wall beside her groaned loudly and exploded into a shower of fast-moving missiles. Willow turned her head quickly and held out her hands, casting a warding spell without even truly having to think. Tara was with her, amplifying her power to a level that was almost intoxicating. The shattered concrete shrapnel that tore her way was cast aside, blasted into powder by the incantation, and Willow looked to where it had come from and saw only the gaping hole where the wall had been a moment before.

No, no other monsters or demony things from the Hellmouth. I said please *didn't I?*

Xander Harris groaned, most of him feeling like he'd been put through a taffy puller. The parts that didn't feel strained felt bruised. He opened his eyes in the darkness and immediately wished he hadn't. Wherever he was, it was dank, smelled of burnt plastic and wood, and was about as comfortable as resting on a bed of nails.

He sensed as much as saw the movement around him. There were small critters skittering over the debris and searching for something. While he studied their movements, he recalled the fight at the factory, remembered being grabbed by a couple of vampires and dragged away into a separate room. *Vampires. I really hate vampires. Also, not big on the whole Xander, the boy hostage deal.*

"Ahhh . . . I see you're awake."

Xander knew the voice. It was smarmy and reeked of confidence. He kept hoping he'd never have to hear it again, but like a bad grade on an algebra test, it just kept popping back up. And the association with a failed math quiz let him realize where he was. The gritty tiled floor, the ruined furniture and smell of burnt remains scattered around him. "Oh crap. I'm at the school and Ethan Rayne is here with me."

"Very good, Xander. You have a keen sense for the obvious."

"Yeah, well, obvious for you. Aren't you supposed to be in a federal penitentiary?" He tried to sit up and felt the reason why his body felt like it was strained so badly. He had ropes tied around his ankles and wrists, and they in turn were apparently tied to each other. Xander looked around and saw Ethan's legs not too far off to the right. Judging by the directions of the toes, the man was looking right at him. Xander couldn't quite strain his neck high enough to be sure.

"That's hardly a concern right now, lad. What's far more important is that you give me the information I need."

"Sure, because I always like telling the bad guys everything they need to know. It just makes life so much easier for Buffy and the rest of us."

Ethan chuckled, his voice moving in the near darkness, his shoes sliding out of view. "Relax, Xander. I'd hate to have to resort to torture."

"No, you wouldn't. You'd love to resort to torture."

"True enough. But I don't really have the time to enjoy it. There's already someone else here, and I really should take care of the interruption."

"Well, don't let me stop you. Just go on ahead and take care of your other business."

"All in good time. First though, I'm a little puzzled. Why are you here?"

"Because some vampires grabbed me and took me away from the fight." He rolled over until he could look at Ethan. The man smiled down at him. "What? You were expecting me to be Buffy?"

"No. Actually, I was expecting you to be the werewolf boy. Oz, isn't it?"

Xander frowned. *Oz? What does Ethan Rayne want with Oz?* "Sorry, no werewolves around these parts. Oz went off to inner bad dog obedience training."

"I sent them to get Buffy's male friend. I never expected they'd grab *you.*" He shrugged, completely ignoring Xander's indignant noise. "Well then, I guess you'll just have to take his place." There were very faint sounds coming from above their heads, and Ethan frowned as he looked toward the ruined ceiling above.

"'Take his place?' In what? Because unless it's the contest to see who can kick your butt the best, I'm really not interested."

"In my army, actually." Ethan looked down at him again and then scowled. "Oh, damn. I think it's your friend Willow up there. I'll have to get back to you."

"Willow? Here? What's Willow doing here?" Xander struggled to right himself and had half-managed it when he heard the loud hisses from all around him. He stopped and looked around, noticing that the little mouse-things he'd seen shuffling around earlier were all looking his way. Even now they were barely more than dark spots in the shadows, but their eyes glittered in a very non-mousy sort of way. *Oh this is just getting better. Ethan has an army of trained demon mice with him.*

"Try not to get into too much trouble, Xander. The Bakemono have orders to restrain you. They probably won't kill you, but I never said they couldn't take a taste or two of your flesh."

Xander groaned. *Okay, that's worse than the demon mice. Those little creeps have some serious claws.* He stopped moving and felt a sharp edge press against his wrists. Something behind him could very possibly be used to his advantage. He moved just his arms, feeling the sharpness scrape his forearm until it caught at the bindings holding him in place. Then he started rubbing as softly as he could, hoping whatever was back there would slice the fibers of the rope instead of just an artery or two.

Ethan looked down at him and flashed that used-car salesman smile of his. "Do behave, Xander. I'll be back for you soon." The man turned away and moved toward the left, out of Xander's view. A second or so later he heard Ethan start climbing a set of stairs.

Xander waited for a few moments, his eyes taking in the positions of the tiny demons that surrounded him. Then he began to saw more diligently at the ropes around his wrists.

Around him the shadowy forms hissed and murmured, but none of them moved. Not yet, at least.

Willow kept waiting for the big, nasty demon thing to come out of the wall, her mind flashing back to the times in the past when she'd been witness to some of the horrors waiting on the other side of the Hellmouth. Something big and slimy should have been coming out of the hole and making the sorts of noises that turned hair white, but so far nothing. The Bakemono hadn't blown out the wall. She was certain of that if nothing else. They didn't have that sort of power, unless they'd hidden it from every researcher ever to write about them.

The ground bulged beneath her, swelling into unnatural shapes and closing around her body like a fist. Thick Linoleum and concrete fingers wrapped around her body, or tried to, but were held at bay by the ward she'd cast with Tara. "If it isn't the Bakemono, then what is it, Willow?" Tara's voice was in her head, her soul, and seemed to be both Tara's and hers alike, the two different voices melded perfectly into one amalgamation. She could sense Tara's body where it lay a few yards and two walls away. The tiny demons were trying to reach her lover but failing. That was good. That was better than good.

"I don't know, honey, but I'm going to find out." She forced the ground away from her, back to where it belonged, though the end result was hardly smooth and natural. Willow pushed on, seeking the source of whatever attacked her, but saw nothing save more of the Bakemono.

This time when another attack came, it was direct. A searing white lightning blast ripped down the hallway and bullwhipped across the walls in her direction. The demons that remained on the walls leaped down away from the roaring current as if expecting it. The cinderblocks blackened and exploded in a long stream of carnage that ran crazily toward Willow, and she countered the deadly bolt with a shield of her own even as the ward she'd created was blown away.

"Somebody's gonna get hurt if they don't show up really soon, and I mean it." She tried to sound confident, even still felt a little cocky, to be honest, but that last one had frazzled her nerves. Fighting demons was what Buffy did, and she made it look easy. Willow Rosenberg was not quite sure if she was up to it, even with Tara at her side. Still, Tara's presence was comforting.

"Now, now, child. No reason to get nasty about this." The voice was familiar, and it only took a second to recognize the source when he stepped forward into the hallway, still a dozen feet from her.

"Ethan Rayne!" He smiled at her, almost like a teacher with a favored student. Ethan Rayne was handsome in a sinister way, an old friend of Rupert Giles back in his early years, back before he decided to dedicate himself to the Watcher's Council and his duties as a Watcher. When Giles had been her age he'd dabbled in a lot of dark magicks, things he'd rather forget about and that he tried his best not to let anyone know of. Ethan had been his friend in those days. The difference was, Ethan still played with things best left alone. He'd given himself over to the worship of chaos and did all he could to bring disorder and mayhem to the world, wherever he went. The worse the situation, the happier Ethan was.

He'd been a problem for Buffy and the Slayerettes

several times and normally managed to get away by
sheer cunning and duplicity. The last time he'd been
taken away by the Initiative. Willow had thought for
sure they'd never see him again.

"Hello, little sorceress. You've grown far more
powerful since last I saw you." He stalked closer, his
smile so innocent and charming. Willow wanted nothing to do with it. She knew him for what he was and
would just as soon have seen him turned into a turnip.

"You have no idea, Ethan." It sounded good, and
with Tara at her side she felt almost invincible. That
was one of the problems with magick: It could be
heady stuff. She had to remind herself of that from
time to time.

"I'm pleased." He stepped closer and she held her
ground, searching for the best spells to deal with him.

"What? It makes you happy that the witch is
going to kick your uptight, English, magick-dabbling,
chaos-worshipping butt?" *There. That sounded properly confident.*

"Sticks and stones, my dear." He stopped moving,
only a few feet away, his eyes glimmering with amuse-
ment, as if he knew the punch line for a joke that she
had never even heard. "Now, let's find out precisely
how powerful you've become."

"Not a problem." Willow shrugged and followed
through immediately with a spell that sent shock waves
running through the air. The Bakemono were thrown
like leaves in a tornado, tossed about and bounced off
the floor and walls. Ethan Rayne merely smiled and
countered with his own ward.

And then the fireworks began in earnest. Tara's voice was not really a separate thing anymore. Willow and Tara merged together into one sentience, or at least that was what it felt like. Ethan cast out another lightning blast that carved the ceiling and walls and floor into new and interesting patterns. Willow cast it aside, blowing away a section of wall in the process, and countered with a fireball that seared the air and left the combatants partially blinded. *When did he start being able to do that? I mean, he's never been big into the whole storm-at-my-fingertips sort of stuff.* Ethan struck again, this time sending shadowy, serpentine things her way that struck hard enough to cut her skin, even through her shields.

Willow lashed out without much thought, almost instinctively seeking the best method to hurt the sorcerer, and once again cast the chain lightning she'd used on the small demons. The bolts of energy danced around her enemy, circling him, bouncing against the wards he used to defend himself and then arching back to strike again and again. While he backed away, confused and scalded by the assault, she threw another at him, this time simply causing a sudden torrential rainfall to soak his skin, even as the lightning lashed against him. *Water and electricity are always a good combination, provided you don't mind frying.*

Ethan staggered back, the water soaking his clothes and the electrical discharges blasting against his shields, illuminating the air around him until she could physically see what normally she'd have only noticed with her awareness of magick. The invisible shields flared with the lightning, and she watched them begin to crumble.

Ethan staggered further away, and it was only when she turned the corner that she saw the wicked grin on his face. He winked at her, *winked*! And then he was gone.

And the remaining Bakemono attacked as one unit, having used the distraction to position themselves. They dropped from the ceiling, they ran from the shadows and clawed madly, tearing at her battered defenses and overwhelming her senses with the loud shrieks and chattering sounds of their teeth clashing together. A dozen, then a score and then what felt like a hundred of the tiny demons tore at her, cutting clothes and skin alike with tiny savage slashes. She felt like she was taking a razor blade shower, the small cuts stinging and irritating more than actually incapacitating her.

Willow staggered. There seemed to be hundreds of them, though a part of her said that was impossible. They weren't very heavy one on one, but after a while the weight added up. She might have actually fallen down and given up or lost herself to panic, but Xander was depending on her, and Tara's presence within her mind was a soothing balm.

Willow pushed and shoved, trying to get a little room to maneuver for anything at all, but they were everywhere. A clawed hand caught her bottom lip and pulled, eliciting a scream of pain.

This time when she retaliated, the creatures were thrown back as if she were a grenade. They slammed into the walls and pulped there, leaking blackish fluids as they fell lifeless to the ground. Several of the ones that had not yet reached her were wounded but only seemed more determined to tear her apart. It was easy to feel cocky when it was one on one or even several on one as long as someone was watching your back. Now, with what seemed almost like an army of the little things tearing at her and—yes, one of them was actually eating what it had torn from her leg—biting in a frenzy, it wasn't quite as cool.

Tara's voice buzzed in her mind, but she couldn't make out the words, she was too busy having a panic attack. When it was just her alone, Willow seemed to flounder. She kicked madly with her legs, more like an aerobic instructor trying to run in place than anyone trying to cause damage, but it worked. Her legs thrashed and threw the Bakemono through the air. Her arms slapped at the creatures covering her body, swatting some aside and knocking others off their perches. But they kept coming, chomping their razored little teeth and snarling in rage. Blood flowed over her arms and body in small streams from a hundred bite marks and cuts. And the whole world seemed to reduce down to a tunnel of the Bakemonos' writhing flesh and glistening eyes.

It's very possible she would have died if the wall hadn't crumbled not far away. Not the wall nearest her, for that probably would have only added to her panic. No, the wall that fell was adjoining the hallway. It was the wall in the Computer Science lab where she'd once taught and been calmer, even in the midst of insanity— had she been happier? No, not really, but she had been

with someone who loved her then, even if that someone had left her a while later—the wall in the room
where Tara waited, trying to calm her down and steady
her in the midst of the obscene danger of the tiny
demons.

She saw through Tara's eyes, felt with Tara's body
as the cinderblock barrier fell inward like a gigantic
hand and slapped down on her. She heard the sound of
the roof of that room collapsing in and falling on Tara
with her own ears and with Tara's as well. And then her
connection to Tara was gone.

"Tara."

For one heartbeat, she felt the world grow cold and
dark.

"Tara?"

The presence that had been in her head was gone,
the warm comforting soul that had been joined with
her by their spell was no longer holding her, touching
her, comforting her even in this horrid moment. Her
heart thudded to a stop and then kicked into overdrive.

"Tara!"

And then she was calm again, her heart filled with
a far deeper terror than the one that had frozen her in
place, but Willow's mind worked again, because it was
Tara in trouble now, not just Willow Rosenberg.

Willow made a gesture and again blew the Bakemono back from her. This time, they caught aflame as
they sailed through the air. Her power was like a
nuclear blast barely contained, barely held in check,
and later she would think about how good it felt, but
for now her only concern was Tara. The demons died

by the dozen, shrieking mindlessly as their bodies were blasted into so much powder.

Willow rose from the ground and cast the wreckage of the ruined hallway aside with even less effort than the demons, knocking papers, soot, ash, and lockers away with casual ease. The wall near the door she and Tara had sealed had fallen inward, covering the very spot where her lover, her reason for living, was supposed to be safe and sound, protected by the powerful ward they'd created. Had she time to think, Willow would have known there was nothing she could do about the cement and mortar and ruined metal that now covered the floor of the room. She didn't take the time to consider, she merely acted. Willow called her power and forced her will upon the debris before her. Thousands of pounds of manmade stone and steel containers sailed away, hurled to the sides of the room with enough force to further strain the walls and shatter the rubbish.

She looked at where Tara had been, where she still was. Tara looked at her, the magickal sphere of protection wavering, faltering, and finally collapsing around her. Another minute and Tara would have been crushed.

"Tara!" She slid across the cleared, damaged floor, pulling at her lover, hauling her into a sitting position and wrapping her arms around Tara before the other girl could even fully realize that she was no longer in danger of being crushed. "Oh, baby . . . Oh, sweetheart, I thought I'd lost you." Willow tried to calm herself on the verge of tears, Ethan Rayne and the little demons forgotten in her overwhelming relief at seeing

Tara. Her vision fractured amid a sting of tears, but she held it in, doing her best to be brave.

Tara's sweet face smiled at her, wide blue eyes almost completely peaceful, her skin pale and marred by three scrapes over her cheek and chin. "I knew you'd get to me, Willow. I knew I'd be okay." She touched Willow's face with her lips and pulled back enough to look into Willow's eyes again. "I'm always safe with you."

From out in the hallway they heard a clattering noise and a grunt. The sound was alien, the voice was one she'd heard a zillion times, it seemed. It was the throaty note Xander made when he was frustrated and ready to scream.

Tara stood up, dusting herself off and moving toward the hallway with that tilt to her head so much like a startled fawn trying to see what might be happening. She had only made half a step through what remained of the threshold when Xander came into sight, looking battered and bruised but intact.

He carried a two-by-four in his hand that had either been soaked in black-green paint or was covered in Bakemono blood. Considering that the art department had been completely leveled by the after-graduation activities the year before, Willow was pretty sure it wasn't paint.

"Yeah, you better run!" He waved his club after a few small, fleeing shapes. One of the Bakemono made an obscene gesture before vanishing into the darkness. Xander looked at Tara and Willow, his dark eyes showing more concern than the rest of his face. Willow looked at Tara's arm and saw the blood flowing down from the back of her shoulder. She moved to Tara's side in an instant. Tara winced, finally realizing that she was hurt now that the adrenaline was wearing off.

Xander stepped closer. "Are you two all right?"

Tara looked from her arm to his face and smiled shyly. "I messed up my shoulder. I think I'll be all right."

"But you're gonna have it looked at." Willow put on her serious face, trying not to let her happiness that two of the people who were most important to her in the world were alive stop her from looking determined and in control.

Tara smiled, her face lighting up and her eyes saying that she would play by Willow's rules. But also saying that she too was happy everyone was mostly unharmed. "Definitely." Her eyes studied Willow and her smile grew more subtle, almost shy and almost dirty at the same time. "So that . . . that Unity Spell. It was nice."

Willow smiled and rested her forehead against Tara's looking deep into those perfect eyes. "Very."

Then Xander did his usual guy thing and broke the mood. Okay, so he was right, but it still sucked. "Hold off on the unity a sec, guys. Not that I don't appreciate the rescue, cuz I do, but what's going on?" He jerked a thumb over his shoulder and shifted his grip on the club in his other hand. "I mean, what's Ethan Rayne doing here? What's he got to do with *any* of this?

Willow looked his way and nodded three times. "A fine question . . . to which we have no answer. Not yet, anyway."

Tara nodded too, but with less enthusiasm. "But we will."

"Well, here's a clue for you and Velma, Daphne." Xander looked at Willow and shook his head and dropped the club, rubbing at his wrists which were chafed raw from where he'd been bound before escaping. "Our good buddy Ethan said something about wanting me, now that Oz was out of the scene." Willow blinked, taken aback by the mention of her ex. "I don't know what he wants me for, but then I'm just here for my looks and muscle. You're the detective." He was grinning as he said it, but it was that puzzled grin that said he was just taking the sting out of the bad news.

Chapter Six

Buffy looked around the Magic Box, astounded by how quickly Giles and Anya had managed to put the place back together again. Oh, there were still signs of a struggle, but aside from the counter that had been covered with particle board where the glass had been, it could have been just another day. She sipped at a cup of coffee and looked over at Giles. His face was strained and tired, but almost always looked strained and tired.

Spike was looking around the place and trying to pretend that he was bored instead of sore. But Buffy could see how he was favoring his left leg, and it was hard to miss the swelling around his left cheek. Anya was sitting near Giles, her face worried, and probably about the exact same thing that Buffy was fretting over. Willow, Tara, and Xander.

Giles spoke up, standing and moving to the coffeemaker. "So, what are your plans now, Buffy?" She'd already filled them in on the Blood Factory.

"Well, first we have to figure out why the factory became a blood bottling place, and then we have to figure out how it just disappeared."

Anya nodded and raised one hand. "I might have an idea about that." Buffy and everyone else present looked at her in silence until she volunteered the rest. "Back when I was a vengeance demon and answered Cordelia's wish that you'd never come to Sunnydale, there was an old vampire who'd pretty much taken over the town, and from what you described, it sounds like what you encountered was almost exactly what he was creating."

"A blood factory?"

"Exactly." Anya nodded. "I think it might not be the Kakistos you knew before, Buffy, and I think that the factory changing around you might be a sign that there is something very big at work here. The Hellmouth is a permanent weakness between the dimensions, but it sounds like what you encountered—with the strange blood plant and maybe even the vampiric Tara—might be a direct result of dimensional bleedthrough."

Giles nodded, his brow furrowed. "That does rather make sense. It explains how Sid and Kakistos could both be back and why Willow and Tara's attempts to discover a resurrection spell for Kakistos were inconclusive. There is a Kakistos running around, but not necessarily the one you encountered with Faith in the past."

Anya scowled slightly. "That's what I just said. Dimensional bleed-through."

Giles stood up and started moving toward the stacks. "I have heard of such things, but they are almost never random events. So the question now is what could have caused this bleed-through."

"A vengeance demon." Anya looked over smugly. "Not that I'm saying it is a vengeance demon, only that I was certainly powerful enough in my day. Also, it could have been a spell cast by a witch who didn't know better. I seem to recall a little problem with a vampiric Willow a while back."

Buffy waved her hands. "Let's get back on track, people. Giles, why don't you see what might be behind this. Spike was going to hit some of the vampire hang-outs, see if he could get a line on Kakistos, figure out how all these vamps are getting into Sunnydale without either one of us being aware of it." She set down her now empty coffee cup and crossed her arms. If she kept moving she could pretend her body didn't already hurt as much as it really did. "And humor me here, let's go over this bleed-through thingie one more time. You said you had theories. Let's hear 'em."

Giles nodded. He set down his freshly filled mug and took off his glasses to clean them, though they were already immaculate. "We've examined every possibility for vampiric resurrection, and Kakistos fits none of the criteria. There are very few ways to bring a vampire back from the dead, but all of them apply only in cases where the bones of the deceased remain after they have been slain. The only time I've seen such a thing was when you killed The Master. But when Faith killed Kakistos, there were no bones. Only dust. There's simply no way he could have been resurrected."

Buffy nodded. "Okay, but you do remember how he's been trying to kill me all night?"

"You might have mentioned it once or twice."

Anya stood up and walked over to where Buffy and Giles were standing. She looked exasperated, which, when Buffy thought about it, was often how the ex-demon looked. "Giles just doesn't want to tell you that his big theory is actually *my* theory."

Giles sighed heavily and shook his head. "I'm sure you haven't forgotten the visit we had from Willow's vampiric doppelganger. We owe that wonderful brush with alternate dimensions to Anya."

Anya managed to suddenly look very defensive and simultaneously proud of her past efforts. "Yay me!" She looked at Buffy and shrugged dismissively. "Well, maybe *you* weren't thinking yay me. But if I hadn't been trying to get my powers back, and brought evil, skanky, vampire Willow into this dimension by accident, we would all be completely lost in this conversation right now."

Sometimes it frightened Buffy that she could understand the woman's logic. "You're such the team player." She looked away from Anya and over to Giles, who had put his glasses back on again. "So, what then? We're dealing with alternate-dimension Kakistos?"

"Our research certainly turned up plenty of precedent for 'dimensional bleed.'"

The door to the Magic Box opened, the bell ringing clearly, and everyone inside turned at the same time. Willow came through the door, her arm around Tara, who walked stiffly and had her arm in a brace. Xander came in behind them.

Xander nodded his greeting to everyone, his face wearing a grin that was worthy of the Mona Lisa. Buffy felt her heart relax a bit, felt the tension slip from between her shoulder blades. "What was that about bleeding? Seems to be a lot of that going around."

Anya was past Buffy in a flash and wrapped her arms around Xander. He got a pleasantly surprised look on his face, as if he was still puzzled, even after all of this time, as to why a woman as attractive as Anya would be interested in him.

"You're not dead!" Anya's voice went up half an octave and for that moment she seemed like nothing more than a young woman who was truly, deeply relieved to see her boyfriend. "I . . . I knew it all the time."

Xander hugged her back, closing his eyes for a moment and savoring the feel of Anya against him. "I'm glad one of us did." He looked over Anya's shoulder to Giles. "Okay, so what's the what?"

Buffy looked his way. "Blurring of the lines between dimensions, Kakistos and Sid actually from other realities . . . blah blah . . . Star Trek . . . blah."

"Check. Thanks for the update."

Giles looked at Willow and Tara. "Tara, are you all right? What's happened?"

Tara nodded and smiled wanly. "I will be. With some rest. And immediate medical attention."

Willow hugged her girlfriend more tightly for an instant and looked around at everyone in the room, even Spike, who was still looking bored. "It wasn't vampires who sneakily absconded with Xander. It was a bunch of stinky Bakemono. And who put 'em up to it?" She got a pouty, indignant look on her face. "Three guesses. Okay, it was Ethan Rayne."

Buffy scowled. "Ethan? What does that oily little snake have to do with this?"

Giles shook his head and raised his eyes to the heavens. "My head hurts."

Willow frowned. "I got the feeling he was testing me, but I don't have the first clue why."

"Could . . . could he be responsible for all of this?" That was Tara, sounding weak and a little worried.

Giles shook his head again, looking directly at Tara. "It's doubtful. This would be an enormous leap forward for Ethan. He's never had this kind of power. I can't imagine his presence is mere coincidence, but if he's involved, it's likely as clown rather than ringmaster."

Xander nodded agreement. "Not to mention, wasn't he in federal custody last time we knew?"

Anya shrugged. "Maybe it's an alternate-reality version of Ethan?"

Buffy groaned. "And now *my* head hurts."

Giles shook his head. "I wouldn't put anything past Ethan Rayne. He's beyond merely crafty, as he's already proven on several occasions. Besides which, with the Initiative disbanded, at least as far as we know, it's possible he was lost in the paperwork shuffle. That's precisely the sort of chaos that Ethan has always taken advantage of."

Buffy looked to Tara and frowned a bit. "Tara, if you were off with Willow, I guess that means you didn't happen to pop by that warehouse where you did the 'Where's Kakistos' spell earlier?"

"No. I was with Willow the whole . . . oh no. Please don't tell me. Alternate-reality Tara?"

"Looks like." Buffy was relieved. She had been trying in the back of her mind to figure out how to breach the whole vampire Tara thing and now she didn't really have to. At least not in the Guess-I-better-stake-Willow's-girlfriend sort of way.

Willow interjected. "Okay, hello. Brain not going there. I'm getting Tara to a doctor."

"There's nothing more to be done this evening. I think we all need some rest at this point." As always, Giles was the voice of reason.

Buffy nodded and moved closer to Willow and Tara. "I'm with you. Pretty soon this place'll be just a hotbed of crankiness. Let's meet back here in the morning and we'll start a search for Ethan, see if we can't force these puzzle pieces together."

"Agreed. I just need to fill one last mail order." Giles moved back toward the counter, ready to fill out the appropriate paperwork.

"You go ahead. I'll wait and walk you home. I don't think any of us should be alone right now. There are too many enemies out there. Too many things we don't understand yet."

Xander put one arm around Anya, who promptly snuggled in closer. "Everyone just be careful." He and Anya left a moment later, taking Willow and Tara with them. It was off to the hospital for a check up.

Giles grabbed up the papers and moved to the table where all of the latest tomes were set out for speedy research. "All right. I'll just be a moment."

"I'm not going anywhere." Buffy settled herself against the counter and crossed her arms. Spike slid out the door, looking her way for a second but not saying anything. She did her best to pretend he wasn't there.

Giles took his papers and moved them again, this time toward the basement. He muttered something that Buffy didn't hear and descended. The words were obviously meant for his own ears. It was something he did when he was thinking and she'd grown used to it over the last few years of her life.

He closed the door behind him. Spike had closed the door as well. For a moment, Buffy stood in the silence and rested her eyes. She opened them again when she heard the sound of someone moving nearby, felt that strange pull she'd experienced before at the warehouse.

She turned, stifling a yawn that quickly became a small gasp of surprise. Kakistos was standing ten feet away. The door had not been opened; she'd have heard the bell ring its usual alarm. But the ancient vampire stood there just the same, a handful of underlings with him, each and every one of them looking prepared for hunting and killing a Slayer or two.

Kakistos smiled, an unpleasant sight at the best of times and certainly not heart warming under the current circumstances. "Hello again, Slayer. Just a quick visit to satisfy my curiosity." He stepped a little toward her and Buffy slid her hands to her sides, two fingers catching the edge of the stake in the back of her pants. "I've been wondering, you see, how well you would function without your Watcher."

Buffy felt herself slide into a combat ready stance, arms loose and relaxed, legs slightly bent and her weight shifting to the balls of her feet. At the same time she looked around the room noticing that Giles was not, in fact, present. He'd already descended to the basement.

She shook her head. "What are you talking about, Hoof-Boy? Giles is fine. He's in the basement."

Kakistos did that creepy-smarmy used car salesman with a surefire gimmick smile of his again, and Buffy felt her skin crawl as he spoke.

"Yes. He is in the basement. And he isn't alone."

Having spoken, Kakistos just faded away, like a ghost in a bad TV movie. His minions, unfortunately, stayed there, solid and deadly as ever.

The first one slid in fast, a skilled martial artist with a gait that said he was prepared to defend himself and kill the Slayer. His right foot shot out and snapped a flurry of blows at Buffy's head and chest which she was obligated to defend against. She ducked the first strike at her face, blocked the second kick which would have likely caved in her ribcage, and slapped his leg to the side as the third kick tried for her sternum. The return blow left the vampire marginally off balance, and as he tried to correct for the sudden change in his body's center of gravity, she slammed the stake through his chest.

As he faded into little more than graveyard dust, she moved through where he had been a second before and shattered the jaw of the next vampire in line. Even with a broken face, this one was tough enough to make it count. While he fell back he used his own momentum and landed a perfect snap kick into her stomach, lifting Buffy off the ground and launching her through the air. She hit the wall behind the counter and sent several fertility statues and jars of rare herbs to the ground as so much ammunition for the garbage pail. Several pieces of pottery cut deeply into her back as she fell in an avalanche of store goods gone bad.

Half of a statue of a rotund Babylonian goddess came up with her and struck Mister Broken-Face in the skull. This time he stayed down. Buffy came over the counter and into the waiting arms of a vampire that had more muscles than brains. As he tried to capture her in a bear hug, she brought her hand in low and pierced his ribcage and heart with a blow she felt all the way up to her elbow.

The next of the vampires came in swinging a thick chain. He knew how to use it, and made his point by cracking the thick links against the Slayer's shins. The chain wrapped three times around her legs and she grunted as the demon hauled back, sending her down to the ground and reeling her toward him like a prize catch. As he started lifting her off the floor by her bound legs, Buffy threw her stake and caught him in the throat. He dropped her quickly, gasping as a wash of cold blood gouted from the wound. Buffy caught the chain and yanked it closer, whipping it around hard to give her legs some slack. Another of the vampires tried to grab her at that moment and got all the fingers on his right hand broken for his efforts. While he was still screaming profanities, she looped the chain around his neck and pulled the links tight. He was crumbling into dust by the time his head fell away from the rest of his body. Buffy took another kick to her ribcage as she ripped the stake from the throat of the one who was coughing blood. She fell forward, catching herself on the palms of her hands and kicked him back into the wall. The vampire fell unconscious and heavily wounded.

That left two vampires for her to fight and only one of them was paying her any attention. The girl was big and brawny, probably the sort that lifted small cars for exercise, but she was also fast. Before engaging the Slayer, she pulled a wickedly sharp rapier from a sheath across her back. Buffy nodded and hooked the chain with her foot. The vampire slid forward, thrusting at Buffy's face. Buffy hopped back, kicking the chain up high enough to catch.

While the female sword fighter was circling her warily, Buffy saw the last of the group, a thin, gaunt male with hair as white as snow, whispering and gesturing. Whatever he was up to, it couldn't be a good sign. She didn't really practice magick, but she knew enough to catch a clue when a practitioner was up to no good.

"Giles! I think I've got trouble up here!" Buffy dodged fast, narrowly missing a serious problem with a sword up her nose, and swung one end of the chain in an arc that bullwhipped across the vampire's stomach. The woman hissed as the chain battered her and staggered her, but she kept the sword and cut Buffy across the forearm as she was backing up.

The thinner, paler vampire smiled and nodded. Buffy heard a rough grating sound and tried to look around, but the chick with the saber distracted her by putting a new cut across her midriff. From somewhere down below, Giles called out that he was a trifle busy just at the moment.

Zorro's undead cousin wasn't going to leave well enough alone, and Buffy turned all her attention to the sword-wielding maniac. The girl grinned at her, baring an impressively wide set of fangs, and moved in for the kill. One of the many things Buffy had learned under Giles's tutelage was that a good chain was practically the natural enemy of a good sword. A sword was meant for cutting and thrusting. It's only as effective as its edge, unless you're dealing with a heavy weapon. The rapier was not a heavy sword and it was meant for quick, efficient thrusts. Buffy whipped the chain around sword girl's elbow and flicked her wrist like a jump roper. The chain rattled and clacked as it spun from the point where it wrapped around the vampire's elbow and looped itself up her forearm and over the length of the rapier. While the vampire was looking genuinely puzzled by the move, Buffy hauled hard on the chain and yanked the vampire straight at her. Before the girl could change the direction of where the sword was going and use it to her advantage, Buffy had stepped aside. The vampire hit the counter and shattered the plywood where it had replaced the glass façade. Buffy gave another tug that pulled the girl back toward her and planted her foot squarely in the vampire's back. The girl's spine snapped with a sound like a branch giving way. Buffy finished her quickly.

And turned to face the pale, older vampire, who smiled at her, arms crossed over his narrow chest.

"What are *you* smiling about?"

He tilted his head a little, dark eyes staring at her. Unlike many vampires, he hadn't changed his face from its human appearance. "My friends are going to beat you to death."

"What friends?" She asked, but just knew she wasn't going to like the answer. And she was right too. The two massive stone gargoyles at the front of the Magic Box turned their heads at the same time with a grating noise. The heavy brows of their foreheads crunched down into angry furrows and their stone eyes suddenly flared with an inner light. They moved, stepping from the short pedestals they had perched on since they were created, and headed toward Buffy, lowering down into crouches as they lumbered forward.

"Oh," she said in a very small voice. "*Those* friends."

The first of the two granite beasts swung a sharp taloned claw at her head and narrowly missed as she flipped back away from the attack. Heavy granite claws cut four deep trenches into the floor where she had been a second before. The thing hissed at her and lunged again. Buffy moved fast, heading for the high ground in an effort to find a good weapon to use against the beasts.

She fairly flew over the ladder until she reached the loft. Unfortunately for her, the huge gargoyles had wings, and even if they weren't big enough to support the weight of the stone demons, they were enough to give them a little boost. The second gargoyle looked at her and grinned, baring heavy gray fangs. It flapped its wings as it jumped and carried itself to the second floor loft, breaking through the banister to get there.

"Oh, crap." The thing stomped across the ground, the weight of its body shaking the flooring and almost throwing Buffy with the vibrations alone. *No way is the floor going to hold for long, especially not if both of the critters get up here.* Buffy pushed one of the book stacks over, aiming at the gargoyle. The books and shelves fell onto the beast and its heavy paws caught the edge of the shelves, books avalanching around it in a shower. The creature flexed and the shelves imploded, sending splinters of wood as long as her arm flying everywhere.

It charged her, feet crushing wood and paper and leather bindings under its weight. There was no way she was going to be able to outmuscle the thing; it weighed half a ton easily. So she waited until it was close and then did a back flip over what was left of the railing. The creature looked almost comical as it grabbed the air where she had been. It didn't look quite so funny as it fell from the second floor and hit the ground like a ton of bricks. It didn't break, which was what she'd really been hoping it would do. Instead it stood back up, shaking its head. She barely had time to acknowledge that from the corner of her eye, however, as its twin was busily trying to bite her face off.

The broad stone face lunged at Buffy even as she regained her footing, and she barely missed having the massive jaws clamp down on her skull. Granite broke and crumbled away from the gray fangs, and Buffy hopped back, her hair flying free of her ponytail and partially obscuring her view.

The elderly sorcerous vampire was watching form the sidelines, smiling smugly. Buffy wanted to punch his lights out, but couldn't really spare the time. The gargoyle closest to her grabbed for her and caught an arm. Buffy let out a shriek as it started squeezing, her muscles feeling like they'd been freshly pulped in an orange juicer. The bones in her forearm actually creaked, and she swung her whole body up, bracing her feet against the stone body and trying to push off. She might as well have tried swimming through a mountain. Nothing happened except that her arm got a little skinned as she pulled.

The gargoyle roared, the cold breath smelling like a quarry and lifting her hair from her face. She lifted one foot and kicked as hard as she could against the stone visage. It felt like she'd broken her heel, but the granite cracked and a heavy chunk of mouth and jaw slid away from the gargoyle and slammed into the ground.

Whatever else could be said about the things, they could feel pain. It let go of her and bellowed as it tried to cover what remained of its face, eyes burning with hatred and a promise to make her suffer. The vampire who'd animated the gargoyles blanched, apparently not expecting that she could do anything like that. She wasn't surprised by his expression. She hadn't expected it to work herself.

Buffy tried to stand and almost screamed at the white-hot pain in her heel. She limped as fast as she could away from the gargoyles, trying to figure out what, if anything she could use to break the giants apart. *Come on! I'm in a magic shop. There better be something here that can turn stone into butter, or I'm not gonna have a good night.*

Down below, in the basement, she heard the sound of something heavy breaking. "Giles! I'm trying to get to you, but I have two really big, really pissed off gargoyles trying to eat my face!"

"Buffy? The gargoyles are alive?" His voice was strained, but it was definitely still him. Better him than some vampire answering.

"Yep. That's pretty much the situation. Do we have a magic jackhammer around here?" She ducked just in time, and the wall next to her head became so much negative space. The gargoyle's arm flexed and he pulled it back out. This one had a whole face.

"Well, don't destroy them too badly! They cost a fortune!"

"Oh. Maybe a half-off sale would be in order?"

"What?"

"Never mind. What should I do here? Not really been studying much on fighting big stone statues that won't stand still."

Just to help her make her point, one of the two turned away from her and stormed toward the stairs. "Giles! Get to the cage! Now!"

"The cage? Oh." His voice faded for a moment. "Heavens! Yes. Of course. Meet you there?"

"I'm on it!"

Buffy hobbled out of the main room and into the exercise area set aside for her. There, in the corner, was a small trap door hidden by the mats she used to practice. Buffy threw them aside as the gargoyles came closer. She lifted the door and dropped down, slamming it shut behind her. They would find it, but hopefully not before she could finish what she had to do down here.

Rupert Giles was a cautious man. Perhaps overly cautious sometimes, but now and then he proved that extreme measures could be the right path. This was one of those cases. There was a narrow tunnel with iron rungs that led down into the lower end of the basement. Buffy used it to get down to her Watcher as quickly as she could.

The main reason for the tunnel was not, however, to take the place of the stairs. It was designed as a sort of hidden vault. Halfway down there was another door. This one was made of thick stainless steel and when Buffy opened it, she dropped down into a small room overflowing with books. She took the time to close and lock the door above her before she went any further.

Not that she could go very far. The small room had heavy gauge steel walls and a floor of the same material. There was a small window with equally thick steel bars every few inches. It would have taken Buffy half a week at least to get out of the narrow room without the key to the door, and the only person who possessed that key was on the other side of the small room, lying down and panting heavily.

"Giles! You okay? Did they ruffle your tweed?"

"A bit worse for the wear, but I'll survive." He was understating his condition. She could see the bruises and the cuts from where she was.

"Thanks to the security cage. Remember when I said you were paranoid for wanting to lock away the priceless occult goodies? I meant it. But here's a big YAY for your paranoia."

"I nearly didn't make it to the cage in time. It took some powerful magick to bring those gargoyles to life."

"Blame Kakistos. He popped by just to rub it in."

"Another puzzle. Even if this is somehow the real Kakistos, he never had any sorcerous abilities that we were aware of."

"If he had he probably wouldn't have let Faith ram a support beam through his chest. But it isn't him. He's got a little sidekick with a little sorcerer's hat and a magic wand."

"Yes, well, my point."

"So now what?" Buffy listened as the gargoyles beat on the separate doors into the room. "These stone-uglies seem pretty unkillable and, no offense, but not really partial to the idea of spending the rest of my life in a cage with you and your *most* valuable books.

Giles shook his head and winced. His face was swelling along the jaw and he had several scrapes. There was a lot of that going around tonight, the face swelling trick. "The gargoyles aren't like demons or vampires. You cannot possibly hope to defeat them, Buffy."

"Okay, then, thanks for playing." She sighed.

"I meant that certain magicks are required to revert them to their natural state. I don't know the spell off-hand, but if you can get out into the store and retrieve my copy of *Bibeau's Compendium of Gorgons and Stone Demons,* I should be able to figure it out."

"Great. It would've been *much* too easy if that was one of the books valuable enough to keep in *here.*"

"Yes, well, I hadn't really thought I'd have much need for that particular volume, Buffy. There just aren't that many cathedrals for them to hide on in this area."

"Good point." She shook her head. "I'm willing to give it a try, but I don't think the granite twins are gonna give me a whole lot of spare time." The door behind Giles shuddered heavily and rocked his whole body.

"Wait a second." For a man who was being rattled like a child's toy, he was remarkably calm. It was one of the things she loved about him. "On the shelves, look for a vial with the words 'gorgon venom' on the side."

"Right." Buffy nodded and then frowned. "Which shelves?"

"The ones behind the counter." Something behind where her Watcher sat fell, and Giles scrambled toward her a bit, his face urgent. "Almost directly behind the cash register and slightly to the right."

Buffy thought about the shattered shelving where she'd hit the wall a few minutes earlier. "Oh. Swell." She stood up and moved to where Giles had been sitting, gesturing for his key. "Will this stuff stop them?"

"Well, it should. It will turn a regular person into stone. I imagine it should very well petrify a gargoyle as it's already halfway there."

"Okay. Good plan." Buffy unlocked the door and threw the key to Giles. Lock up after me." He nodded and moved into position as Buffy slid through the opening, taking the gargoyle waiting there by surprise. She used the door to whack it in its stone face and slammed it shut as quickly as she slithered out. The gargoyle roared and came after her. Buffy hobbled faster, moving up the stairs as quickly as her heel would allow.

She limped up the stairs and back toward the counter with the gargoyle in hot pursuit. She hit the floor with a clear view of the ruined wall and the collection of vials on the floor and then got helped in that direction when one of the gruesome twins hit her from behind. Buffy hit the wall again, this time face first.

The vampire said something in a language that meant nothing at all to her, but by his tone she knew he meant for the gargoyles to stop her, and immediately if not sooner. Buffy started looking through the remaining bottles, vials, and clay containers, frantically searching for the right one. *Eye of newt—is he kidding? Blood of something called a mandrake root. Wolvesbane.*

Cemetery Mold. There! She grabbed the thick stone container and pulled out the stopper. The fluid was as heavy as syrup and smelled even worse than the zombies she'd dealt with earlier. She flung a few drops through the air at the gargoyle coming for her, the one that was now kicking its way through the countertop. Giles was going to be very, very upset about that. As soon as the liquid hit the gargoyle, it reared back, as if prepared to scream, and froze. The other gargoyle—the one with the big chunk of face missing—came at her from the actual open end of the counter, but pushed everything aside and broke half of what was left as it came. She hit it fast with the whole bottle. The stone vial cracked like an egg and spilled the remaining gorgon venom. The gargoyle stopped moving, perched on one thick foot like a cherub from Hell. The only thing missing was water spilling from its mouth and it could have been part of a nightmarish fountain.

Giles came limping into the room from her workout area, his leg looking freshly clawed. She could only assume it had been the gargoyle who caused the damage before he came after her. Buffy looked a question at him: *Are you okay?* He nodded and pointed to the white-haired vampire.

Buffy got around the statue warily. It didn't move. That made her very, very happy. The crusty old vampire that had brought the gargoyles to life looked at her with wide, wide eyes.

"You wait right there," she said. "I am *so* gonna beat you to death."

He didn't listen. He moved for the door faster than

little old men should be able to move and reached it before she'd limped half the distance to him. Buffy looked around for a good stake to throw.

He grabbed the door handle in his hand and yanked hard. The door was locked, but that didn't stop him. He hauled back with both hands and broke the lock. Even withered old vampires were stronger than the average bear.

The creep looked at her and smiled, ready to say something rude and possibly moderately witty, but he never got the chance. A startled expression came over his face, and he looked down at his own chest where a stake had punched through him. He looked back at Buffy again and collapsed into a pile of dust.

And standing where he had been a second before was Faith. The other Slayer stood looking fresh and clean, not even a speck of dust on her too-revealing clothes. Faith pulled back the stake she'd used to kill the little weasel of a sorcerer and nodded.

"Faith?"

Faith gave her a little half grin. "Hey, B. What's shakin'?"

Buffy felt her lips press together in anger. "What's shakin'? Simple as that? Last time I saw you, you tried to take over my life, went all Body Snatchers on me. Then there was the L.A. rampage. Now you break out of prison and I'm supposed to say, what? Welcome home?"

Faith stood just past the threshold and shrugged, looking bored with the conversation already. "I was thinkin' more along the lines of 'pull up a chair, grab a beer,' but yeah, basically. We don't gotta hug or nothin'." She looked directly at Buffy, her dark eyes unreadable. "I'm not looking for forgiveness, B. Just doin' the job." She shrugged again. "Say what you want, I'm still a Slayer. Bad as you might want to, you can't take that away."

Buffy nodded, hating that she couldn't quite get a neutral look on her face. "Fine. But I'm guessing the jailbreak wasn't just 'cuz you missed the stellar Sunnydale nightlife. What the hell are you doing here?"

"Long story, chica." And now Faith smiled knowingly. Giles came forward and placed his hand on Buffy's shoulder. Faith winked at him by way of saying hello, but Buffy knew that at least was all bluff. "But I got the answer man right here."

Faith pulled her arm into view, and at the end of it, held firmly in her fist, was the collar of the shirt on Ethan Rayne. For a man who had been up to no end of causing Buffy grief, Ethan looked remarkably intact. She thought about fixing that for a second.

Ethan smiled sheepishly. She trusted that saccharine grin not in the least. "Hello, Slayer."

"Oh, for . . . forget it. Look, I need to get Giles to the hospital. And now."

Faith gave a Mona Lisa smile; seductive, amused, and secretive all at once. "Convenient. That way when you're done whaling on Witch Boy here, they can patch him up."

Buffy shook her head and then reached back, helping Giles come forward. "Let's go. Doctors now. Answers later."

Chapter Seven

The hospital room was as sterile as any hospital room, and Buffy hated it on sight. She pretty much hated all hospital rooms. They were meant to cure illnesses and ease suffering, but mostly, they seemed to be where people came to die. Oh, she knew it was irrational and she did her best not to think about it too much, but there it was. Sadly, she knew a lot of the people standing around Giles's bed felt the same way.

And there were a lot of people in the small room. Aside from herself and Giles, there was Willow, Faith, and, of course, Ethan Rayne. She might have felt a little uncomfortable, but Ethan was positively squirming. That was a big plus in Buffy's book. Okay, that he was squirming because she had her hand around his throat and had him pinned to the wall like a butterfly in a display case . . . well, that was just dreamy.

Right at the moment, he was turning the most delightful shade of purple red, almost like the color of a really ripe plum. Normally, Giles would have been cautioning her to calm down about now, and she would have been listening. Giles felt that too much gratuitous beating on a baddy was a bad thing. Of course, where Ethan Rayne was concerned, that particular rule didn't apply. Right at the moment, Giles wasn't feeling too much of anything. He was asleep and doped to the gills with enough happy medications to stop his battered body and recently sewn up leg from hurting too much.

Just before she would have let him go anyway, Spike and Xander stepped into the room.

Xander took one look at the scene and moved over, placing a hand on Buffy's arm. "Whoa, camel. Hang on. Anya's home asleep, but I stopped to get Spike like you asked, just in case Kakistos attacks the hospital. But you promised not to beat Ethan to a pulp until I got here."

Spike shook his head and mumbled. "A bloke can't get a decent hour's kip around here."

Buffy looked over her shoulder at Xander and smiled. Ethan stayed where he was, but she eased up enough to let him get a little air. "Right. And now you're here. Let the beating commence."

Xander nodded and looked past Buffy to see Willow. "How's Tara?"

Willow, looking a little like a witch who'd been in some serious fisticuffs with little demons and was now in need of a few weeks sleep, smiled faintly. "Upstairs, resting. They don't think it's serious, but they want to X-ray her shoulder."

Buffy hauled Ethan away from the wall and then slammed him back into it. "Talk to me, sconehead."

Ethan smiled a nervously smarmy smile. "Happily, darling." Buffy set him down and he did his best to look cool about the rather unfortunate turn of events. "During my captivity, I prayed often to the lords of chaos I had worshipped for so many years. But my pleas for aid fell upon deaf ears. Eventually I turned my devotions elsewhere. I began to worship the being known as the 'First.'"

Buffy frowned. She had met the First before. "You're joking." She studied his handsome, crafty face and shook her head. "No. Of course you're not."

Faith tilted her head and squinted a bit. Xander looked decidedly uncomfortable around Faith. "What the hell is this thing? The First. The First what?" Faith shrugged and indicated Ethan with a nod of her head. "He said you'd know."

Buffy sighed. She looked at Faith and then back at Ethan before she spoke. "The First is the very First evil on the face of the Earth."

"Serious?" That had Faith's attention.

"Deadly." She nudged Ethan to get him talking.

Ethan smiled patiently and spoke like an instructor sharing important information on motorcycle safety. "The First is as old as the primordial darkness. It existed on this planet before the sun shone down . . . before the Lord said 'let there be light.' It's absolute evil, older than humanity *or* demonkind. Even amongst many demon tribes it is considered a myth." He looked at each person in the room, excluding only Giles, who remained asleep. "But it isn't. It's a power that transcends reality, time, and space. Which means it can tap into all *possible* realities as well as all *times*, accessing the past and future."

Xander nodded and crossed his arms. "Which is where you get your major dimensional bleed."

Ethan smiled as if he'd just heard the local idiot boy make an important connection. "Score one for the boy."

Willow's scowled and shook her head. "So chaos wasn't enough? Now you're playing bootlick for the thing that gave Evil its capital E?"

Ethan shook his head, obviously fully warmed to his subject. He was, Buffy knew, enjoying this immensely. "Not precisely. The First *did* agree to help me escape, but I also wanted power. So much power that I would be nearly a Lord of Chaos myself. The First enjoys a challenge, and so I challenged it to a contest, with that very power as the prize."

Spike yawned and looked at Ethan. "I'm sorry. Still half asleep. You did *what*?" He shook his head. "You really *are* as bloody stupid as you look. You give evil a bad name, mate, you really do."

Ethan smiled indulgently. "It's simple really. A contest of will and cleverness. The First and I each choose five individuals as our champions in combat. I'd thought of the Slayer first, of course . . . or more properly, the *two* Slayers." He held up one hand and started ticking off fingers, adding to the count as he went. At first he put up two fingers, but more followed quickly. "Willow's a witch. Spike's a vampire with marvelous credentials. I'd originally planned to use the werewolf as number five, but he's skipped town apparently, so young Mr. Harris will have to do." Xander looked at him with an expression that promised to make him eat his words. "I broke Faith out of prison against her will, but she, at least, was reasonable."

Faith grinned and shrugged her shoulders. "Sounds like a party, actually. More fun than prison, anyway."

Ethan nodded, liking to have at least one person in agreement with him apparently. "I abducted Xander so that I could observe the witch, test her." He looked toward Willow and almost managed an apologetic smile. Like him, it lacked sincerity. "But when I realized Kakistos was here in Sunnydale, I realized two very unsettling things. Number one, that the First is not confined to choosing from *this* dimension. He can pick his combatants from any reality he wishes. I also realized that the First was cheating." He looked around at his chosen five again. "By sending Kakistos after you, he has begun the contest early."

Xander stepped closer to Ethan, who, wisely, took a half step back. "Okay, so I get what happens if you win. What if you lose?"

Ethan almost looked like he hadn't given the notion any thought, but his words made a lie of the expression. "If I lose? I'll suffer eternal torment as the whipping boy of the lowest toadies in the First's dark dimension."

Willow lowered her head and let a small and rather nasty smile play around her lips. Buffy would have never told her best friend in a million years, but she could look positively intimidating when she wanted to. "Oh, and we wouldn't want *that* to happen."

Buffy looked at the other Slayer, shaking her head. Her disappointment was obvious. "Faith, I can't believe you're willing to go along with this. The girl I knew would have just kicked Ethan's ass and let the First make him a soul-slave."

"Hey, I figure if I get to stomp the granddaddy of all evils, that's gotta be major karma points, right? It's all good."

"Not hardly." Buffy looked back at Ethan. "You can forget it. Boggles my mind that you'd even think any of us would help you."

Giles made a low noise in his chest and shifted a bit, his eyes opening blearily. "Buffy?"

Even as Buffy started toward Giles, Ethan laughed and shook his head, his eyes glancing to the ceiling before looking back to Buffy. "You really think I'd tell you all this if you had any choice? I've already named you as my champions. I've *told* the First that I've chosen you. It's done, Buffy."

Even as the words left Ethan's mouth, Buffy felt that pulling sensation again, felt the odd tug of reality around her shifting. The hospital room began to fade, and the other people Ethan had chosen began to fade as well, each looking puzzled and wary as the room became translucent.

"No! Ethan, we're not fighting the First for you!" Buffy's voice was angry, but even to her own ears it sounded tinny, like it was being transmitted on a really crappy radio with a lot of static. Giles sat up in his bed and reached for her, his pale face alarmed.

"The First? Oh, no . . . Buffy . . . listen . . . you cannot combat the First directly without the Dagger! It can only be harmed with Hope's Dagger." Giles voice sounded even more washed out than her own, and Buffy had to strain hard to make the words out. *What's Hope's Dagger?* She had no idea.

But she knew who did. Her hand reached out fast, and she grabbed Ethan again, yanking him half off his feet and toward her. She wasn't going alone, not if she could help it. Luckily, she could. "You got us into this. You're coming along for the ride."

Ethan's voice became clearer as he screamed and was pulled to her. What started off as a distant panicky protest became crystal clear as the room faded away completely. "What? No, Buffy! Noooo!"

The hospital room was empty then save for Rupert Giles, who looked around at where his young friends had been a moment before. He rubbed the bridge of his nose and sighed. Even that small movement left him feeling weak and drained. "God help you all." Giles slumped back down, the painkillers in his system murking his thoughts, muddying even his ability to worry. A moment later he struggled in vain before falling back into a fitful sleep.

• • •

The hospital was gone and an instant later, Buffy stood in the Magic Box, confused and disoriented. It was the same shop she'd been in earlier, but the furniture, the banister, even the floor, were in much worse shape than they had been only an hour earlier. Ethan's voice continued its loud denial for half a second before he looked around as well, just as surprised.

The counters and shelves were broken into fragments small enough to pick up with a dustpan. Several bodies lay scattered around the room, most of them dead for at least a few days.

"It's the Magic Box." Her voice sounded faint again, but for entirely different reasons. She was having trouble catching her breath.

Ethan nodded. "Or this world's version of it."

Buffy shoved him, and Ethan stumbled, falling to his hands and knees. "You are *so* dead."

Before she could demonstrate, Buffy caught movement from the corner of her eye. Several figures stepped toward her from the darkness, shadow shapes that seemed to have little real form. They moved with a grace that was unsettling, but not as disturbing as the sounds they made, noises like a deep sigh and a scream mixed into one.

Ethan scrambled away from her, heading over to the ruined shelves behind the counter, where he immediately hid himself away. The dark forms, little more than blacker smudges in the perpetual twilight in the Magic Box, ignored him completely, slithering closer to her instead. Buffy scanned the room quickly and saw a decent-looking axe resting in a delicate skeletal hand.

The axe was actually familiar, one of her favorites. She didn't let herself dwell on the hand that held it.

Buffy rolled across the ground, moving from where she'd been a second before, and came up with the axe held firmly in her grip. The shadows made a new sound, a noise not unlike laughter, though distorted and unsettling. Apparently they'd played this particular game before.

The first shadow shape lunged at her, and Buffy tried to dodge. Where its hand touched her flesh she felt a deep, numbing cold. She stepped back fast and swung the axe. The shadow limb fell off with ease, hitting the ground and sinking into it, like a spray of water returning to the ocean. The dark shape made a new noise that hurt her ears but made her smile. She liked hurting the bad things. They *could* be hurt and that was half the battle.

It was the other half that proved to be a problem. They didn't play nicely and they didn't like being fair in a combat situation; the things surged toward Buffy and merged, like shadows crossing over shadows. The darkness swarmed across her body, solid, bitterly cold, and trying very hard to push her skin aside as if seeking to steal her soul. Buffy felt the cold licking at her flesh, almost freezing it with every touch. She swung the axe and kicked with her legs, feeling the numbing force of every contact.

The good news was still the same: They could be hurt. The bad news was that there were a lot of them, and every single contact made her feel weaker, more disoriented, and less like a Slayer.

She did what she had to do and began hacking madly at the darkness that was trying to smother her. The darkness grew more complete and still she struck and bashed against it. And eventually—it could have been mere moments or a few eternities—she saw light again, felt warmth again, and then the ruined Magic Box was around her. The room was filled with evidence of death and mayhem, and the bodies looked a little too much like they might have belonged to her friends and possibly even to her, but there had seldom been any place that looked as fine as that horrid mirror of her own world in that moment.

Buffy shivered in the twilight, the last echoes of the shadow things' screams fading away. Ethan stood nearby, his normally calm composure broken for the moment. When he realized that Buffy could see him, he put on his best poker face.

Buffy stared daggers at him. "Where are the others? What is this dimension?"

Ethan shook his head. "This isn't some alternate reality, Slayer. This is the First's own dimension. It controls everything here. Everything you see it has created for your battlefield. As for my other champions, I'd guess they're scattered about. While you were busy keeping us alive however, I made this."

His held out a plastic bottle that said Holy Water on the side. Judging by the glowing green stuff she saw inside it, she guessed the ingredients weren't just blessed tap water.

Buffy took the bottle and looked at Ethan dubiously. "And this is. . . ?"

"It's a potion, dear girl." He shrugged. "A little bottled relocation spell, if you will. I can't send any of us back home, but I can at least get us all in one place, and if push comes to shove, there's enough floating around in this establishment to let me defend myself until you return." Ethan gestured at the ruined products strewn around the Magic Box and then pointed to the bottle in Buffy's hand. "Once you find them, splash them with it and they will immediately be transported back here."

Buffy nodded and slipped the bottle into her jeans. "Did I mention how dead you are?"

Ethan nodded and tried to smile. "You might've." He looked around the area and out the shattered window to the street. "Now you'd best find your friends, before *they're* dead."

"Any idea where they might be?"

Ethan shrugged. "None whatsoever. But I have a suspicion that if you find the loudest noises, you'll find your friends." He shrugged. "It's just a hunch, mind you, but I'm of the opinion that they aren't being welcomed as old buddies."

"So dead." Buffy moved to the door and out into the street. "So dead that you can't even begin to imagine how dead you are . . ."

Ethan watched her leave. He didn't say a word, but a smile still played at his lips, even after she was gone.

Buffy followed Ethan's advice and found it useful. The streets were almost completely empty. She could hear sounds from place to place but would have bet that this particular mirror of Sunnydale wasn't really a party kind of town. Buffy walked down the street and listened for where the most racket was being made.

And she kept telling herself that this wasn't her Sunnydale, which helped make it a little less painful to walk along. Because, real or not, it looked like her Sunnydale, if everything that could go wrong had already done so with a vengeance. The sky was dark. Not black, but deep, deep gray with an almost bruised appearance. She couldn't say for sure if the gray was clouds, merely that there were no stars to be seen. What illumination she had came from the street lamps and fires that burned at odd intervals. The light was just enough to let her know that she didn't want to see anything more.

The Magic Box had been bad, but the carnage in there had appeared older. What she saw on the streets and in the Town Square was fresher, and that made it much, much worse. Bodies were hung everywhere, their entrails draped over lampposts and through the bushes like some psychotic's idea of fleshy Christmas lights. There were no living people that she could see, though she'd already spotted one car in the distance, its windows tinted black and the engine roaring like a bear as it tore down the road. It had looked a little like a Ford Thunderbird, the sort of cherry classic that made Xander all but salivate. Only she was pretty sure most Thunderbirds didn't have bone in place of the chrome in the detailing. She didn't flag it down to find out for sure. There were screams coming from a few places that sent shivers down her spine. Not because they were unnatural, but because they sounded all too human. She felt an urge to seek them out and try to save the people behind those wretched wails, but couldn't. There wasn't any time and she had people from her own universe to deal with.

Before she even got to the movie house, the façade came down and she had to find a new way in. There was a fire escape that was mostly intact. She scaled it and slid inside the building, moving past the projectionist's booth without bothering to look inside. Whatever was in there made wet sounds and cried out softly from time to time.

She found the source of the real noise in the lobby. There were five bodies on the ground that were fresh. None of them were human. These things looked around five feet tall and at least as wide, with thick-plated hides that could probably resist the average bullet. They had more trouble with standard-issue fireballs apparently, and Willow was proving it to the rest of the things surrounding her. If they had heads, they hid them well, but they made enough noise to at least have mouths somewhere. In addition to the heavily armored hides, the creatures had pinchers big enough to take off an arm with ease. Buffy didn't try to get close enough to find out. She watched Willow blast two more of the creatures into big hard shells filled with exploded guts and then slipped in closer through the opening that particular explosion left behind.

"Willow!"

"Buffy! Thank God! I can't keep this up much longer."

"Could have fooled me." Willow leaned past her and made another gesture. A thick bolt of electricity ran from the witch's fingers and flash fried two more of the creatures. The rest stepped back warily, apparently having learned to respect the power if not the shape that wielded it.

"You're out of here." Buffy pulled the bottle from her back pocket.

"Can't really go anywhere right now, Buffy. I've got crab thingies trying to eat me." Willow nodded at the monsters not far away. "I think they think I'm popcorn or something."

Buffy splashed a few drops of Ethan's potion on Willow and her friend disappeared. *If Ethan lied about what that little formula does,* she promised, *his death will be extra special painful.* Having to trust Ethan Rayne was right up there with kissing an electric eel.

She didn't bother trying to fight the demons. She ran for the roof and was happy to note that they weren't really very agile on stairs. The wet sounds kept coming from the projection room, but the cries had stopped. Buffy tried not to think about it. By the time she'd made it back to the fire escape, the crab things had maybe managed the first flight on the way up.

It didn't take Buffy long to find the next place to look for trouble. The liquor store just down from the cinema was burning at one end and surrounded by an angry mob of vampires and much, much stranger things at the other. Buffy crept up, staying to the shadows as best she could and quickly found Xander in the basement. The window was too small even for her to climb through and barred besides. Xander looked to be holding his own, but only because he'd barred the door with a few kegs of beer. The kegs were sliding a bit, but not enough to let the things on the other side through. *Judging by the way they're all fighting to get inside, I figure fresh human is something of a precious commodity.* She'd always felt that way herself, but not at all for the same reasons.

While the crowd of demons, vampires, and other things was fighting a bottleneck of traffic to reach their prize, Buffy moved into the bar proper, coughing on the smoke. She didn't have to look far for weapons. A few cases of high octane liquor were sitting behind the bar, and she made full use of them. *Funny thing about high-proof alcohol: It burns very nicely. Funny thing about high-proof burning alcohol: It burns demons nicely.* Buffy launched Molotov cocktails made from bourbon and dishrags at the horde trying to reach Xander. The resulting firestorm left a lot of dead monsters and a bar that was hot enough to bake a cake. Buffy kicked past the demons unfortunate enough not to get out of the way and called to Xander. "Xander! It's me! Open the door."

Xander peered out at her, his face bearing an expression of deep relief. "Buffy! Have I ever mentioned how great it is to see you when I have a horde of monsters trying to munch on my butt?" He started hauling kegs out of his way.

She had to step back from the blaze she'd created while he worked and met up with two of the local vampires who weren't really all that eager to lose their meal before he had the path cleared. They both burned nicely when she kicked them into the growing conflagration, but not before they managed to push her into the flames for added insult.

Thirty seconds after Xander opened the door, she sent him on his way with a splash of the potion Ethan had given her. They didn't talk. They were both too busy coughing. She got out of the bar a few minutes before the entire structure started collapsing. Her hair was a few inches shorter by the time she managed to get out and her skin was red and blistering in a half dozen places.

She found Spike one street over, pinned down in the Espresso Pump. The place was closed for business, at least that was the first impression one got if one considered the heavy steel rolling door that blocked the glass door where she normally went in. There was no way she was going to get through that thing. Not a chance, not as tired as she was.

Through the grating, Buffy could see Spike was doing his best and holding his own against a group of vampires who apparently didn't like strangers coming into their neck of the woods. The problem wasn't so much that he couldn't defend himself, it was more that getting anywhere was a bit of a challenge and they had the home field advantage. Spike was cut and bruised and battered. But he was grinning from ear to ear and roaring out obscenities if she had to guess what he was saying behind the thick glass barrier. Even as she watched, he swung himself over a table and kicked one of the younger vampires into a wall hard enough to crack the plaster.

Much as she wanted to let him have his fun, business had to come before pleasure. After checking the side and back of the building, she was forced to go into the sewers to gain access from below. The sewers in her Sunnydale were nasty, just like sewers anywhere were pretty much guaranteed to be disgusting. But these sewers had things in them that moved and chewed at you when you least expected it. They might have been rats, but she didn't think so. Several of them bit at her and a few broke skin before she managed to climb into the basement of the coffee shop.

By the time she actually got into the main part of the Espresso Pump, Spike was standing alone. His clothes were torn and his body bleeding from a dozen places. He looked so happy it was unsettling.

"Slayer. Nice of you to join me."

"Spike." She looked around and tried to count the dust piles. "Shouldn't you be fighting someone?"

He shook his head. "Not when all they have around here is newbies. Most of these pups couldn't fight their way out of a mosh pit." He grinned again. "Looks like you've been doing a little dancing yourself, Buffy. You all right then?"

"Good enough." She pulled out the bottle again and looked at him. "Sending you to the others now. Get a little rest. You're going to need it." Before he could say anything else she'd splashed him with the vile fluids in the bottle and he vanished.

"I must be getting the hang of this. It's almost been easy." She slid back into the sewers and discovered how mistaken she was. The things that liked to chew on her hadn't been rats. They'd been babies. The mother of the things took it personally that she'd killed a few. At least she guessed it was the mother. Whatever it was, it had big claws and a serious attitude problem. Buffy caught only the briefest glimpse—enough to know it had fur and very large teeth—before she was forced under the rancid waters.

The paw that held her down pressed with enough force to keep her pinned to the algae-slicked cement. Buffy's hands tried to pry individual fingers away from her chest and stomach where the massive paw held her, but with no luck. Her heart raced and thudded like a drum, and her vision started blurring as she fought to just get the scaly paw away from her long enough to let her breathe.

The curved base of the tunnel pressed against her head and shoulder blades, limiting her movement. Her fingers could only just barely get the thick claws on her body to move at all, and she finally gave up trying. Instead she pivoted her hips upward and kicked out of the water with both feet. Her left foot touched only air, but her right foot hit something that felt like a grapefruit and then suddenly gave in, exploding under the impact.

Just as quickly as the weight had pinned her down it let her back up, and Buffy sucked in a lungful of air as the thing shrieked like a stuck pig. The shape reared back, both of the heavy paws scratching madly at the left side of its wet, furry face. The low-slung, fat body of the beast trembled and it turned, lumbering away at high speed, crushing its own young, or whatever the little things were, as it went.

Buffy sat in the cold, filthy water coughing and sputtering for a few seconds before standing up and climbing back up to the street. "Got to remember to never say how easy things are going. I knew that rule, just forgot it."

When she was back on the street she could hear the sound of still more violence not far away. She knew she was headed in the right direction when she heard the sound of Faith screaming out a profanity. She moved closer and soon found the source of the commotion: a bar called the Twilight Show. It must have been a particularly classy place in the eyes of the First because there were even bouncers in tuxedoes at the ornate double doors. Buffy looked the two guys over and wondered just how many yards of silk it took to fit tuxedoes on the likes of the two nightmares guarding the place. They were only a few inches taller than she was, but they were also almost five feet wide at the shoulders. Broad, flat faces stared back at her under brows covered with barbs and a nest of hair that writhed across their scalps. Their skin was a deep blue, mottled with patches of what looked like mold in the oddest places. If they had eyes, they were too dark for Buffy to see. One of them turned toward her and shook its head.

"You got ID?"

Buffy blinked. "I'm sorry?"

"I said, 'You got ID?'" The demon turned its head toward her, the voice that spilled out—higher in pitch than she would have expected from something that big and that brutal looking—sounded bored.

"Um . . . no?"

"Then you can just go on your way. No ID means no entry."

"Look, I really need to get inside, just for a minute. One of my friends is in there and she's underage." She shook her head and held her breath. *Now I have to worry about being carded in Hell? What is the universe coming to?*

"Well, your friend is on her own. No ID means you don't go in. End of discussion."

Whether she felt silly about it or not, Buffy wasn't really in the mood to take no for an answer. "Oh, I don't think so." She moved forward and prepared to slide between the two apish things if she could. She barely made it into their range before a hand as wide as her shoulders pushed against her chest. "Hey!" She slapped the hand away from her and scowled. "Watch where you're touching!"

The demon snarled and backhanded her. Or would have backhanded her if she hadn't been expecting that reaction. Buffy ducked under the massive arm and popped back up on the other side of the offending limb. She braced her hands against the double doors and kicked at the now exposed side of the demon with both feet. The mountain of flesh grunted and stumbled a bit but did not fall down.

Oh yes, this is not going at all the way I'd planned. The other bouncer, the quiet one, grabbed her by her ponytail and hauled her backward. Buffy hit the wall hard, and probably would have fallen to the ground if not for the firm grip on her hair. He kept his hold on her ponytail and swung at the waist, lifting her through the air like a rag doll and swinging her toward the wall on the opposite side of where he stood.

Buffy reached up with her hands and caught her own hair higher up the ponytail than the demon's hand. As soon as she got a grip, the pressure from where he was pulling eased up substantially. At the same time, she twisted her body and pulled her legs in, so she could use them to take the blow when she hit the wall. It worked too. She wound up crouched against the stone exterior and then she kicked off as hard as she could, swinging her legs out again until they were in front of her. Buffy swung hard, her hands the only thing that stopped the pressure on her hairline from scalping her, and shot both feet into the dark blue face of the demon that held her.

The bouncer bounced hard when he hit the ground. Along the way he was forced to let go of her and she took full advantage of her freedom. The first bouncer had returned to finish their little debate, and she slammed her elbow into his wide nose, cracking the bones in his face. His head snapped back, but that didn't stop him from finding her with his massive hands. One blunt-fingered paw caught each of her arms and squeezed hard enough to make her gasp.

"Your problem is you got no respect for authority." That too-high voice grated on her nerves. Those too-big hands held her arms wide apart and then started pulling in opposite directions. Buffy let out a scream as the muscles in her arms, back, and chest stretched tight and started straining further apart than nature intended. She could feel tendons and ligaments drawing further apart and gritted her teeth.

"Your problem is you talk too much!" Buffy brought both legs up close to her chest and flipped her body backward, hot flashes of pain lancing through her shoulders as she made her move. Both knees crashed into the demon's throat and he let her go instantly, reaching up to protect his airway. Buffy landed on her back, unable to maneuver fast enough to correct her fall. She grunted again, the wind half knocked out of her, and kicked upward with one leg, connecting at the juncture of his pant legs. He was male, and happily, one of the sort of demons that had the same sort of sensitivities that most males have. He dropped to his knees and doubled over, his hands leaving his throat and moving down to protect his groin, once again a little too late to make a difference. She kicked him twice in his head and dropped him to the ground. He didn't move and that suited her fine. The other bouncer was just standing up. She used both of her fists on the back of his skull to convince him to change his mind.

Her arms felt like they were three inches longer than when the fight started, and her back was going to bruise in a major way, but she was standing and they weren't. Buffy pushed the door into the Twilight Show and stepped into the bar.

The line of devastation was incredible to behold. Mostly because it was all so obviously fresh devastation. Whatever the demons might have done to the rest of this mirrored Sunnydale, it was obvious that they had set this bar up as a place where they could relax.

Faith had rectified that situation. There were three pool tables in the main room. One of them was on its side, the legs broken off. The second was broken in half, part of it covered by the unconscious or deceased body of a monster with eight legs and more eyes than should have been possible. One of the legs from the previous table was sticking through its abdomen. The last table was surrounded by the dead and defeated. But on that table was Faith, held in place by six demons, all of whom looked radically different, except for the expressions on their monstrous faces that said they were perfectly ready to carve the other Slayer into filets.

Faith was pinned in place, her body thrashing violently. Her face was bloodied and her clothes so torn and disheveled that the situation could have been considered erotic by some people. But it was obvious right away that there was nothing remotely sexual in what was going on. It looked like the demons were planning to carve her heart out.

And Faith, despite the desperate situation, looked like she was having a blast. When it came to death and destruction, Faith almost always looked like she was up for a party. That was, maybe, one of the reasons she spent most of her time in a prison cell these days. Her dark eyes were wild, her hair scattered around her like a tarnished halo, and the expression on her face was one part desperation and two parts almost animalistic glee. *I hope that look never shows up when she's dealing with humans again.* Buffy wanted to believe that Faith was reforming, learning from past mistakes, but the look on the other Slayer's face made her have her doubts.

Buffy took in the situation and walked over to the wall on the right, where the pool cues normally rested. A lot of the cues were missing, but that was okay, there were still enough of them. Buffy grabbed a four-foot long wooden shaft and tossed it with deadly accuracy, nailing one of the demons in the back. The shaft rammed through and broke the breastbone in the front. Most times that was enough. This time, the demon turned and snarled, the vulpine muzzle on its black furred face peeling back to reveal teeth as big as Buffy's fingers.

The rest of the demons turned to look at Buffy. She grabbed another pool cue in her left hand and cupped a 12 ball in her right. The first one that moved in her direction learned the same lesson that David taught Goliath: Little round things can hurt when slammed into a thick skull with sufficient force. The round missile shattered against the heavy brow, but left a new dent where it had been. The demon dropped like a cut fishing line.

Faith planted her hands on the green felt and pushed back, launching her legs up into the air. She caught the demon who'd been drooling on her face, her feet hooking around his neck, and let her weight drop back down to where it had been before. The demon was catapulted over the billiards table, and into the back of another slimy-looking thing that had about a dozen too many writhing tentacles where its head should have been. Both of them fell to the ground, angry and ready for a fight. Happily, the thing with snaky arms instead of a head decided it was all right with beating the tar out of the Mad Drooler who landed on it.

"Hey, B. Nice to see I'm not the only girl in town." Faith sounded moderately winded, but that cocky smile was still in place.

Buffy snapped her pool cue against the bull neck of the thing jumping and bouncing in her direction. It landed on her anyway, fists swiping at her body, and pounding into her ribs like sledgehammers. She took the pointy end of the cue and rammed it down the monster's snarling maw. This time it didn't break off. The demon reared back, shaking its head madly, and Buffy caught it a solid blow to the throat.

Something that looked like it was oozing green oatmeal grabbed Faith by her hair and hauled her off her feet. Faith took that about as well as Buffy and broke its neck with a side kick to its head. Her foot made a wet, slurping noise when she pulled it back.

The demons backed off a bit, snapping at each other in a language that made the two Slayers want to cover their ears and hide from the nauseating tones. Instead, Buffy spilled a dose of her potion onto Faith, catching the girl off guard. One second Faith was there and the next she was gone. Buffy poured the last of the potion on herself and followed suit.

Chapter Eight

One second there were butt ugly demons making unsettling noises in what wanted to be a decent neighborhood bar. The next, there were friends and a few not-so-much friends in the dark ruins of the Magic Box.

Buffy manifested in her workout room. Through the door she could see the rest of the gang. They were not yet aware of her. She counted heads, just to make sure they were all present and accounted for.

Sometimes Buffy hated the idea of waking up every morning.

Xander was leaning against the ruined countertop, his eyes focused on the skeleton not far from where he was resting. It was wearing the exact same clothes he had on. Willow was rifling through a small stack of archaic books, her brow knitted in concentration. Spike was cleaning under his black-lacquered nails with a wicked looking dagger. He was facing away from her. Faith was standing with her legs apart and her head tilted just slightly, staring at Ethan Rayne as if he were, perhaps, the ugliest bug she'd ever seen. Ethan was looking a little nervous. He was also looking a little smug. He was one of the only people she'd ever met who could manage both at the same time. The only other one Buffy had ever seen carry off that look had been Willie the snitch. Willie managed to look nervous whenever she was around. He also managed to look smug when she brought along a few of her friends, like Xander. Somehow Ethan managed to make the expression look classier, but that didn't take a lot of effort.

They were all there. Ethan got to live without knowing what having his legs torn off would feel like. *For now.* Later, Buffy made no promises.

A dark, furtive motion caught Buffy's eye. She turned her head a little and looked down. Sid the Dummy was looking up at her, his face unreadable.

"Hey, sweets. I was wondering when you was gonna get here."

"What are you doing here?"

"Waiting for you, kid. I figured maybe you could use a little help."

"You knew where to find me?" Sid nodded, his glass eyes staying on her face in a way that was unsettling. She'd have maybe liked him a little better if he blinked a little more often. "How?"

"I have connections, cupcake. A demon hunter learns a few tricks after a while." Wooden shoulders shrugged with a slight rattling noise.

"You couldn't have explained all this to me the last time I saw you?"

Sid shook his head and again his eyes stared at her, unmoving in the motion of his shake. "The Big F's been keepin' an eye on me. The First knows I'm sneaking around, but can't put a finger on me just yet."

"You mean the First didn't bring you here? You're not from some alternate reality?" Buffy frowned, puzzled by the dummy.

"Hey, now. There's only one of me, babe."

"So how are you here? After you killed the last of the Brotherhood of Seven, your curse was broken. Your soul was supposed to move on."

Sid stepped closer, his wooden shoulders shrugging with a creaking noise. His eyebrows lifted for a second and fell back. It was amazing how little she could understand of his facial expressions and how little she could empathize with him. The human face has muscles that just don't exist in a ventriloquist doll's, and those muscles offered so many ways to express a thought or a feeling. She didn't really think about it all that often, until she met up with someone like Sid, who barely had facial expressions.

"Well, that's true, see, but, see, I ran into the First a long time ago, back when I was still human and huntin' demons, and I royally pissed him off." He shrugged again, making due with what he could show for expression. "So when my soul was finally free, goin' on to a paradise of calendar girls and good whiskey, the First got hold of me and trapped me here, caged my spirit in a duplicate Dummy body he whipped up like it was nothin'." The doll head looked down, away from her, and in that simple gesture she understood his pain better than she ever could by reading his face. "Bastard." Sid looked back up at her. "Anyways, when I got wind of what was going down, this whole contest thing, and I saw that the First was trying to get a head start by sending Kakistos and all those vamps through . . . well, I figured I'd sneak through the "bleed" to give you a hand."

"And now we're trapped here with you."

Buffy thought about Dawn and Giles, Anya and Tara. Half of the people who made up the core of her world, and they might be lost to her forever if she didn't do Ethan Rayne's dirty work.

"How's that old song go, doll? If you were the only girl in the world and I was the only Dummy? Naw, that ain't it." He shook his head again, the emotion raw in his voice.

"Thanks for trying to help, Sid, but my friends and me, we're out of here. Just as soon as I can figure out how."

"Willow's magick won't do it, Slayer." Sid looked away again, his short arm pointing toward Willow in the next room. Something about his gesture caught Spike's eye, and the vampire stepped closer, his expression hard to read. "She's not powerful enough to take on the First. He won't let you go home until you win or you die, whichever comes first."

Buffy shook her head, denying that possibility.

"There's got to be another way to do this. There's no way I'm going to be a chess pawn for Ethan Rayne. If we win, he'll just be more powerful and crueler than ever."

"What choice do you have? Somebody's gotta win the contest. Better for you if you survive it."

"Maybe there is a choice. If we can destroy the First, then we all get to live and Ethan doesn't get the power he wants." Buffy looked not at Sid, but at Spike as she spoke. She turned back to Sid a second later. "Giles said something, right before we phased into this place. . . . He mentioned Hope's Dagger. Have you ever heard of it?"

Sid nodded his head vigorously, his eyes shifting to look at Spike and then back at Buffy. "As a matter of fact, I have." Sid whispered and Buffy listened. A few minutes later, they entered the Magic Box proper.

If Spike was disturbed by the idea of a ventriloquist's dummy walking around, he didn't let it show. He just got that rare look on his face that said he was honestly interested. "Right, I heard a few bits and pieces of that, but start again. What's this Dagger now?"

Sid spoke. "Hope's Dagger. It's some kind of blade, constructed from the very first ray of light ever to shine on the Earth. We're talking biblical 'Let there be light,' light here. Seriously powerful stuff. Legends call it the Light of Hope. It was magickally gathered in the twelfth century and forged into a blade by Cassandra Rayne."

"I'm sorry, did you say Rayne?" Ethan looked over, his face curious.

"Yes, Ethan." If her tone was clipped and short

with the man, it was only because she wanted him dead. "Your ancestor. Seems she was a warrior for the Powers That Be at that time. Let's hope the Bad Guys' union doesn't find out or they might revoke your membership card. Sounds like there might be a little fate at play here, doesn't it?" Ethan's expression said the idea didn't sit well with him.

"So what happened? With Cassandra and the First, I mean?" Xander had stopped looking at his rotted mirror image on the floor and looked decidedly happy for the interruption.

Buffy gave him a quick smile. She understood what he was going through. "They fought. Cassandra hurt the First, but before she could kill it, it took her down. Hope's Dagger had changed her, though. She was immortal. Since the First couldn't kill her, it tore her apart and scattered the pieces of her body throughout the world of its own creation."

"So . . . if we put Humpty Dumpty back together again?" Faith's face lit up.

Buffy nodded. "Exactly."

Sid stepped forward and ran his eyes over Faith. If he wanted to make one of his usual lewd comments, he kept it to himself. "Hope's Dagger can't be destroyed either. The First hid the dagger here, just like it did Cassandra's body parts. Her soul is tied to the Dagger, so if we can resurrect her, she should be able to find it."

"Then not only do we win, but we destroy Big Daddy Evil forever, and Ethan doesn't get shit." Faith's smile increased in wattage. "I like that idea, B. Just sounds like a good way to end the day, if you know what I mean."

Ethan shook his head. "I don't think I like this plan at all."

Spike sneered and loomed over Ethan. Buffy would have bet a pint of blood that the only thing keeping Spike from ripping the man's head off his shoulders was the chip in the vampire's head. "Yeah, well I don't remember you asking us our opinion of your brilliant scheme. Wanker."

Willow moved up, placing herself between the vampire and the sorcerer. "Um, not to burst anyone's macho bubble, but how do we know where to even begin looking for the scattered remains of a twelfth century warrior woman? Evil realm big. Very big."

"Oh, I already know where to find a piece of her." Every person in the room looked at Sid as he spoke. "Well, two actually. Word in the shadows says Cassandra Rayne's *eyes* are in the morgue at Sunnydale hospital."

Sunnydale Memorial Hospital was not looking its best. Everything that Buffy hated about hospitals was defined, distilled, and purified in the building, and then it was made even worse. The walls of the hospital were a much darker brown than the tan color Buffy was used to. She knew why instantly. The entire exterior of the place had been soaked in blood, a hellish red wash instead of a white wash. The windows were darker too, as if the idea of letting the light in was simply repugnant.

The inside was far, far worse. The slaughterhouse smell of the place made the blood factory she and Spike had visited seem positively mild in comparison.

These scents were those of a charnel house, not merely a slaughterhouse. There was death and disease in the very air, and even Spike—who normally did a Pavlov's dog trick at the notion of human blood—was looking put off from the idea of eating.

There were people inside . . . or at least parts of people. The lobby was furnished with chairs made of bone and sinew frames and finished with thick, rotting slabs of human skin. The welcome desk was covered in a collection of doll's heads each degraded in one way or another and stuck in place with wads of rotting meat. On the far side of the lobby an ambulance had broken through the wall some time ago, and the occupants were still there, though parts of them were missing.

Buffy looked around, her face tight and grim. Something that had a vaguely feminine shape walked past pushing a gurney. A man who'd been carefully opened up and peeled back layer by layer was screaming, his exposed lungs inflating and his heart thudding madly, on the moving table.

A long lean female form in a candy striper's uniform moved past, with choice cuts of raw meat laid out on a snack cart. She looked at Xander, Spike, and Ethan Rayne and smiled broadly, exposing multiple rows of teeth that looked like they belonged on the business end of a few hundred rusty scalpels. Buffy stopped Faith from moving in closer to knock that smile into the next decade. The renegade Slayer's face was pale and shocky, but not from fear so much as outrage. Buffy knew exactly how she felt.

Buffy and the rest of the group moved further into the hospital, past the lobby and into the first waiting room. Though there were signs of violent death in the past, the room was empty.

· "There are too many demons in here." Buffy made sure to look each of her friends and associates in the eyes as she spoke. "Sid and I'll have to move fast. I don't want to waste time with fights we can avoid. Stay here. Don't move. We'll be back." Most of them nodded. Ethan Rayne remained pouty. Faith merely kept quiet. She had a few doubts about Faith, but only a few. Less than she actually expected to have.

She and Sid left the room a few moments later, moving as quietly as they could and avoiding the places that sounded busy or overly violent. Every door they encountered looked to be solid steel and several inches thick. Whoever had done the redecorating had decided to add a little security along the way. Probably not to keep anyone put, just to keep them in. After ten minutes of searching for a good way in, they discovered that none existed. At least not for someone as large as Buffy.

"Looks like I'm gonna have to find a way to get one of these doors open for you." Sid looked around. "Give me a boost, kid. Slide me up to the ventilation shaft. Looks like I can squeeze through there if I try."

Buffy looked at the opening and shook her head. "No go. We'll have to find another way."

"Just boost me up there. I'll have a look on the other side."

She thought about it for a moment and nodded. "I'm not exactly thrilled with this plan, Sid." She grabbed him by the seat of his pants and lifted the doll up to peer through the vent.

"Hey, hey, easy on the merchandise, sister. I bruise easy, y'know." His voice had the teasing quality she'd come to know and to remember fondly from the past.

"Just hurry, Sid. And be careful."

"You forgetting I was at this before you were even born?"

"No. I'm just worrying about what we're going to do if a few hundred of those nurse things come looking for me."

"Just keep your pants on, kid." He looked back at her and waggled his eyebrows a few times. "Or better still . . ."

"Go. I'll wait here for you."

"That's what the girls always say." The dummy slid up into the vent, the grate hanging from where he'd pulled it aside, and vanished into the tunnel.

Buffy listened, fretted, fidgeted, and did her best not to go crazy with impatience for the next ten minutes. During that time she dodged a total of four nurses and a few orderlies wearing leather aprons that were heavily bloodstained. The orderlies also had tusks that were elaborately carved with runes that she remembered from her one meeting with the Harbingers, the high priests of the First. They bore little resemblance to anything she'd seen so far in the weird reflection of Sunnydale, but there was a certain wild boarishness about them, even in their narrow eyes and the wide nostrils that flared when they stopped to scent the air. The good news was her sweat apparently didn't cut through the reek of the entire place around her. She didn't have to fight any of them, much as a part of her wanted to.

Just when she was certain that something had happened to Sid, the lock on the door disengaged from the other side. The slight creak of the hinges was nothing when compared to the distant screams echoing down the corridors.

Buffy stepped warily through the door. The area smelled even worse than the hallway. Sid held up one finger for silence and they moved down the hallway, the dummy showing her where to be extra quiet. After another few endless minutes, they were in another hallway, this one both better lit and quieter.

"So where's this morgue?"

"Well, toots, that's the problem. I don't really know. I know it's down this way, but all the signs have been taken down . . . or covered with stuff I don't want to think about."

Buffy looked at the intersection just ahead of them. There were signs on the walls, like those found in the Sunnydale hospital she was used to, and Sid was right: She really didn't want to think about the strange substances that were covering them. Whatever the stuff was, it moved ever so slightly, like grass in a breeze that she couldn't feel. It had also corroded the signs into obscurity and blackened the wall behind for a dozen feet in every direction, including the floor.

"Okay," she said, nodding. "New plan. You go left and I'll go right. Meet back here as soon as we can."

Sid craned his head up to look at her and stayed

silent for a moment. Then he nodded. "Be careful, Slayer. I'm thinking it will only get worse the further in here we go."

"Now *that's* scary."

"What?"

"You and me thinking the same way."

Buffy went to the right and soon discovered that the only two doors down that wing led to a very large laundry area that was obviously not being used by the new employees, and a stairwell leading down. There was more of the black fungal stuff on the walls as she went down the stairs. The air smelled stale and felt cold and damp. That might mean she was heading in the right direction, but it might mean she was just going to find more storage facilities. Only one way to find out, so she opened the door.

Wherever she was, it was dark and stank like a week's worth of leftover beer bottles at pretty much any of the frat houses on U.C. Sunnydale's campus. She hadn't been in school long, but she knew the odor well enough. Stale beer had a special reek, and this was it. Only more so.

She touched the wall to the left of the door, hoping to find a light switch. The feel of something deathly cold and furry made her yank her hand back. "You'd think I'd start carrying a flashlight, even one of those little penlights sooner or later, but no. . . ." Her voice echoed, the whisper coming back to her, barely intelligible but obviously her voice. Wherever she was, it was a big open space.

She reached to the right, fingers lightly probing the

wall, and just when she thought she'd never touch anything other than cold concrete, came across a smooth plate with switches. She flipped them all, and squinted as the stark, sterile overhead lights flickered to life.

Buffy looked around at the parking deck of the hospital and sighed. The wall to her left was covered in more of the black gunk as far as she could see, and it looked as if parts of it had sprouted reddish flowers ready to go from bud to full bloom—until she realized that the red circular forms were actually eyes that stared at her blindly, unseeing as far as she could tell. There were plenty of cars, all of them torn and battered or even beaten flat. The columns holding up the next level were broken and cracked, as if they'd been through a rough earthquake. And the very center of the deck was gone, nothing but a massive hole that was lined by the black sludge she'd seen growing on the walls. On the ground at her feet someone or something had written:

NYAR' HARISH
DEVOURER OF ALL THAT IS PURE
HAS MADE HIS HOME WITH US
WE ARE BLESSED
LET US ALWAYS REMEMBER TO PAY HOMAGE
LEST WE BE HIS NEXT SACRIFICE

The handwriting made Xander's scrawl look like fine calligraphy, and an arrow led toward the hole in the ground.

"Nyar' Harish?" Buffy frowned, trying to recall if she had ever run across the name anywhere. Best to know what you might bump into whenever possible. Best to know if it could be killed. "Sounds like a cafeteria special." She tried to keep it light, but the smell of the place and the hole in the ground had her worried.

Something hissed lightly to her left, and Buffy turned in time to see the thick black mass on the wall move, slithering across the ground and toward the hole. The door she'd come through blasted open and more of the blackness undulated from the stairwell and toward the pit.

The ground shook below her and Buffy stepped to the right, where the cinderblock wall was untouched by the nasty-smelling stuff. She stared, uncertain what to do as the columns cracked a bit more and the ceiling groaned. Whatever that dark ooze was, she would have bet Mr. Pointy it wouldn't be good to be caught by it. So she waited as it continued to spill through the door. The shattered concrete beneath her bucked and heaved again, and Buffy clutched at the wall, feeling like a trapped rat. Then the hole that dominated the center of the place simply wasn't there anymore. In its place a massive, writhing shape spilled out, flowing upward toward the ceiling.

It did not speak, but Buffy sensed its intelligence, the malignant hatred that spilled from it as it took form. Thick ropy vines of darkness seethed around each other, every one of the tentacles ending in a bulging red orb, almost like a spider's eye. Along each of the serpentine bodies were endless faces, distorted and wailing silently in pain, eyes opened in rage or closed in sorrow, the faces twisted along the prehensile outgrowths, moving even when the heavy tendrils did not. None of the faces were complete, merely vague shapes that resembled the half-formed visages of fetal deaths. That made it worse somehow than if they'd been fully distinct and finished.

When the voice spoke it was in her head, a violent and foul presence caressing the folds of her mind, seeking to understand what she was and not at all impressed with what it found. *You have called and I have come. Offer to me your sacrifice.*

"Oh, no, I did *not*. I would have remembered if I'd called you." The worst of the tremors seemed to have stopped, and Buffy slid toward the door, eager to make her departure.

You have spoken my name and summoned me. Give me what you will or pay with your own miserable life.

"Listen, I'm sure lots of girls would just love to give you what you have coming, but I'm a little pressed for time. Got a date with the First and he just hates it when I'm late." Buffy reached the door and found the handle. It was locked. *Of course it's locked. It's a rule: All of the doors are locked in hospitals, especially when they have what you wanted, like freedom from the bogey man's ugly uncle, for instance.* "So, I'm just gonna be on my way now, and you can go back to being wall mold, or whatever you are."

Before she could grab the handle and force the door open, a thick column of dark flesh as wide as her entire body smashed itself against her only way out, blocking it and warping the steel security door in the process.

I am Nyar' Harish. You will obey me.

"I am Buffy. You will get a clue."

Impudent! The black mass heaved itself further from the pit in the ground and the twisting shrieking faces that seemed to cover every inch of the thing opened their mouths wider, baring fangs that would have left Spike feeling inadequate. Buffy ran hard to the right and jumped at the last moment as a thick pillar of the stuff separated from the central mass and swatted the wall where she'd been. The wall didn't so much crumble as explode where the thing hit.

"Geez, lighten up! It's not like I was teasing you about your waistline or anything." Buffy dodged again as the part of the thing that had smashed through the wall split and writhed in her direction; two separate bullwhipping cords of warped faces and burning eyes that tried to do to her what they had done to the wall. Thing was, she knew the walls were pretty tough. She wasn't sure she was going to keep standing if the things managed to punch a hole through her. Buffy ducked under the first one and leaped over the second. The latter of the two struck a Buick that had last seen a good day some time before Buffy was born, shredding the metal in a shrieking tortured thunderstorm of noise. The car just slid into the wall and crumbled like so much aluminum foil, spilling gasoline and oil as it went.

Buffy nodded to herself and started thinking about math problems as she ran. Giles had warned her that certain things could read minds, and she'd once had a little problem along the same lines, back when she'd accidentally gotten the Aspect of the Demon from one of her kills.

Whatever Nyar' Harish was, she was pretty sure it could actually catch her thoughts as it spoke to her. So she tried to remember the calculus she'd forgotten at the end of high school and hoped it would work to keep the monster from reading what she had in mind.

Buffy climbed on top of a Camaro and stood on the hood, looking for the best way to escape, when the next tentacle came for her. The cancerous thing at the center of the garage quivered and roared in her head, then threw out a pile driver of a swing, from somewhere in its mass, that slapped down at her from close to the high ceiling of the parking deck. The Slayer jumped and kicked off the column next to the cherry sports car, wincing as if the pain was her own when the Camaro was whacked through the column, shattering the support and spilling its fluids all over the spot where the car had been.

"Come on, my little sister can hit better than that!"

Buffy ducked behind another column, peering around to watch for the attack. She missed the thinner snaking tendril that hooked around her ankle and yanked her back around the edge of the concrete post. Her fingers tried to catch the fractured concrete of the floor for purchase, but all she got was a few small pebbles of the stuff wedged under her index fingernail.

This time when Nyar' Harish roared, the sound was physical as well as mental, and loud enough to make her bones vibrate in her body. The small mouths on the mass that was clinging to her calf opened and started biting, chewing at her flesh. Buffy cried out and grabbed the tentacle, ripping harshly at the black cold flesh. Her strength was well beyond normal human, even for an athlete, still the hide of the thing almost refused to yield. She dug in with her nails—wincing as the concrete chips dug in deeper—and strained until finally, the flesh parted, bleeding out a sour-smelling gray fluid that left her gagging. The ground shuddered as she tore and the monster humped more of its mass out of the crater, sending vibrations rippling across the surface of the place and buckling cement and steel rebar alike.

When it let go of her leg it thrashed hard enough to slap Buffy against the post, which refused to move away from the impact. Places where she'd already been battered reminded her that she needed time to heal, and her lungs decided to give up her breath for her.

Buffy fell to the ground and tried to remember how to breathe. Her vision got gray for a second and then she pushed herself back to her feet, dodging hard and fast as another pseudopod of the thing tried to smash her into the column again. The post broke into powder, exposing the steel rebar framework inside and cracking from the floor all the way to the distant ceiling. Buffy flipped backward to avoid another tendril as thick as her waist and then ran as fast as she could, weaving between a station wagon and a Ford Bronco. This time it came in low, a massive black snake of flesh that lifted the station wagon off the ground and flipped it in Buffy's direction.

Buffy rolled under the Bronco and out on the other side of the truck even as the station wagon rammed into it. With a deep roar of frustration, Nyar' Harish launched even more if its central mass at her, hauling the wagon away and slamming into the truck with a half dozen tentacles that pounded the truck into the floor and into the support post next to it. The truck scraped along the column, sparks skittering away like fleas from a dead dog's corpse. As the Slayer did a fast crawl across the ground, the gas tank tore open and spilled fuel all over the floor. The fumes met the shower of sparks and decided they should stay together for a while. That was when the gas ignited and sent a fireball rolling across the garage in a blast of heat and air pressure that threw Buffy halfway back to the door.

The flames licked greedily at whatever they could find, from massive demon to gas-soaked concrete, everything in the vicinity was suddenly ablaze. Buffy grabbed for the door again, this time wrenching the lock open, as Nyar' Harish roared in pain and pushed more of its flabby mass into the parking deck. The hole widened even more, and the burning truck slid toward the ancient creature, hooking the station wagon along the way. Fender kissed rear bumper and the two vehicles fell together into a burning wall of super-heated metal.

Flames and several tons of Detroit's finest export fell into the hole, or rather against the flesh of Nyar' Harish. The monster roared again, a high-pitched wail of sound that left Buffy half deafened. She got through the door and into the stairwell just as the monster rose high enough to hit the ceiling, and just as the fuel tank of the station wagon caught the burning bug and went up in flames.

The broken columns gave up their pretense and

fell away, the ceiling above collapsing without the added support. Nyar' Harish let out a different sounding scream this time and even the closing metal door wasn't enough to weaken the cacophony. Buffy turned and looked back as the concrete from above the monster fell down and onto it, bringing several cars from the next level up down with it.

Buffy didn't wait around to see whether or not the creature survived, but she had her doubts. She also made sure she was out of the stairwell before the rest of the cars that had pinned most of the thing in place began to burn and then to explode, one gas tank after another.

Her head felt like someone had used a meat tenderizing hammer on it, and her nose was bleeding. But after a few minutes, the greasy-feeling pain subsided, around the same time the screams from the parking deck faded to obscurity. Buffy sat in the upper level hallway for almost two minutes before she felt she could walk again.

She made it back to the place where she was supposed to meet up with Sid. He was there, waiting for her. His face was scratched in a few spots—revealing the wood under his lacquer—and his clothes were bloodied. "Looks like you've been having a good time too, toots."

"Well, it's not every day I get to fight a killer pudding." Buffy winced a bit, moving closer to him.

"Gotta watch that stuff. It'll go straight to your waistline."

Buffy managed a smile. It was nice knowing there

were others out there who used humor to hide a bit of terror. "Did you find anything?"

"You mean other than vampires? Yeah. I found the blood banks. And then I found the morgue. And then I found these." He held out his right hand, and the handkerchief that held two perfectly normal-looking eyes, complete with optic nerves but missing eyelashes.

Buffy made a face. "Okay, Sid, that's just disgusting."

The demon hunter shrugged. "They may not be the prettiest things ever, but they're what we're looking for."

"You go ahead and keep them, Sid. Let's just get to the rest of the gang and get out of here."

Sid slipped the bundle into his jacket pocket and nodded his head. "Yeah, let's do that. I gotta tell ya, Slayer, I've never much liked hospitals. They're creepy."

Buffy nodded and started walking. Creepy. That was a good word for it. As good as any she could think of.

They sat in the waiting room as patiently as they could. For around two minutes. That was when Faith started pacing, and Ethan began filing his nails. Spike just stared at the wall, his face unreadable, his body seemingly relaxed and comfortable. And Xander? Well, he kept looking at Faith from the corner of his eye, and Willow watched him watching the Slayer and knew he was probably thinking of their rather checkered past. Faith was his first . . . physical encounter with the opposite sex, and Willow understood that to some guys—guys like her best friend Xander Harris—that meant something. Whether or not they really wanted it to, that moment in their lives marked a transition. Well, that was all good and well as far as it went, but not every person you had your first experience with almost killed you a little while later.

And here was Faith with them again, doing her best to behave. She'd actually turned herself in to make amends for what had happened in the past, including the accidental murder of Deputy Mayor Allan Finch, back when she'd still been on the edge of becoming a full-scale Scooby Gang member. *And, okay, she's doing all the stuff she's supposed to, but no one really knows her well enough to know if she's* sincere *in what she's trying to do*. They'd all tried to be her friends—*well, maybe not succeeded, but tried at least*—and she'd done them a dirty. It was hard to accept that she might really be trying to set herself on the right path and it was harder still to think that she might just be doing it to look like she was trying to get herself in on the right side of things.

It was just a question of whether or not she could be trusted, really. She'd shown up with Ethan Rayne, after all, and that was not a good sign. But she wasn't exactly getting all touchy-feely with him either, and Faith—the old Faith—hadn't minded touchy-feely at all, as Xander could attest to.

Which brought Willow right back to the looks Xander kept shooting at the Slayer when he didn't think anyone would notice.

Spike lit a cigarette and blew out smoke. Like Faith, he was getting restless.

"Sod this. I hate waiting."

Xander looked at the vampire and lifted one eyebrow

slightly, that sarcastic little half-grin on his face. "Hey, maybe we'll get lucky and one of the nurses and a few doctors will come along and set us up in a more comfortable room."

Spike looked ready to make a rude comment, when fate proved Xander right. The door to the room opened and a nurse stuck her head in. The reptilian eyes narrowed as the demon looked at them. "You aren't supposed to be here." Her words were full of accusation and maybe just a little excitement at the idea of having something new to play with.

"Oh, bollocks." Spike swatted Xander on the back of his head and grimaced as pain lanced through his skull. Near as Willow could figure, sometimes Spike decided it was worth fighting the chip. Sometimes it was just reflex he hadn't unlearned after a few centuries as a blood-thirsty monster. This one was maybe a little of both as far as Willow could tell. Xander got a guilty, sheepish look on his face, like a guy who'd just been caught with his hand in the cookie jar. Ethan started to stand up and then rethought his strategy: Standing up would mean exposing more of his creepy body to possible injury. Willow tried to think of a spell that would help them out of the situation, but she'd been so busy thinking about Faith that she was caught unprepared.

Faith whipped a really, really big knife from God only knew where and pinned the nurse-demon to the wall with it. You could say what you wanted, but there was no denying Faith knew how to put a hurt on the average bad guy. The long blade whipped through the air and slammed into the nurse's shoulder with enough force to knock the portly demon off balance. It did not, however, stop the nurse from screaming bloody murder.

Faith's foot took care of that a few seconds later when it made the nurse-thing's head kiss the wall.

"Well, that's bloody perfect." Spike threw his cigarette onto the carpet and stormed toward the door. He pulled the unconscious nurse-demon off the wall—taking a bit of plaster with the blade—and peered out into the hallway beyond. Faith slipped up behind him and looked over his shoulder. Then she dropped down to the ground and pulled her knife out of the demon, taking the time to run the blade over the monster's exposed throat in the process.

Spike backed away from the door, his monster face in place, and looked at Willow, then at Faith. "We're screwed. We've got a small army of nasties coming this way."

Faith nodded and let a small smile creep along her lips. "Guess we better find a new place to hide out, guys."

Ethan stood up again, his eyes looking for possible exits with almost instinctive speed. There was only one door, and right at the moment, it was the door most likely to be opened by a small army of nasties. "Damn, why do I let myself get involved in the dirty parts?"

Xander stood up and pushed Ethan in the same gesture. "Just shut up and get ready to fight."

Willow moved past them all, calling her power, drawing it into herself and preparing the words she'd say to focus that power into a weapon. Faith stepped

out of her way and so did Spike. Part of her acknowledged that simple gesture for what it was: respect for
her power. She looked down the hallway and saw several of the orderlies moving toward them, piggish faces
snarling and lots of blades that had nothing to do with
hospitals bristling from their hairy hands.

She unleashed the forces she'd gathered together
and spoke the words and felt satisfaction as the wave
of power rolled from her. Satisfaction changed quickly
to horror, however, as the power grew bigger and bigger, changing the fireball she'd meant to catch the
demons off guard into a massive searing wave of flame
that scorched the walls and burned the very air.

The demons didn't even have time to be frightened
before the overgrown spell caught them and blasted
them into burning writhing figures that were little more
than bones and charred meat before they hit the ground.

Faith looked over Willow's shoulder and nodded
her approval. "Damn, Willow. You got bitchin' strong
when I was away." High praise from Faith, but Willow
barely heard it.

"I didn't mean to. I mean, I meant to, but it wasn't
supposed to be so . . . BIG."

Ethan Rayne moved up behind her. "I think the
witch has just learned a lesson in physics." He put a
hand on her shoulder that would have been comforting
from Giles and merely felt creepy and dirty coming
from him. "The rules aren't quite the same here, apparently. You've grown very, very strong. I'd be careful
about which spell I cast around anyone I wanted alive
if I were you."

"But, before, when I was fighting, that didn't happen! Everything was the way it was supposed to be!" She shook her head. "I didn't blow up a building or anything!"

Ethan slid past her to look down the hallway. "Then perhaps it's *you* that is more powerful here, Willow." He looked at her, his face calm and pleasant, his eyes cold and calculating, no doubt figuring how best to use this new knowledge to his advantage. She pulled her shoulder away from his grasp and reminded herself that he was the reason they'd gotten into all of this. "Either way, we should be going."

Faith moved forward and pushed Ethan into the hallway. "Not that I like to agree with this loser, but it's not gonna be safe here. We need to get someplace that isn't here, and now."

Faith led the way and the rest followed. Xander kept Ethan close by, but didn't speak. He didn't have to. Willow had noticed the same thing that was probably bothering him. Neither of them really trusted Faith, and surely Spike had no reason to trust her, but they were all three following her. For the exact same reason they followed Buffy. Maybe it was a Slayer thing, that ability to lead and have others follow. Maybe it was just that both of the Slayers were so strong willed. *Small wonder they never got along. In a lot of ways, they're alike. Not so much in the way they think or feel about things, but more because they're both the Slayer.* That seemed to do something to them that was more than just speed and strength.

• • •

"I know we left them around here somewhere." Sid's voice sounded frustrated. Buffy understood how he felt.

"Willow! Xander!" Screaming was, maybe, inviting extra trouble, but no way was she going to leave without them.

Willow's voice sounded in her head, just like the big ugly monster had before, only without the feelings of violation. *Buffy. We're in the operating theater down the hall. Hurry.* Buffy touched her temples. Willow's voice seemed much louder than usual. Normally it was a little uncomfortable—real or imagined, it seemed like a pressure built in her head when Willow talked to her this way—but this was different.

"What's the matter, Slayer? Migraine?"

"No. It's Willow. She's cast a spell . . . a mind link. She's done it before. It's just kind of weird having someone else inside your head."

"Oh, wonderful, she's hearing voices now."

"Follow me. I know where they are."

Sid and Buffy followed the trail of carnage down the hallway where their friends should have been. First was the big spot where someone had played Hiroshima on the hallway—up to and including a few silhouettes where the walls weren't burned, like negative shadows of demons on the walls—and then there was just more standard death and destruction. A few things in doctor's coats were splattered against the walls. A dozen or more nurses and a handful of candy stripers added to the broken forms and three more of the freaky-looking orderlies finished off the list of ex-demons.

They found the gang together in an operating theater,

with Willow, Ethan, and Xander in the very center, and Spike and Faith on the perimeter, mopping up the last of the hospital staff that was still standing. Spike snapped the neck on something that looked like a gorilla with no skin and around two hundred pounds too much muscle. It fell dead to the ground and stayed there, which was a nice thing for the nasty monster to do. Faith rammed a skeletally thin doctor into the wall until his skull broke open. Thick wormy things crawled out of that cavity and died as soon as they were touched by the light.

"Hi, guys."

Willow smiled relief at seeing them. "Buffy! And I see you brought Sid back again. Hi, Sid." She climbed over a dead candy striper and moved closer. "Did you find them?"

"Sid figured out which corpse to take the eyes from. He's good at detective stuff."

"Comes with the territory, ladies." He looked over at Faith, then Willow, then Buffy. "I'm into exploring new things."

Faith snorted lightly. "And that makes you different from other men, how?"

Sid looked back at her. "I can fit in tighter spaces." He pulled the package from his jacket and opened the kerchief to reveal his prize. "We got the eyes, just need to know how to use them."

Xander did an almost comical double take and then shook his head. "Um, guys? I'm thinking we could maybe have this discussion elsewhere." He moved past them and grabbed an IV stand, shoving the narrow end through the door handles. "Because unless

I'm seeing things, we have more of the natives looking to make us into lab specimens."

"No time, Xander. We have to get this finished. Besides, where else will we go that isn't just as bad?"

Spike grabbed the operating table in the center of the room and heaved toward the doors. The table was heavy and would at least slow the Unwelcoming Committee. Just as he settled the table in its new location they heard voices coming down the corridor.

"Willow? How do we make these things work? We need to know where the rest of Cassandra Rayne is." Buffy took the eyes from Sid and handed them to Willow. Willow, for her part, looked appropriately disgusted. "Have a look."

Xander leaned against the operating table, looking at the young witch. Behind him, something heavy slammed against the doors and made slobbering noises. "Gettin' any mojo vibes, Will?"

Willow frowned, concentrating. "I don't know . . . it's almost like I can feel that using them should be simple, but I don't know how. I don't know of any spell for something like this." She looked at Buffy and blanched a bit. "Not really a section in my books of magick on holding squishy eyeballs." She looked up, her face saying she hoped someone would have an easy answer. "Anyone else have any ideas?"

Faith looked at her for a second and shrugged. "Hell, they're not *my* eyes."

Spike lit another cigarette and shook his head angrily. "Oh, this is ridiculous. What'd we all come here for, anyway? Should've just sent the sodding puppet."

Xander stood up and tilted his head. "Wait a minute. We said before it seems like Fate's playing a part here. We're all here for a reason. Well, the rest of us are here because Ethan picked us. And Sid just wants to get away from the First. But what about Ethan? Maybe *this* is why he's here."

Ethan snorted and shook his head. "Don't look at me. You're trying to keep me from getting the power I've worked for all these years, and you want me to help? You're all daft."

Buffy shook her head and looked at the sorcerer. "No. I think Xander's right. She's *your* ancestor, Ethan. You've got to take the eyes."

Willow held the eyes out at Ethan with a look that said she was just fine with giving them up, the sooner the better, thanks just the same. Ethan looked at the eyes and made a just-smelled-something-icky face. He had no desire to take them. Faith, Spike, and Buffy all crossed their arms and looked at him. The look promised just about every sort of painful thing he could think of and a few besides. "Bloody hell." He reached out and took the eyes gingerly from Willow. The gesture said he wanted to get dramatic and snatch them away angrily, but they were squishy eyes, after all, and more than that, they belonged to one of his ancestors, so at least a modicum of decency was required.

As soon as his flesh touched the eyes it happened. Ethan went completely rigid, his every muscle twitching, his eyes going wide in his face. A brilliant kaleidoscopic wave of colors spilled from the eyes in his hand like a film projector on an acid trip.

Faith nodded. "Now we're cooking with gas."

The room darkened around them and grew bitterly cold. From somewhere behind Ethan a blackness spread, like ink in a glass of water, and it began to grow even darker than it had been. Beyond merely black, and deeper than the darkness between the stars. They all turned to look, save Ethan, who was frozen in place. The side of the room where the darkness was simply ceased to be, stretched away by the growing darkness. And from within that pit of endless, ancient black they felt the presence grow. High up above their heads, far higher than the ceiling of the room, a pair of eyes exploded into fiery existence, bathing them in a hot red radiance. They could not see it clearly, but they could see it just the same. Evil stood in the room with them. Evil strong enough to make even Spike's worst sins seem trivial. The eyes loomed above them and looked down with contempt and cold, merciless malice.

Xander spoke in a weak voice, trying to find the courage to speak at all. "Pay no attention to that man behind the curtain."

The voice of the First was a frozen hiss, the whisper of a razor cutting innocent throats in the darkness. "You are a fool, Slayer. Did you truly think that you could do such a thing, in *this place,* without me knowing your every move?"

Sid moved forward, craning his wooden head up as high as it would go, his voice casual and sarcastic. "You know, for a being that likes a good wager, you seem awful eager to disrupt the contest before it's over."

If the First's words could have actually dripped

venom, the dead demon hunter would have been reduced to toothpicks by the first drop. "Little matchstick man. Do not try my patience. You are not even a part of this contest. The only reason I do not destroy you is that I am savoring the nurturing of hope in your heart, just as I will enjoy bearing witness to the destruction of that hope."

The First collapsed into itself, growing smaller, changing its shape and its voice, but losing none of the powerful malice in its tones. When it was done with the transformation, it looked like the Master, the ancient vampire that had once killed Buffy. Somehow it wasn't any more comforting than the big fiery demon thing from a few moments before. "Now, Slayer, it is time for the contest to begin."

Buffy shook her head and crossed her arms. "I don't think so."

Sid shrugged and looked at the new incarnation of the First. "She's right. Ethan made it clear that the rules of the contest don't say a damn thing about his champions not trying to destroy you."

Faith flipped her thick brown hair back and stepped up next to Buffy. "And let's not forget you were the one playin' fast and loose with the rules before, dragging that alternate dimension Kakistos into town."

The First looked at each of them with the Master's face and eyes that would have made the Master cringe in terror. The malignance there wasn't doing much for Buffy either, but she managed not to flinch. She'd seen the First before, dealt with it when it tried to corrupt Angel and later, after failing that, when it tried to kill him before he could find out why he had come back from the dead. The First looked at Faith and changed again, becoming a perfect image of Kakistos. Faith remained as stoic as Buffy had.

"You speak true. I cannot stop you from attempting to destroy me, but wherever you go, wherever you search on your quest, you will find the champions and arenas I have chosen awaiting you." Kakistos was wrapped into shadows, his features fading away, leaving only a Cheshire cat grin and a few parting words. "I think I am going to enjoy this." And then it was gone.

Buffy looked around at her friends and made sure she looked at every last one of them, letting them know that this was the big time now, that everything else had been a warming up exercise. "Ready?"

Xander shrugged his shoulders and looked sheepishly at her. "Can I go home now?" His eyes made a joke of what seemed like cowardice.

Buffy smiled at him. "Let's go."

Buffy, Faith, Xander, Willow, and Spike stepped toward the remaining light that spilled from eyes of Cassandra Rayne. Sid slid closer to Ethan Rayne, his hand touching something else in his pocket. "Good luck, kiddies. I'm gonna stay here and keep Mama Rayne's little boy in one piece for a while."

The five stepped forward, all but Spike looking back at the dummy before they passed into that scintillating brilliance. And then they were gone.

Sid looked at Ethan Rayne and sighed. "Just me and you, buddy." Ethan made no response. "And I can see you're not gonna be much company."

He heard the noises from up above a moment later, the sound of breaking glass and whispered curses. Sid looked up in time to see the windows on the second floor of the room shattering. A moment later the demons came down in an angry swarm, dropping from the windows of the observation bay with growls of protest.

Sid pulled the handgun out of his pocket and released the safety. There were only a few bullets, but they'd been bathed in holy water. After that it was just him and his trusty knife again. "This just isn't my afterlife."

Then

For eight years Cassandra Rayne had waited and prepared, practicing with Hope's Dagger and studying the movements of the Enemy.

The First Evil had been busy.

The Crusaders spilled across Europe and into lands as far away as Jerusalem, bringing with them the word of the One True God. Some of them fought for what they believed was right, and that was all well and good, but many also fought for what could be taken. The worst of that lot lived in the castle over the next hill. If he had been merely a man she would not have considered him an issue, but he was tainted, touched by the First's taint and a willing servant of all that was wrong with the world.

There were claims that he was undefeatable. Cassandra was here to prove that claim false, even if she died in the proving. Besides which, this was personal. The fiend had been the very one who killed Lars and left her a widow and her two sons fatherless.

The children were safe now, in the care of her sister and her sister's husband. If she failed to return they would still be safe. And as her sister was barren, at least good people would care for them. They would be raised in the traditions of the family.

Alexander, her second, looked to her. "We are ready."

"Nonsense, Alexander. We will never be ready. But we will do what we must." Cassandra looked over the landscape, noting the bitter cold in the air and the damp that wanted to sink hungry fangs into her joints and slither merrily beneath her skin. This place was vile to her, and she did not want to die.

Alexander shook his head and smiled. Sometimes she feared their quest had driven him insane, but if so, he was at least loyal in his madness. "We have nearly a hundred men and the castle is open and waiting. What could we have to fear?"

Cassandra stared at his dark gray eyes until he looked away, his smile fading into nervousness. That was good. It might keep him alive. "We have to fear that a hundred armed warriors are riding up to a castle and the people inside have not even sounded an alarm."

"Yes, Milady."

"We have to fear that the First is waiting for us, and even if I am strong enough to wield Hope's Dagger there is always the chance that the Beast will outthink me and use what he can to distract me." She spat and took a deep breath before looking at him again. "The First has cost every last one of us more than most could ever understand, Alexander. Did he not kill your wife, your whole family? Did he not take Lars from me as well? There are tales that the First can use the forms of the dead to haunt your mind and steal your spirit. That is what we have to fear!"

Alexander looked away, his face confused and lost for a moment, and Cassandra placed one gloved hand on his shoulder. "The First has already tried, Milady." His voice was a hoarse whisper and his body shook slightly. "I saw Elizabetha last night."

She studied his face, saw the lines that were fresh, lines crafted by worry and lack of proper rest. She saw the gray in his hair that had not been there only a week earlier. "Be strong, Alexander. Be strong, but not foolish. 'Tis death we are about this day."

"Aye." He looked to the slope that led to the castle and sighed. "And I suspect we had best be about it. They are coming."

Cassandra looked and saw them, the Bringers. They were dressed in black robes and did not so much walk or run as slither from the front of the castle and down toward her and her small army.

"To arms!" she called loudly, her voice as clear and loud as thunder. Her men listened and obeyed, drawing weapons and calling out their battle cries. Most of them called her name as if for strength. She hoped it would be enough.

She had heard of the Bringers but never seen them. They came fast and silent, never speaking, never calling out, merely moving and attacking, the scars where their eyes should have been staring blindly even as they struck with deadly accuracy.

One hundred men and only a dozen of the Bringers. She soon learned why they were the high priests of the First. Their savagery was renowned and their skill was legendary and both were earned well. Still, only a dozen? She and her men would have them down and dead before the first minute of combat.

And then the screams from behind her. Cassandra parried a blow meant to take her head and retaliated in a flurry of motion that would have explained to any man why her soldiers allowed themselves to be led by a mere woman. The Harbinger who dared try her for sport died quickly, though she took no satisfaction from the kill.

She turned her horse and looked back the way they had come and felt her heart sink. A dozen? Nay. Half again a hundred. Outnumbered by demons as they sought to find the Beast who ruled over these fiends!

Alexander beside her grabbed her arm to get her attention.

"Go, Milady! Do what you must and leave the foot soldiers of Hell to the likes of us!"

"Alexander! I cannot abandon you here!" She shook her head, angry that he would even consider that an option.

He grabbed with his other hand and, strong as she was, when he shook her body she felt it from her feet to the crown of her scalp. "We will die this day in either case, Cassandra! Go! Drive your blade into the Beast's cold heart!"

Before she could reply he pushed her away and turned, his horse rearing on hind legs to strike down on another of the Bringers. The Bringer finally made a noise, a scream, which was mirrored both by Alexander and his steed. Hooves slashed down onto the demon's head and broke bone and meat alike. But the monster's sword drove up through the horse's side and into Alexander's thigh in the same stroke.

Alexander and his favorite warhorse fell down, crashing over the Bringer and crushing him completely. Alexander rolled away from his horse, standing, but barely, his thigh bleeding openly and his face pale but furious.

"Do not let me die for nothing, Cassandra!"

He turned away and swung his sword, the blade cleaving air and flesh alike. Cassandra turned her steed and charged away from the battle, her heart heavy. The sounds she heard were familiar enough, save for the voices of her men screaming as they died, her name still on their lips.

The path to the castle was open and clear, Cassandra Rayne drove her horse hard, the stallion's hooves chopping through the ground and throwing clods of dirt behind her. The courtyard was empty, save for the bodies of those foolish enough to come to this forsaken place and try to take it by force. Still, none barred her way. She grew chill with the knowledge that she was expected.

Cassandra did not dismount, but instead pushed through the massive oaken doors into the castle proper, riding as hard as before, with Hope's Dagger in her right hand, where it was meant to be.

"Come forth, Demon! This time, this very day, come to me and meet your final end!"

She looked around the massive room, her eyes adjusting to the smoldering darkness that hid here from the sun's rays.

And before she could speak her challenge a second time, the darkness responded.

Chapter Nine

Xander blinked as he looked around the hallway of Sunnydale High School, thrown by the sudden change in scenery and the bright light that almost burned his eyes after the semidarkness of the operating theatre. It took him a second to realize that none of the others were with him. The school looked the same as always, at least from before the whole Blow-Up-My-High-School-and-Kill-the-Evil-Mayor thing.

"Oh, man . . ."

The school bell rang, a loud Klaxon sound that he had dreaded for years, only amplified. Then the doors of the classrooms opened and Xander had to pinch himself to make sure he wasn't asleep. The pinch hurt, it wasn't a dream. It just felt like one. From every classroom they came, short skirts and long, luscious legs spilling across the floors and, as an added bonus, the rest of the bodies attached to the legs looked pretty darned tasty. A pair of six inch spikes ran up to a pair of black fishnet stockings, and Xander felt his mouth go dry as his eyes trailed up the muscular calves to the perfect knees and shapely thighs. His eyes got to the black leather panties and he remembered how to swallow, though there wasn't really any saliva in his mouth to get rid of. *Yep. That's a nice pair of legs and the hips are looking mighty fine too. I thought this was supposed to be a bad place. Oh, wait. Sunnydale High School and gorgeous girls . . . that almost never worked out well for me in the past. Why should now be any different?* He shrugged, even as his eyes kept looking over all the women in the area. *Anya. Remember Anya.* Like they were pulled straight out of his favorite fantasies.

"Gotta be a dream and I swear if you wake me, mom, I'll never forgive you."

The hips crawled at a nice leisurely pace—not really hidden but rather emphasized by the plaid skirt that didn't even reach the end of the leather undergarments—to a flat, perfect belly with a cute little inny navel and then to a bodice that covered narrow ribs and the sort of chest that made him feel absolutely giddy with schoolboy hormones. His eyes moved past the chest—with a modicum of effort, granted—to the graceful curve of a perfect shoulder and the long neck that practically begged to be nibbled. Thick curls of dark red hair spilled down in two pigtails framing a face that was designed solely, he knew, for the purpose of being smooched. He looked at the full, pouty lips and reminded himself to breathe. The perfect little nose with just the slightest upturn to it, and the wide, smiling blue eyes below horns that split the otherwise unmarred skin.

"Wait, horns?" He blinked. And that was when the whip cracked across the edge of his cheek and left a welt. His hand moved to the searing sting on his face as his brain registered the horns and the wickedly hooked barbs that took the place of fingernails on his fantasy girl made flesh.

"On your knees, pig!" Her voice was a nasty harpy's screech and ruined the image completely. Even more than the whip and the claws for picking flesh from bones.

Xander backed away and bumped into a delightfully curvaceous body. The girl-demon behind him slashed at his back, sending knives of pain running from his shoulder blades to his hips in eight stinging cuts.

Xander hopped forward, letting out an involuntary yelp, and looked over his shoulder at the demoness that scratched him. She was dressed almost the same, but with a crisp white schoolgirl blouse over a black leather bra and thick, platinum-blond tresses pulled back in a ponytail. "Ow! Damn, what is it with beating on me?"

She smiled, her perfect lips peeling back to reveal teeth that ended in razored tips. Unlike her counterpart, this one had a voice as pretty as her face, when she wasn't baring those nasty chompers. "I don't believe we gave you permission to speak, dog." She swiped at him with her claws and he leaned back away from the deadly strike.

Enough was enough. Xander Harris had dealt with this type of girl in school far too many times, and because she was a demon and technically not just another pretty face that wouldn't give him the time of day, he did what he'd been wanting to do for a very, very long time. He hauled his fist back and landed a punch square in the center of her perfect nose. The blonde's head snapped back nicely, and when she looked at him again her lips and nose were bloodied.

"I've about had it with snotty little bimbos who think Xander Harris is supposed to be their stepping stone. Bring it on, you skank."

"Skank?" She hissed. "I'll flay the hide off your pretty boy face!" She roared, her fingers growing longer, her nails longer still, until the thick, sharp ends looked like they could impale him with frightening ease.

"Who are you calling a pretty boy?" He looked around for another likely suspect and realized she had to be talking about him. "You must have some *serious* losers in this dimension."

Then common sense won the day and he ran, dodging another swipe from talons that cut the air with a whistling sound as he went. The redhead snapped her whip at him, grinning a challenge, and he blocked it with his arm, which promptly began to bleed. Xander lowered his head and charged like a bull, wincing at the pain running from his wrist to his bicep. The demon schoolgirls of his dreams might have been mean but, happily, they only weighed in at around a hundred pounds soaking wet. Working construction paid pretty well and taught him a lot. It had also been adding some heavy muscles to his body, though he wasn't really conscious of that fact. His shoulder caught the cheerleader from Hell in the stomach, and he lifted her off the ground, sending her sailing through the air. In a perfect world that would have been the end of it, but Xander Harris did not live in a perfect world and the one he was visiting made home seem like Nirvana. She came back down hissing and using profanities that made Faith look like a nun in comparison.

The two demons opened their mouths wide and screamed, the sound moving in almost palpable waves down the long hallways. Xander cut a hard left toward the auditorium, hoping that he would avoid any more of them. The floors were slick, not from the diligent work of the janitors—which, like in his own reality, wasn't very diligent—but with fresh blood, and Xander slid and slipped as much as he ran. The door to the principal's office opened and out stepped another demoness, but this one was different. This one looked almost familiar.

Xander came to a complete halt, looking at the female demon with the long auburn hair and a form he'd come to know very well. She was not looking at him, and if she noticed him at all, it was not as something to be worried about. With her back to him, the young woman in the black leather outfit walked across the hallway to where there had been a water fountain once. The ground there was built up slightly, like a small pedestal. The stone used to make the addition was as black as pitch except for where it glowed hot and red like a burning coal.

"Anya?" His voice was barely a whisper.

She turned, the girl he was thinking seriously about marrying, and he saw the demon visage where her pretty face should have been. Her flesh was wrinkled and warped, the features sharper and more angular than usual, and the eyes infinitely crueler, but it was Anya, or more accurately, the vengeance demon Anyanka.

"Oh, Anya, honey. What did they do to you?" His voice sounded ragged, even to his own ears, and Xander felt a sting at the edges of his eyes. He blinked a few times and forced the threatening tears away. Crying wasn't going to solve anything.

Anyanka looked at him and stepped up to the small pedestal, putting her body over the glowing coals that looked, from his perspective, like a pentagram drawn by a lunatic. The energy glowed brighter and the air around her seemed to sizzle for a second before Anyanka breathed in and took the wavering, heated air into her lungs, her body.

When she was done inhaling the power, the small dais was cold and dark. *There's something wrong with this. This can't be the Anya I know. She'd have told me about stepping on little pedestals to get her strength back. And where's the amulet she needs to do stuff? Maybe this Anyanka doesn't work the same way. Maybe she—*

"Do I know you?" The voice was hers, but the tone was cold and bitter. Xander had heard stories from his Anya about what she'd been like, but if this was her handiwork she'd understated her own power. "You don't seem familiar and yet you call me by my familiar name. Did I eviscerate you in the past? Or are you someone just playing games with me?"

"Sorry." He could barely breathe and speaking loudly seemed beyond his abilities. "Sorry. Wrong girlfriend."

"Girlfriend?" She scoffed. "Please. I've never been anywhere near *that* desperate."

"Oh, yeah." He forgot himself, forgot that this wasn't really Anya, just a shadow of what she had been once. "Well that isn't what you said last night, baby. Or the night before either."

"You're a very annoying little man. I think I'll tear you apart myself." She stepped from her small pedestal and moved toward him with a predatory grace that usually meant it was time for some lovin'. Not this time.

"Oh. Look at the time. I've got that save the world thing to do." Xander slid along the wall, his feet squelching in the blood of the hallway. "Don't mind me, I just have to find something and then I'll be gone, honest."

Anyanka moved in his direction, and he took that as a sign that he should start running. "Wait, come back, little man, I haven't had time to flay you."

"Listen, maybe next time, okay? Right now there's that thing, with someone else. Anyone else."

The auditorium was just up ahead and he hoped it was empty. There were lots of seats to hide under and probably a few props he could use to pretend there was a chance he was getting out of here alive. He pushed the doors open and moved in, grateful for the silence and the lack of carnage.

The auditorium was dark, but there were a few

lights working overhead. Xander moved toward the stage, wondering where he was going to find the part of Cassandra Rayne that needed finding and whether or not he could maybe locate a good machine gun with maybe a million rounds of ammunition.

He breathed deeply, telling himself again and again that the thing in the hallway had not been his Anya. She just looked a little like her, in an evil demony sort of way, and had a penchant for cutting the skin off any man she noticed. *Not really a problem, not if I'm very, very careful.*

When he reached the stage he saw that something was already going on and groaned with recollections of past traumas. There were dozens of things on the platform already, props and much, much worse. There was a large, tacky plywood box painted with the words "The Amazing Jonathan" on the side. Next to the coffin-sized magician's box was a table with a magic wand and a top hat. Not far away a tuba sat in its case beside a collection of bowling pins that were probably just for juggling. He reached for a pin and hefted the weight. It would have to do as a weapon.

He saw the movement in the back right corner of the stage before he did much more than swing the pin while testing it for balance.

Anyanka was there, just *there*. She hadn't been there a minute before and he knew that for a fact. She hadn't followed him down the stairs leading to the stage and she hadn't slipped around to the back and climbed up through a hidden compartment. She just appeared out of nothing, her face set in a twisted reflection of the pout he found so fetching most times. A murderous, sadistic reflection, but still close to the woman he loved.

She stepped closer and tilted her head just the slightest bit. "I believe I said I was going to flay you."

Xander backed up a pace for every step forward she took. "Listen, I gotta tell you, I'm allergic to flaying. Makes me break out something fierce." He cocked the pin back and got as ready as he could.

Apparently Anyanka didn't find him intimidating in the least. She reached out one almost delicate hand and caught him by the throat, easily lifting him off the ground. "Gah!" It was the best he could manage to say in his defense.

But the bowling pin worked better. He swung it around and felt it connect with the side of her head, the impact sliding from his fingers all the way to his shoulder. Anyanka dropped him and he stumbled back, the bowling pin falling out of his hand and leaving a trail of blood behind it.

"That hurts." The voice was pure Anya and not at all happy. Anyanka looked at him, the side of her head caved in, blood and worse leaking from the deepest part of the dent he'd made.

"Oh, Anya." His voice weakened, and despite what he knew, his heart broke a little looking at the demoness as she came for him. Then his brain clicked back into action and he crawled back, knocking over the magician's table and all the props in an effort to get away.

Anyanka grabbed his right foot and hauled him off

the ground again, swinging him like a cowgirl with a lasso. Xander was glad no one else was there to hear the girly scream that peeled past his lips against his will. When she let go he hit the magician's box and felt it break under his weight. The wind was gone from his body, kicked as senseless as the plywood magician's aid. His fingers curled and uncurled as he tried to stand up. Not two feet away from him, a pedestal rose abruptly from the floor of the stage, another black step with a shimmering red pentagram.

Anyanka stepped onto the pedestal, and again she breathed in the resulting wave of energies. As she inhaled, the wound on the side of her head began to heal. Xander grabbed something that had a soft edge and stood up, hoping whatever he was holding could be used as a weapon. He'd have checked, but he was a bit busy looking at his alternate-reality lover and the promise in her eyes that he was going to die very badly.

"Stay back, Anya . . . I mean it!" He grabbed his weapon of choice and held it out in front of him like a cross. Unlike a cross, the top hat did nothing to repel the demon coming his way.

"Or what? You'll do a song and dance routine?" She smiled a little as she approached, refreshed by her strange energy bath and ready, apparently, to rip his face clean off his skull.

Xander held the hat out at her and backed away. "Maybe I'll just pull a cannon out of here."

"Nonsense. A cannon wouldn't fit. Besides, I don't sense much by way of power on you, boy."

"Well then, maybe I'll just run." He was about to

make another comment when the hat suddenly dropped a bit in his grip, the weight of the thing tripling in an instant. "What?"

Anyanka froze, looking at his expression. "What is it?"

"I think I know. . . ."

"What?"

Xander reached into the hat, his face breaking into a smile. "A little something I know you don't want to miss." He felt the fur and pulled, lifting a large spotted rabbit from the top hat's interior. While he'd wondered several times about Anya's fear of rabbits, he'd never really tried to solve the reasons. Right then he didn't care as long as the fear existed in this version of Anya as well.

She jumped back faster than a vampire kissed by the sun's warm caress, her eyes flying wide with fear. "Noooo!"

"Oh yeah, baby! Daddy Xander's got a little bunny for his sugar girl!" He walked toward her, the kicking rabbit held in front of him, and Anyanka backed away, terrified beyond the ability to do more than panic.

Anyanka turned and ran and Xander started after her, ready to get this done with once and for all. She cast her eyes back and ran faster, pushing out the stage door and fleeing from him and the rabbit that was twitching in his hand, eager to get away.

Xander followed, sliding into the hallway near the cafeteria and grinning ear to ear. It was nice to have the upper hand for a change, and a feeling he could easily get used to.

Anyanka pushed into the cafeteria and Xander followed. Half a second later he wished he hadn't. All of the students he'd seen, even those spotted at a distance, had been girls, albeit skanky demon girls in leather. Now he knew where the males of the student body were hanging out, and in this case he meant that literally. Chains dropped from the ceiling of the room, falling a few short feet until they met up with the wrists of the boys who hung from them. He saw faces he'd known in high school, many of them friends and even more of them the sort he'd tried to avoid being victimized by. He could recognize some of them easily. But with others, the ones who'd had parts of their faces cut or chewed away by their attending demon-bimbettes, it was a lot harder to see who was being tortured to death.

It wasn't the nice, neat Hollywood sort of torture he saw in the movies, it was more like a slaughterhouse where the animals were sliced into thin pieces of tender meat without the mercy of being killed first. In every single case the thing that most of the boys would have claimed made them men had been removed first. Xander dropped his bunny and let out a weak breath as the demonesses in the room looked from the panicked Anyanka to him.

Anyanka pointed toward Xander with a shaky hand. "Kill him! Kill him now!"

"Oh, damn. Mom! Mom! Wake me up now! This dream *sucks*!" Xander ran the other way, swinging the hat in one hand and running for all that he was worth. The demonesses started after him, their high heels tapping against the bloodied floors.

As Xander ran the hat grew heavier from time to time and another bunny appeared. The first one sat in the hat, looking remarkably calm about the entire affair, as he pelted down the hallway and toward the stairs. Maybe the library would be a better place to hide. He had some fond memories of the library, give or take the whole Hellmouth thing.

Up ahead he saw another of the glowing pentagrams burning on its short pedestal. He had no intention of touching the thing, being pretty sure that what helped the demon Anyanka was not exactly going to do him any good. The bunny in the hat had different ideas and jumped from the brim of the hat onto the bloodied Linoleum. It bounded over to the pedestal and landed on the pentagram, and Xander caught sight of the flaring light as the bunny did exactly what Anyanka had done before. It drank in the explosive heat from the flaring symbol and remained unscathed.

Xander stopped long enough to look at the rabbit and gape before the sound of the Dominatrix Cheerleader Catholic High School Girls from Hell reminded him that he was about to be turned into so much bloody confetti. He ran again, an angry stitch already starting in his side, and held onto the hat for dear life. He cleared the science wing of the school in record time, losing two more rabbits from the hat that were suddenly there and then jumped away from him when they found the pentagrams where there had once been water fountains.

Somewhere behind him, he heard the sounds of the girl-demons chasing, and then he heard a loud, shrill screaming noise that set the hair on his neck and scalp rising like hackles on a frightened dog. The sound was not human and it didn't come from one of the Cheerleading Cannibal Demon-Girls either. He knew that sound, sort of. When he was just a kid, maybe four or five, his neighbors had had a massive Rottweiler. The dog was as friendly as could be and Xander had considered him fine company. But Thor, the big friendly oaf—liked to chase small animals. Normally they got away and that was that. Once he'd caught a rabbit. When Thor started tearing into the poor bunny's flesh, the dog had made a screaming noise almost exactly like that. Almost. This one sounded much, much bigger and a lot meaner too. He didn't want to know what the bunnies he'd dropped off looked like. He just did not. All he knew was that the screams afterward sounded like they came from frightened cheerleader demon girls and that was enough for him.

Xander hit the library doors and slid to a halt once he was inside. Another of the little pedestals was there and glowing. He let the bunny do its thing and sat down at the mirror image of the table where he'd spent many a night doing research, instead of homework, with his friends. Sometimes it seemed like a miracle to him that none of them had died so far helping Buffy with her duties as the Chosen One. Most of the time he made a conscious effort not to think about it.

Anyanka swept into the room, her face terrifying in her rage. She saw the rabbit on the ground and froze as sure as if it were a cobra reared back and ready to strike. The rabbit looked at her and Xander waited, wondering when the monster bunny that hid inside would rise and devour her.

"Monster bunny? Come on now, get up out of that cute little body and kill the bad thing." He licked his lips. The rabbit twitched its nose and preened, looking very disinterested at Anyanka, who, for her part was moving around the rabbit slowly.

"Those things make me want to run screaming, boy, but I don't really think they can turn into monsters." She looked at him and shook her head. "You do, don't you? You think it's going to grow great big fangs and eat me alive or something. Look, I'm the one with the phobia here, not you. What's with the bunny?"

He knew it wasn't his Anya talking, but she managed to carry off a perfect alternate-reality imitation of her. "But I heard these horrible sounds, like a giant bunny getting nasty, and I heard all the Catholic High School Girl Hot Mama Demons screaming. . . ."

Xander looked around and moved behind the desk in the library, hoping he would find something, anything he could use as a weapon. Anyanka was still moving past the bunny, which continued to preen.

"Really loud screams, kind of like fingernails down a chalkboard only more offensive?"

"Yeah." He found the fire extinguisher on the wall behind him and decided the little plastic thingie that stopped it from working would be too awkward. She'd be past the bunny by then and he'd be in deep trouble.

"Oh, is *that* all." Anyanka waved a dismissive hand and finally got around the rabbit. "That was Beatrice. She screams a lot and her voice has never been very pretty."

"What?" Xander looked at the rabbit, feeling oddly betrayed by it. "But what about all the other girl-demons and their screaming thing? That wasn't the sound of them dying horrible deaths?"

Anyanka laughed and shook her head, and for a second he fully saw his own Anya inside that simple gesture. Not even the warped flesh could completely hide her away. "Not hardly. I told the girls there would be special treats for whoever brought you back in one piece and Beatrice gets a little competitive." She looked at him and walked closer. "She also pulls hair."

"Oh. Crap." Xander ran around the side of the desk and reached for the top hat. Anyanka caught his hand and hauled him back toward her, then slapped him hard enough to make him see stars.

"I meant it. I'm going to kill you personally and make it last a long time. There's just something about your smug familiarity that pisses me off."

Xander hit her back and felt his knuckles make unhealthy crunchy noises against the side of her jaw. Other than the hot throbbing pain in his hand, there was no noticeable effect. "So, can we talk about this?"

"No." Anyanka slammed him into the table where he and the gang had done research and eaten more donuts than any mere mortals should ever consume. Xander made a loud WHOOOOF noise and tried to get some air back into his lungs.

"Definitely like you better when you aren't all demony." The words were weak, but then so was his ability to breathe just at the moment.

"What are you talking about?" She put her hands on

her hips and leaned a bit toward him. "You see? You're doing it again, acting like we should know each other."

"Well, see, where I'm from, we've been sort of dating for about a year now."

"Oh, I can't see that working out at all."

"Yeah, well, just now? I'm having a few doubts of my own." Xander sat up and looked at the demoness. She in turn looked at him, her face unreadable.

"So what are you saying? You're dumping me?"

"Hey, I said I'm dating *human* you, not *demon* you."

"So it's because I'm a demon?"

"Not just a demon, Anya. You're a vengeance demon and you have a thing about turning guys like me into shredded wheat." And why was he feeling so defensive? It wasn't like he was actually dating *this* Anya.

She crossed her arms and looked at him, her head turned to glare menacingly. "That is just so typical. Judging a woman by stereotypes. I'll have you know I've had several lovers who were amazed by my sexual prowess and thought I was a fun date to boot."

"And that's just what I need to know! I so need to hear you going on and on about how much other guys like your style! Don't you think I have enough troubles in our relationship without you bringing up the past again?"

"Oh, so it's all my fault now."

He lifted his hands and held them in front of his face as the demoness came closer. "I'm not the one that started this, Anya. You're the one who always has to go on about how much other guys like you. If it's not about money or how great it was to torture thousands of men to death, it's about how much other guys like you or how my best friends are all women."

"Wait a minute. I'm *still* a vengeance demon, and I don't need any money."

Xander looked at her and blanched. "Oh. Yeah. Well, you just sounded so much like *my* Anya, I forgot for a second."

"So you talk to her this way too?" She sounded incredulous.

"Well, not all the time, only when she starts going off about her past life and glories."

"Well maybe she wouldn't go on about them if you were treating her the right way." Anyanka looked at him, her lips pressed down into her normal thin line of anger and frustration.

"I treat her like gold!" Xander bristled, offended by the demoness's tone. "She's the best thing that ever happened to me. She's the only reason I ever moved out of my parents' house and got an apartment, and she's the number one reason I got a decent job. There's nothing I wouldn't do for her!"

Anyanka blinked and backed away from him. "You say that like you mean it."

"Of course I mean it! Sure, we fight, but that's just a little thing. Most of the time when we're together I'm happier than I've ever been."

Her demonic face broke into a look that was also familiar to Xander. It was the look his Anya got when they were ready to make up and then make with the big sweaty roll around in the bed and on the floor. Of course, his Anya didn't exactly look like a, well, like a vengeance demon when they got to that stage. It was a cold slap on the face that brought him back to reality.

Anyanka moved closer still, and he swore she looked like she wanted a hug. He grabbed the top hat and held it up in front of him. "Oh, hey, listen. You're *not* my Anya. No offense, but she'd kick my ass if I let you hug me."

Anyanka looked puzzled, then angry, and then like she was going to rip his head completely off his shoulders. Then she let out a bloodcurdling doozy of a shriek as a snow white bunny jumped from the hat and landed on her black blouse. Xander backed up, horrified, as bunny after cute little bunny leaped from the hat, streaming out at a terrifying pace. And every last one of them landed on Anyanka the vengeance demon. For her part, the scourge of foolish men who'd spurned their lovers fell on the floor paralyzed with fear.

Xander dropped the hat and moved to help her, not thinking again, just reacting to the sound of Anya in pain. He pulled at the rabbits, yanking them away from her and shooing them aside. His fingers found warm fuzzy bodies and then found her nasty-looking demoness skin, and his right index finger found a chain around her neck that had dropped low into her blouse and remained hidden earlier.

The one thing that used to drive him crazy when he first started dating Anya was her incessant complaints about how crappy her life had become since she'd lost her necklace. It only took Xander a second to catch onto what the chain was tied to. He found the small amulet at the end of the chain and closed it in his fist, then yanked back as hard as he could.

Anyanka screamed again, her voice even more panicked, and reached for him as the chain came free. "No! That's mine! I need that!"

"And that's just what Anya used to say too!" Xander smashed the amulet against the corner of the hard wood table and felt it break in the palm of his hand with a brilliant flash of white-hot heat. He pulled back his hand and looked at the damage, saw the heavy blisters already forming on his palm and moaned. "Ow! Oh, I just know that's gonna leave a scar."

The non-demoness Anyanka rose to her feet and ran from the room, a flurry of bunnies in hot pursuit. She looked like his Anya, but he knew better. Maybe somewhere out in the warped mirror of his own world there was a Xander waiting for her, but it wasn't him.

Xander looked over the room. Almost everything there was where it belonged, as if the school had never been blown to smithereens and he could expect to see Giles come through the door any second now. But in the locker where Giles held Oz the wolf boy during full moons there was a torn, preserved arm with long feminine fingers.

Xander looked at it for several seconds, dreading what he had to do. He touched the door to the cage and found it locked. He walked over to Giles's desk and pulled the key from the second drawer, where it was always kept.

Xander stepped carefully past the rabbit that was preening itself not five feet from the door to the library and opened the metal mesh locker. He closed his eyes for a second before grabbing the arm. It felt dry and dusty, like it was maybe made of wood, but it weighed about as much as he figured a woman's arm should weigh.

"If I get out of this alive, I swear I'm gonna beat your descendant into the ground at least three times." He looked at the arm as he spoke while carrying it back to the table. Happily, the arm made no reply.

Faith looked at the old stone manor in front of her and shrugged. It was old, it was stone, and it was a house. Aside from that, it meant nothing to her. Had anyone told her the Quarryhouse had a history, she would have stared blankly. It was a history that meant nothing to her at all. But she could admit that it looked properly intimidating silhouetted against the full moon.

She moved toward the house, her skin tingling. There was no way this was going to go easily. That was all right. Part of her wanted a fight, wanted a little mayhem, because the last few months in prison had been rough. Nothing she couldn't handle, but it was going to be nice being able to do more than work out constantly in an effort to relieve a little tension.

At least none of the old gang had ragged on her too hard so far. Couldn't be easy for Xander. She closed her eyes for a second, remembering the look on his face when she'd almost choked him to death. Even thinking back to that time made her feel a little ill. It was the past, sure, and she was trying to make amends, but she had felt his eyes on her, could almost read his mind without any supernatural help as he looked at her in the hospital waiting room.

They'd had sex, so what? It hadn't meant anything

to her. That didn't make her feel any better about the way she'd treated him when he'd been one of the few guys she'd ever met who hadn't basically used her like a dishrag and tried to throw her away afterward. He was a good person and she'd done him wrong. Maybe someday she'd find a way to apologize to him.

Not today though. She had other things to worry about. The manor was big, and it was old, and she didn't like the vibe she got off it. Naturally that meant it was where she had to be. She could sense it well enough.

Up on the roof she saw movement. It was furtive and careful, but she saw it. Slayers don't live long if they can't use their senses. She decided to play along, looking around as she spoke, but she kept track of the figure on the roof.

"Ooh, spooky. Just the kinda place I'd expect someone to hide hacked-off pieces of a dead woman. Time for a little Recon. Faith's gotta bring home the bacon."

He took the bait, waiting until she appeared to be looking off toward the ocean before dropping down from the roof. Kakistos hit the ground and bent at the knees, absorbing the impact effortlessly. "Yes, Slayer. By all means, come in. I've been waiting for this day."

"Kakistos!" Faith took a step back, her heart thundering in her chest. She forced herself to look as calm as she could, but her stomach was burning and her skin felt clammy. "Shoulda known you're what the First would pull outta the air to go up against me. Only thing I've ever been afraid of."

Kakistos grinned, moving toward her, a predator with easy prey. "With good reason, girl."

Faith shook her head, licking her lips. "Yeah, says the guy still wearing the fancy scar from the axe I buried in your face." She thought about the way he'd screamed and about how he'd screamed again when she killed him. "I killed you once. Ain't afraid of you anymore."

He shook his head, his smile flashing white in the night's darkness. "I hear the quaver in your voice, Faith. You'll have to convince yourself before you can convince me." He stepped forward again, his bestial face almost serene in the darkness. His dead white eye—the one she'd put an axe through once, shone like a gemstone in the moonlight. He sniffed the air and his smile grew again, a feral, vile thing on his ruined visage. "I can smell your fear from here."

Faith shrugged, her heart racing, her hands sweating. The wind cut across the cliff side where the house stood crouching and dried the worst of her fear sweat away. "Maybe you need to get a little closer, then." Her hand slid back to touch the stake she had tucked into her back pocket.

Kakistos laughed and backed away, pointing to the dark pit of a front door on the manor behind him. "Oh, I plan to. Come in, girl. I've got a little party planned for you, just like the old days in that Missouri swamp."

Faith swallowed, breathing in the rich tang of the sea air. She flipped her head and knocked a stray strand of hair away from her eyes. She licked her lips and forced a thin smile onto her face. She tried not to think of Missouri and what the freak in front of her had done to her first Watcher. What he'd sworn he would do to her if he ever found her again. Thinking about those things only made her angrier and more afraid at the same time. That way was the path that had led to her being in prison in the first place. She had to be calm.

"You know me. I'm always up for a party."

Faith moved toward the door, her eyes looking everywhere they could.

There was a sudden pressure in her head and she heard Willow's voice. *Faith. It's me, Willow. You gotta know this is a trap.*

Faith shook her head angrily. "Get outta my head, girl. Now." The last thing she wanted or needed was anyone knowing how scared she was. "I've got it covered. Everything's five by five."

But Faith . . . She could hear, could feel, the concern in Willow's thoughts, but that was part of the problem. The concern was distracting and she couldn't let herself be distracted not right now.

"I mean it!" She shook her head and stopped moving. "I know you want to help. And thanks, seriously, but get the hell out of my head." Willow stopped talking and she thought the witch had vanished. She couldn't be sure, but she thought so.

Faith kicked open the door and dropped into a crouch, fully expecting a surprise. She got what she expected. Something cold and wet jumped over her head and sailed out through the open doorway. She turned fast and saw a scaly shape land in the lawn ten feet away, already preparing to come back her way.

Ophidian eyes glared at her from a face that was more like an alligator than anything else, and the thing

charged at her, running on surprisingly fast bowed
legs. Grayish-green scaled skin glistened wetly, and
the claws on the thing's feet tore tufts of dead lawn
from the ground. It let out a croaking roar and leaped
for Faith, mouth open in a display of rancid breath and
sharp, yellowed teeth.

Faith kicked the door closed with all of her
strength. The wood connected with the gator-man's
head and exploded into flinders under the impact. The
gator thing started to stand and Faith drove her stake
through the scales between its eyes, pinning it to the
ground.

It thrashed wildly, the head pinned but the body
going mad and the tail cracking against the sides of the
doorway. Faith stepped back, and then spun around,
catching the next of the things across the face with a
roundhouse kick. Bones broke in the jaw of the creature
and her foot felt like she'd been practicing on a train
engine. The thing was dazed for a moment and she took
full advantage, catching the broad snout in her hands
and clamping the mouth shut as hard as she could.

"Unnn . . . no! You aren't getting away that easy,
frog boy. You and me, we gotta dance to the finish."
The creature bucked hard and she held on just as
tightly as before, lifted from the ground by the strength
of the monster's thrashing. She waited and timed it as
the creature tried to throw her again, then used the
momentum to her advantage, swinging over its shoulders and taking the long snout with her. The creature
fell backward and Faith landed on its cold, muscular
back, driving her heels into the flesh where kidneys

would have been on a man. The scaly hide around the muzzle bit into her fingers, but she pulled back anyway, stretching the neck taut and bending the monster over itself backward.

She forgot it had a tail. Really, not that many of the demons she'd seen did. The alligator-man's thick appendage slapped her across her back and neck, sending her halfway across the room, where she fell into a wooden table that broke under the impact. She couldn't be sure but she thought maybe a rib or two of hers went the same way as the table. *Stupid! Stupid and sloppy! You aren't gonna get away with anything tonight or ever if you're dead, girl!*

She'd been cocky and she knew it, now she was paying the price. The first of the monsters had been down so easily that she had taken it for granted that they weren't intelligent. Bad, bad mistake. The one she'd almost managed to break in half let out a deep croaking roar and dropped to all fours, keeping low and protecting its belly.

Faith moved back, her body pressed to the wall. If she could dodge any charge it made, the thing would have no choice but to run into the marble wall behind her, and that just couldn't be a bad thing.

Or maybe it could. Her hand touched something, a trigger of some kind, and the wall behind her dropped down suddenly, taking her off guard as she stumbled back into a room that shouldn't have been there. She rolled with it, came back up on her feet and prepared for a fight, but she was disoriented now, unaware of where everything was in her new environment.

Which was when Kakistos grabbed her from behind, his powerful arms wrapping around her chest and arms, pinning her, crushing her in a grip like a constrictor's. She could smell him, a musky, musty odor like a stuffed animal display. His lips pressed to the side of her neck, a mocking kiss that left her skin crawling and her pulse doing double time.

"Faith." He purred, his voice deep and almost pleasant if you didn't know what he was, what he looked like, and what he was capable of. Faith knew all of that, and hearing his intimate whisper in her ear left her terrified. He held her against him and licked his cold, dead tongue over the side of her neck. "I told you we'd have a chance to play. Do you remember that night? The fun I had with your Watcher?" Kakistos sighed, a sound of pleasure that repulsed her even more. "What I do to you will make her time with me seem trivial." His fangs brushed along her nape and she felt his body against hers, his arms slowly increasing their crushing strength.

Faith leaned forward as much as she could, her body pushing back against him for leverage, and then snapped her head back into his face with every last bit of strength she could muster, a scream escaping her lips at the same time.

Kakistos grunted in surprise and his grip loosened. Faith head butted him again, feeling the blow on the back of her skull, the touch of one of his fangs breaking the skin under her hairline just before the fang itself broke free from his mouth. His arms let go completely and she dropped from his grip, wanting to wash her body for hours in a hot bath and instead satisfying herself with a brutal kick to his privates. He was not a human being, had not been for some time, but she knew it hurt like hell.

Kakistos grunted and stepped back, and Faith sprang at him, ready to tear his head off his shoulders with her bare hands if that was all she had to work with. Kakistos roared and swiped at her with an open claw. His fingers found her midriff and cut across her belly, even as her left leg moved up and connected with his chest, kicking him away from her. Had she not been attacking, he would surely have gutted her.

Faith rolled back, bleeding lightly from the wounds on her stomach. Kakistos came for her, all pretense of kindness or anything remotely human taken away by the pain she'd inflicted. Before she could gain her feet, he was there, his thick, powerful leg kicking her in her already tender midsection and knocking her out of the hidden room and back into the area where the gator-things were waiting.

There were more of them now, five or six that she could see as she slid across the marble floor and hit the Persian rug that passed for carpeting. She needed a weapon or twenty and all she had was her knife, the stake she'd earmarked for Kakistos still stuck through the head of the one monster she'd managed to actually take down.

One of the things charged at her, its body moving in a weirdly graceful sideways sway as it attacked. Faith tried to dodge and failed, the heavy body of the freakish beast slapping into her and knocking her across the room again. She felt like a football at the Super Bowl.

This time when she finally stopped rolling, she was near the massive fireplace that dominated one interior wall of the room. *And why does anyone need a fireplace in sunny southern California? Because they could have one*, she guessed. The good news was that the fireplace came with the requisite number of tools, including a poker.

Faith grabbed the sharp-ended tool in one hand and the small shovel for clearing out ash in the other. As one of the lizards charged her again, she hooked the stand used to hold the implements with her foot and shot it through the air. Just as she'd hoped, the beast reacted quickly and swung its mass at the missile. The claws grabbed the stand and squeezed, crushing metal as it hissed a warning in her direction.

Faith ignored the warning and attacked, breaking the blade from the shovel deep inside the thing's chest. Brilliant red blood spouted out from the monster's rib cage and Faith jumped up, planting both of her feet in the area around the wound and sending it sprawling away from her. As it fell, the monster managed to land on an end table that broke into fragments around its dying bulk. With the handle from the small shovel still in her hand and the poker held in her other, Faith spun hard and impaled the next demon through the throat. Not exactly a winning blow with a vampire, but it did the job in this case. The alligator-monster reared back, a wet gurgle replacing the hissing roar that had been spilling past the deadly teeth.

Another of the damned things hit Faith low and

from behind, sending her to the ground with around three hundred pounds of scaly abomination snapping at her head. Faith grunted and shoved the poker past her own ribs as she fell. The blow hurt when her head slammed into the marble floor, but a second later she was rewarded by the hellish shriek of the creature on top of her as the poker ripped through its lung and heart. She managed to get her arms under her and lift herself out from beneath the dying monster, but it snapped its teeth down and scraped through her shirt and into the meat of her arm in the process. Faith hissed herself, the pain enough to wake her out of the half-daze her head blow had caused, and kicked the thrashing monster the rest of the way off her body.

That left at least two of the things, but when Faith looked around the room she couldn't see them. They were gone, or hiding very well in the dark shadows all around the unlit room.

She often tried to forget about her Watcher and the death the woman had endured, but she never forgot the lessons she'd learned. Faith closed her eyes and listened, letting herself grow comfortable with the darkness. There was a slight breeze pulling into the room from the fireplace, and to her left the demon she'd just killed was doing a slow, twitching death dance. The hard scaly skin whispered and creaked against the marble floor. The front door was still open, and she could hear the surf from below the cliffs in the distance. Her own pulse was too fast, too frantic, her body not in tune with her mind's attempts to relax and her senses' desire to expand. She made herself block out the thundering beat of her heart and listened carefully to the faint whisper of long black claws and scaled feet moving toward her at high speed, just there, to her left, near the dying thing, and over there almost behind her, and then gone as the demon left the ground and prepared to tackle her up high, the air now whispering over the body that sailed in her direction.

Faith turned, reached out as quickly as she could, her eyes still closed, and caught the monster by the forepaw, grabbed and pulled as she twisted her body back, added to the speed the thing already had going for it, pushed it faster still as she threw it toward where the other one was moving closer.

They both let out roars of frustration and surprise, their reptilian faces barely capable of actual expression managing to show at least a little of the shock they had to be feeling as they collided. The two forms spilled across the floor, claws seeking some sort of purchase as they fell, trying to stop their momentum any way they could. Faith grabbed the ruined end table top as she moved, lifting the broken marble sheet above her head and bringing it down with all the strength she could muster on top of the two writhing forms. The marble broke. So did the monsters. One of them was unconscious or dead, the other was croak-roaring loud enough to make her head hurt.

It tried to crawl away, still making that deep wet sound as it moved, sliding toward the fireplace and leaving a heavy trail of blood and other fluids as it went. When it reached the base of the massive fireplace, it touched a slab of marble at the corner, and

Faith watched it suddenly drop down, the floor beneath it disappearing with a loud slamming noise.

Faith panted, her arm and ribs on fire, and looked at the trapdoor as it swung back up and clacked shut.

Faith behind you!

Willow's voice almost exploded in her head, and she let her knees go slack beneath her, just in time to avoid having Kakistos body slam her into the mantle of the cold hearth. Faith cursed, Kakistos cursed. Faith got up, Kakistos slammed into the marble facing and broke it with the impact. He turned back toward her, his mouth open in a roar she barely heard, and charged like a bull.

Faith was terrified. The thing coming at her was still one of the worst nightmares she had ever experienced and had come back from death for her, ready to do things to her that would leave her begging for death as surely as her Watcher had.

She rolled toward Kakistos, her body tucked in and her legs drawn tight to her body. As the ancient vampire came toward her she kicked out, catching his left knee as all of his weight landed on it, his visage comical with surprise.

Something crunched in the vampire's knee and he howled in pain. Faith didn't wait around to see how badly she'd hurt him. Instead she struck the exact same stone the gator-thing had hit and caught a deep breath as the ground vanished from beneath her.

It wasn't a long free fall, but it wasn't exactly short either. If she hadn't landed in water, she might have been seriously injured. The water was very, very deep and surprisingly cold. Faith gasped as she went under and came up coughing. There was little light in the area, but she'd already adjusted to darkness and was prepared for that.

She had to tread water. There wasn't any floor that she could feel. But she heard the water lapping against stone to her left and swam that way. In a few moments she felt porous rock and realized there was a ledge. She dropped under the surface of the subterranean lake for a moment and then kicked with her feet, flipping up and onto a relatively dry, flat surface.

There was light here, faint but real, spilling from lichen that grew on the walls and produced a soft luminescence. She could see the shape of the thing she'd been fighting where it lay on the wide ledge she stood on. It did not move, but she wasn't foolish enough to think that meant it was dead. Several items rested on the mantle, pressed to the rough wall. There was a small steel chest and a few torches that had probably been left behind by whoever owned the place before Kakistos came along. *Makes sense that the owners of the place knew they had a secret trapdoor, so why not be prepared to use it?*

Faith grabbed one of the torches. It would do as a weapon if it was all she could find. She had to be resourceful, but that was hardly a new thing for her. She'd been doing resourceful for years, a side effect of living the way she always had.

The gator-thing let out a long, mournful note and shuddered, its tail thrashing weakly for a moment. When the note ended, it was a soft sigh that seemed to go on forever.

Faith?

"I told you to get out of my head, girl."

I know. I'm sorry I didn't, but I had to make sure you were okay.

"Didn't know you cared, Willow."

Hey, you're with us on this thing, and that means you're all the way on the team. Of course I care.

She lowered her head and smiled in the darkness. "Thanks, I think."

Kakistos is coming for you.

"I know. I'm waiting."

Faith knelt down and looked at the rest of the junk along the edge. There was a bolt of cloth that could be useful. She unrolled it quickly and stifled a scream when the arm came out from the center, a fleshy spool for the bolt of fabric.

"I think I found Cassandra."

I think you did. Listen, Faith . . .

"Yeah?"

Oh. I gotta go. Something's—

Willow was gone, just like that. The silence was almost complete. There was just the gentle lapping of the waters below and the sound of her own breathing. She moved back toward the water, stretching out the silk as she went. It wasn't as good as a chain saw or a flame-thrower, but wetted down it would make a decent whip once she twisted it into a rat's tail. Any weapon in a crisis situation was better than none, and she would take whatever she could find to fight Kakistos.

She lowered the silk, feeling it touch the water and start to soak in the moisture she needed. And then she felt it pulled hard and she felt herself caught in that pull and hauled into the waters.

She hit the surface and broke through, water forcing itself into her nose and mouth and a deeper darkness washing over her. Her hand sought a purchase of some kind as she was grabbed and rolled, like a fresh piece of kill for a crocodile. She didn't know up, she didn't know down. There was no gravity in the whirlpool that dragged her and spun her and left Faith wondering if she would ever see daylight again.

Faith scissored her legs and regretted it almost instantly as she ran into the side of the deep pool. She put her hands around her mouth and breathed out a little air, feeling the pull of the surface as the bubbles moved hard to the left. She turned her body in that direction and paddled as hard as she could, using her hands above her to protect from any other unexpected barriers.

Her hands found air first and then her face found the surface. Faith sucked in a deep breath and looked around, trying to orient herself again in the darkness. There, ten or fifteen feet away, she saw the ledge, the faint glow from the lichen clear enough to let her know that she had to move in that direction. Her hand caught the waterlogged silk she'd been soaking and she wrapped it several times around her wrist, determined not to lose it again. Her right foot bumped an outcropping and she reached up, finding a spot to grab with her fingers as she put her weight on the stone underneath the water.

Somewhere below her, one of the gator-things was waiting. She had to get back on that ledge and right away if she wanted to fight the monster. Just a few feet. She could swim it in no time and get back up there.

Faith kicked off from her ledge, grateful for the strength that let her actually cover about half the distance she needed to before gravity took control. She sank fast and then bobbed back up toward the surface. The ledge was close enough that she could get it with ease once she went back under. Simple kick with the legs and she'd be airborne all over again.

This time, Kakistos hit her from behind, dropping from the outcropping above her head just as the first drop of water fell from his body and splashed across her face. The impact drove her down, deeper than before, and his claws tore at her, his teeth tried to slash. Faith sought the topography of his body with her hands, found his shoulder by feel and then the thick circumference of his neck, cold and muscular and tensed against any attempt she might make to strangle. Not that it would matter. Vampires didn't need to breathe. Faith found his hideous face, found the bared fangs and broken tooth that had cut her scalp earlier.

She couldn't breathe, didn't dare exhale, could barely figure out where she was, if not for the fact that his claws were scraping down her back, across her rear end and digging trenches into her thighs. The pain was a supernova of torn nerve endings and slashed flesh. Her lungs felt like they were ready to catch fire in the frigid waters.

Her hands crept up his face, past the thick, flat nose and over the scar she'd given him as a parting gift a few lifetimes ago. His eyes were closed. She didn't care. She punched her thumbs deep into them anyway.

Kakistos let go of her and clutched at his face, blinded by the attack. Faith swam around him, her hands brushing his thick wrists and the claws that covered his countenance and shielded his eyes from another attack. She could hear her own heartbeat getting faster, more frantic, not only because of fear but because she'd been under water for too long. She needed to breathe, to take in oxygen, or she was as good as gone.

She felt the backs of his shoulders with her hands, felt him thrashing in pain in front of her and grabbed his neck for purchase. Her legs slipped around his chest, her feet hooking together in front of him, holding her to his brutal body. He bucked and thrashed between her thighs and she spun the wet silk from her wrist, caught it with her free hand and slid it almost lovingly around his throat. A moment later she pulled the silk tight, catching his neck in a noose of fabric and pulling back, her left arm taut. The deadly scarf still around her wrist and now curled into her fingers, her body arched out away from him. Her freed right hand reached back and found the crude wooden torch. Kakistos roared again, the sound loud and clear as no bubbles left his mouth, no air escaped with the noise. Faith rode back hard, pulling the silken cord tighter still and leaned forward with her right arm. She stabbed again and again, driving holes into his chest a half dozen times before she found his heart in the darkness.

Kakistos was old, he did not die easily and he did not merely crumble into dust. It took several seconds for her legs to suddenly scissor back together, for the noose she'd made for him to simply slide free of where his neck had been. Faith broke the surface of the water and expelled the dead air in her lungs, sucked in a greedy, hungry breath and slid toward the ledge. It took three tries for her to get out of the water this time. She crawled over the dusty rock and gasped, panted, breathed. A few moments went by when she was in total darkness, not even sure if she was really conscious. Then she moved again, taking the silk and placing it loosely around the human arm where it lay on the uneven ground.

She sat in the darkness, her face wet from water and tears, and looked back at the calm surface of the subterranean lake. "This time was better, you bastard. It lasted longer."

Spike was not having a good time. Spike was having the worst time he'd had in several months, since the first time he'd been down in the sterile halls where he found himself now, fighting for his life.

He didn't normally fancy weapons much. They took the thrill out of a good kill as far as he was concerned. But he held onto the oversized blade in his hand as if his life depended on it, which it very likely did.

Funny thing about alternate realities: They almost always wound up being altered in a bad way. Take this one for instance, where the Initiative was still going strong under the less-than-gentle administration of one cybernetic demigod named Adam. Hadn't taken Spike long to recognize the bloke: big guy, green and silver patches, and a penchant for tearing apart and rebuilding anything that struck his fancy. He couldn't have said for sure, but he guessed that maybe in this reality Buffy had never started dating a strapping young farm boy named Riley who also served as a soldier in the Initiative. He thought maybe he'd seen a few pieces of Riley among the monsters that Adam had made, but he couldn't be certain and, frankly, didn't much care.

Right now he was a lot more worried about staying alive.

There were all sorts of bells and whistles and flashing lights going off and that helped a bit, but around every bloody corner there was another of the G.I. Jokes that Adam had built, and each and every one of them wanted to slap Spike down and use his best parts to make more beasties.

Spike would have already been dead if Willow hadn't been hanging around in his head and warning him about some of the nastier things coming his way. As it was he was already battered and bruised and cut in a few more places than he was really comfortable with.

But Willow seemed to be on to something. He had to get to the main control room and let her see the bloody computers with his eyes so she could tell him what to do next. He'd been around the complex a few times, had been able to figure out most of the trail all by his lonesome.

Now all he had to do was get past Adam to finish his task and find whatever little gobbet of Ethan's grandma was waiting in the tool shed.

Of course, there are those bloody soldiers everywhere trying to make it worse. Not that he needed any help in that department.

Spike slipped through the air vents, his clothes tearing on screws where they hadn't been torn on soldiers, and wished the little puppet was along for the ride. He didn't much fancy Sid, but at least the wooden munchkin was good for tight places.

He was lost in thought when the tin soldier with the metallic face and warty demon hide shot him. The electricity made him do a dance the likes of which he'd never have attempted on his worst drunken binges and then he was out cold.

He woke up to the sound of a woman humming softly. Spike opened his eyes and felt the world swim in and out of focus a few times. The voice was lovely, familiar, and filled his dead heart with joy.

"Drusilla? Is that you, luv?"

"'Course it's me, Spike. Who else would it be then?"

He felt a smile spread across his face, felt something like joy for the first time in months. "Dru! How did you find me?" He tried to sit up and discovered that his arms were bound.

"I didn't find you, Spike. You found me. Dropped in like an angel falling from the sky." She turned and faced him, moving closer, her face as lovely and mysterious as ever. Behind her he saw a collection of her dolls, as elaborate and eclectic as ever. She gestured with one delicate hand, her index finger indicating a doll that stared at him with blue eyes the same color as the last daylight sky he'd seen. "Miss Tina says you've been naughty, slashing and breaking all of Adam's lovely little tin men."

Spike blinked slowly and shook his head. "What?

What do you know about Adam? Dru, pet, you have to let me out of these cuffs. I love a little bit of the rough and kinky now and then, but this isn't the time."

She tilted her head, her eyes getting dreamy and distant. "Adam is the savior of us all, the messiah of pain and lingering sins. He touches us and our world grows darker." She touched his face, her fingers lingering over his beaten features. Her expression grew suddenly mischievous and she ran her tongue over her teeth. "He also knows every way imaginable to pleasure a lonely vampire." Her hand abruptly slapped Spike's cheek, from a caress into a stinging attack in one instant. Some things never changed.

Spike felt his arms go limp. His hands stopped their futile struggles. Dru was with Adam. He thought she was here to save him, to take him away from the damned pain, but no. She was working with the very monster that had betrayed him last time. Okay, so he'd betrayed Adam as well, but he'd at least tried to deliver the goods. Adam had merely made promises and never kept them.

"Dru, what d'you think you're doing, luv?" It broke his heart to see her again and not be with her.

Dru looked at him, her face suddenly tight with anger. "Don't call me that. You haven't the right."

"Come on, pet. Enough with this. Keep it up and one of us is leaving here in an ashtray." He tried to smile, to be reasonable, but knew the words were falling on deaf ears. When the madness took her, it was almost always bad. And now, judging by the look on her face, she was not just being held by it but practically crushed.

"I loved you, Spike, but you betrayed me." Her voice was petulant, a child's voice.

Spike snorted. "Me? Well if that isn't the pot calling the kettle a filthy slut. With your track record . . . never mind that you're all lovey dovey with Robocop, wherever he's gotten off to."

She clutched her hands to her head and closed her eyes. "La la la, you're making the glass shatter in my head and the sparrows are crying. They've blood on their feathers."

"You're out of your mind, Dru. Always have been." Now and then there had been a glimmer of lucidity in her twisted mind, that was part of the fun of being around her, not knowing how much of that sanity would sneak up to the surface. Right now it seemed that she'd strangled her inner sane self.

"At least I'm not in love with the Slayer." Her voice dripped with hatred at the mention of Buffy.

Spike stared at her, jaws agape, and shook his head, not believing he'd heard that properly. "In love with the . . . hell's bells, woman. You really are from another dimension. Sure, Buffy's a cute little Barbie doll, but there's no one on Earth whose blood I'd rather drain. I didn't have this chip in my head, she'd be my first meal as a free man."

She slapped him hard across the face and hissed, backing away from him. "Liar! All the voices say you lie." Then she turned in a flurry of skirt and hair and skipped out of the room, leaving him dangling from the chains.

For a while there was darkness again, and when he

opened his eyes he saw Adam staring at him. It took him a moment to realize he'd been zapped again. The dead giveaway was the new scorch marks on his arm.

"Doesn't anyone here understand the concept of caught? You don't bloody need to fry my brain when I can't go anywhere."

Adam stared at him for another moment and then looked away. That was just as well; Spike hated looking into his mismatched eyes. It was like a flashback to the sixties: too many colors and none of them making much sense. "You've distressed Drusilla. I find I don't much care for that notion."

"And I find you a pompous git."

Adam reached out with one hand and caught Spike's jaw. "I think I'll like you better once I've killed you."

Spike spit at the monster standing in front of him. Adam ignored the spittle and tore the manacles holding Spike in place from their anchors in the concrete wall. "I suspect Drusilla would be upset if I simply killed you. She would recover from her emotional state, but I would find myself on the wrong end of her wrath. I would rather not have to bother with it."

Spike looked down at the metal cuffs now half warped by Adam's strength and rubbed at the painful scrapes. "What? You're letting me go?"

"Don't be foolish, Spike. We both know you're capable of actual rational thought. I am giving you a head start. Once you've gone far enough away I will find you and destroy you, thus giving myself an excuse that even Drusilla can understand, especially when I mention the Slayer and your desire to get back to your new lover."

"You've both lost your bloody minds. I'm no more with the Slayer than you're the same man your mother gave birth to."

"Denial does not change the facts. Run now, make your attempt at escape. I'll find you soon enough."

Spike took the head start but did not try to leave the building. Instead he called out to Willow in his head. *Willow? You there, darling?*

I'm here, Spike. She sounded very, very tired. Spike didn't much care as long as she could help him get the job done.

Listen, you said something earlier about shutting down all the robot boys. Can you do it?

I think so. But you have to get to the control center, where Adam set everything up.

Right, I know the place. He rounded the corner and moved to the very door she was speaking about. *Got it. What do I do now that I'm here?*

Spike felt her in his head, felt her looking through his eyes. *That panel, to the left. Open it for me.* He did as she asked. *See those wires, the red and blue ones? You have to tear them out. I'm pretty sure the other soldierbots are controlled by the system he's got running through there. They aren't separate sentient beings, they're just extensions of Adam's consciousness.*

Right. Whatever you say.

Spike grabbed the wires and yanked hard, tearing them loose from their connections on one side of the panel. Sparks flew and electricity hissed in the air and arched across the ground. Spike cursed and backed away, grabbing one of the chairs in the command room and slamming it into the open panel. The chair stuck into the mass of wires and the shower of electrical sparks grew almost as bright as the sun for a moment before the entire room went dark.

Okay, Willow. I think that did something then.

Yay, Spike. Now, see if you can find a very big gun. I think Adam's coming your way.

Of course he is, pet. He pretty much has to, doesn't he?

He could hear Adam's heavy tread coming his way, like a walking tank with an attitude. The big boy was going to be plenty upset. Spike thought of the monster touching Drusilla, holding her in his arms and doing plenty more than just holding, and he got a bit worked up himself.

The thing was, at least with Adam he didn't have to behave himself. The damned chip couldn't explode his head for beating on another monster, now could it?

Adam hit the door hard enough to knock it off its hinges and lunged for Spike. Spike tried to block the blow and felt his hand knocked aside like a toy. The next second he was lifted up, his back slamming against the acoustic tiles of the ceiling, and he let the Big Bad out of the bag, forgetting everything about tactics and just cutting loose on his bigger opponent.

Well, almost everything about tactics. Spike tore at flesh, clawed at the soft, human flesh around all of Adam's hard metal and thick demonic hide. He had no chance in hell of winning, but he wasn't going out without at least putting a few marks on the freakish hybrid.

Adam threw Spike away from him, or at least tried to, but the vampire held on, his fingers digging into the meat and gristle beneath the pink flesh. What spilled from the wounds wasn't blood, but a thick synthetic fluid that smelled more like motor oil than anything organic.

Spike screamed as the barb in Adam's wrist punched through his side, working in and out like a saw, cutting and widening the wound. His hands tore more frantically and his feet kicked and swung. Somewhere deep beneath the skin, his fingers caught a metal coil that surged with energy and burned his fingertips. Adam yelled and spun hard, battering Spike into the wall. Spike fell down, stunned. Adam looked at him and twitched for a moment.

"How did you find that?"

Spike had no clue what he was talking about and couldn't have cared one way or the other. He got back up, his mind still wrapping around the idea of this behemoth touching Dru. Adam looked at him but did nothing about it as Spike got up and moved toward him again, growling low in his chest.

Then Adam turned away, ignoring the vampire. When the manmade monster spoke, the words weren't meant for Spike but merely for himself. "An unfortunate coincidence, but one that has to be rectified immediately. I will make the necessary repairs."

Spike hit the monster from behind, once again tearing with his fingers, attempting to do the most damage possible, to inflict the most pain. Adam staggered, taken off guard. Somewhere in the recesses of his mind Spike knew that shouldn't have happened.

Whatever he had accidentally done to Adam had apparently caused more harm than he'd initially guessed. Adam reached back for him, his heavy hands seeking to dislodge the vampire before he could cause any more harm. Adam's foot touched down on the heavy wires that Spike had pulled before, and he guessed there must have still been current going through them, because he was thrown off of Adam like water off a hot frying pan. He felt almost as fried too.

There'd been something Buffy had said about Adam absorbing energy that was used against him. Whatever she'd heard was either not true in this reality or Spike had managed to gum up the works. Adam stood perfectly still, every muscle tight and tense, and then he began to cook. His flesh blackened, first the human and then the demon, while fingers of electrical current played slowly over his shiny bits.

Spike sat back against the wall and watched, taking great satisfaction in the way the monster fried in his own synthetic juices.

And then Dru showed up and put an end to the fun. She looked at Adam with deep horror on her lovely face and then turned to Spike, her face shifting until the demon inside all vampires revealed itself. "You can't let me have anything at all, can you, Spike."

"Dru, pet, don't do this."

She chose to ignore him and did it anyway. On a good night, when he was well fed and well rested, Spike figured he had a decent chance of beating Drusilla. Under the present circumstances, he accepted that he was as good as dead.

She moved fast and came down on him like an avalanche, her hands tearing at his body and her teeth biting savagely at his face. Just as he had done himself a few moments before, she let the monster inside have free reign and attacked without regard for personal safety or even for the pain she felt when he defended himself.

There was no finesse to the fight, certainly no pleasure for Spike. He loved Dru and he wanted nothing more than to step back in time and be with her again, reveling in the simple pleasures of being the Big Bad and dancing with her through the endless nights of carnage and destruction that had filled them both for centuries.

Sometimes there is no going back. Dru bit deep into his shoulder, trying for his neck, and her claws raked down his back again and again. At some point it was inevitable that he fight back, truly fight back, and not merely try to defend himself.

Spike managed to get his legs against Dru's chest and kicked her back away from him, hoping to get a chance to recover, to reason with her. Dru sailed backward, her face a snarling mask of rage and pain and loneliness that wrenched at his heart. Whatever she had done to him he forgave her and he knew he always would.

It was harder to forgive himself, to take away the pain that he felt when she struck the panel he'd torn open and then fell forward, her body falling just right, just in that perfect way that let Adam's burned arm spine punch through her chest and pierce her heart. By the time Spike reached the spot where Drusilla died, she was only ash at the feet of two monsters. The one she'd once killed with and the one she'd died for.

Spike did his duty. He found the damned leg of the damned woman who was going to save them all, if the bloody puppet could be believed. When Willow tried to speak with him to make sure everything was okay, he didn't answer her.

He wondered about death. He thought about it and toyed with it for a long time, his heart aching, his body tender and broken, cut and gouged by the hands of the woman he'd once have done anything for.

He told himself it wasn't tears that fell from his eyes. He told himself that the sprinklers above him were just trying to control the fire that was slowly spreading through the Initiative's headquarters.

The Big Bad didn't cry. It wasn't becoming.

Sunnydale Mall was closed for business. At least it was supposed to be. Right now it was sort of overflowing with nightmares from the worst depths of Willow's psyche.

She could have accepted the werewolves running around. That was okay, sort of, especially since with a simple spell she's masked her presence in the place and, hey, no rooms exploding in big fireballs to make her feel bad. But she kept having to move and to look for a random body part, and she didn't really like the idea of touching a dead thing if she could avoid it, and she wanted so badly to be back home, with Tara and everyone else, safe and sound, and not to be freaking out about the end of the world stuff again.

Right now she was trying to talk Spike through a bit of a problem with Adam, and she was worried about whether or not Spike was going to live through everything he was going through. She tried not to pry when she was mind-touched with someone, but there was always a little bleed-over and she could feel his confusion and his pain and she could sense that he was definitely not a happy little vampire.

She didn't let herself think about the vampire part too much. It creeped her out. There, Adam was dead. Again. Now if Spike could just get out and find whatever he had to look for, she could do the same and then—

"Oh, Spike. Not Drusilla again."

"No. Not Drusilla." Willow half jumped out of her skin. She hadn't realized she was speaking aloud, and now she'd given herself away. The spell was still new, still a tentative thing, and speaking ruined it. She turned to the feminine purr of a voice that had spoken and looked to see that her nightmare had just gotten worse.

"Tara? Oh, no . . . please no. Anything but this." Her eyes stung and started tearing as a vampiric doppelganger of her lover walked closer, smiling through the demonic visage that altered her in hideous ways.

"What's the matter, Willow? Aren't you happy to see me?"

Willow backed up a bit and heard a growl. She turned fast and saw a pack of werewolves slinking toward her, their maws open and salivating at the idea of a fresh kill. Tara shook her head and the pack stopped advancing.

"How did you do that?"

"I'm a witch, remember? You're not the only one

who can do magick." Tara moved closer, her walk blatantly seductive in a way that she would never have used in public. "Come on, lover. Let's get this over with. Which do you want? Eternity with me?" She turned her head slightly, hellish yellow eyes looking to the werewolves behind Willow. "Or maybe you'd rather be meat for the beast?"

"How can you do this, Tara?"

"The First says he wants you out of the picture. I get that handled and I get more power. Power is good. It makes me feel like singing."

Every word, every gesture was wrong. This wasn't Tara; this was a freakish nightmare Tara that could never be good or kind. This was what was left of Tara's memories, corrupted and warped by the demonic presence that filled her soulless body after death. But knowing that didn't make it any easier to look at her, or to think about having to destroy her.

And, yes, Willow would destroy her. She couldn't let a bastardization of her girlfriend walk around freely. It was like condoning her worst nightmares.

"No answer for me? Well, the First said you might be fussy. He said you were strong and he had plans for you later, but if he had to, he could help me find new ways to make you suffer and die."

Vampire Tara shifted her face, looked like she was supposed to again, except for the gloating, contemptuous expression of glee on her face. Tara clapped her hands and the sound carried supernaturally through the entire mall as if projected through a PA system.

Throughout the mall the small army of werewolves

froze, craning their heads, sniffing the air and listening. And then a howl came in response from over near the Macy's. The mall was full of werewolves, people cursed by magick to become monsters during the nights of the full moon. They loped everywhere, randomly tearing things apart, and Willow didn't like to think about what they'd done at the pet store. But even with all of them around her, she could recognize Oz as soon as he came toward her. Even as a monster he was still Oz and she still loved him. She wasn't *in love* with him, not like she was with Tara, but she loved him.

Apparently he didn't feel the same way.

"Oz?" Her voice trembled as she spoke his name. In response he let loose with a roar and charged toward her, his head lowered, his eyes murderous, and his claws cutting at the tiles of the mall floor.

Willow burned him. She made the familiar gestures and spoke the words without even really thinking. The fireball that exploded from her fingertips hit Oz square in the chest and he ignited into a shrieking funeral pyre before her eyes. "OZ! Oh, god, Oz!" She stood paralyzed and watched in horror as he leapt through the air and ran, trying to escape the burning pain that roasted him alive, his eyes already blinded by the flames and his whole body engulfed in a supernaturally hot pyre that devoured skin and muscle greedily.

Tara next to her laughed and moved back away from the running, flaming mass of what had, in another reality, been her competition for Willow's love. "He's right, Willow! You have a mean streak! What a team we'd make! We could rule here!"

"No! It was an accident, I didn't mean to do it!" Willow backed away, shaking her head in denial. The magick was so easy here. She'd just meant to startle him, to singe his fur and make him leave her alone. Maybe a simple display of power and she could have had all the werewolves running away, giving into their survival instincts. Instead, one of the best men she'd ever known, one of the kindest souls, was dying, falling in a boneless heap of roasted meat in front of her. And the woman she loved was *laughing* about it.

She looked toward Tara and glared. "You're not Tara."

Tara backed away, her face shocked. "What—what happened to your eyes?"

"Tara is good and sweet and kind. Tara would never laugh at my pain or anyone's. You're just the monster that killed her and took her place."

Power. Raw, anger-fueled power. Willow summoned it and drew it into her body, pulling it from the air, from the land, from the essence of what dwelled beneath the ground in Sunnydale.

"Willow? Honey?" The soft, beautiful face of her Tara was in front of her, begging her for mercy and asking that Willow forgive whatever horrid mistake she might have made.

Willow wasn't fooled. "You took Tara's life and I hate you!" Vampires are powerful creatures. They can survive traumatic damage and eventually heal almost anything short of decapitation, too much time in the sunlight, or a stake through the heart. Willow thought about that fact as she created a miniature sun in front of the vampiric monster that looked like Tara. Some-where, some when, her Tara was alive for the moment. That thought helped bring her back to herself as the evil twin of her lover screamed and burned.

She looked around her, the power still singing in every fiber of her body, and stared at the werewolves who still stood around, watching the fireworks. Most of them had fled the fire that incinerated Oz. When she spoke, her power spoke as well, a deep resonance that shattered windows throughout the inside of Sunnydale Mall. "LEAVE HERE. NOW."

The werewolves took the hint. Roaring, snapping at the air and scurrying with their tails between their legs, the cursed lycanthropes tore away in all directions, going anywhere they could to get away from the witch who sent cold fingers of terror around their hearts.

Willow stood stock-still for several minutes, forc-ing herself to calm down, trying to erase the thoughts of what she had just done. What she had just become for a moment. There was a demon by the name of D'Hoffryn. He'd said something to her once about her potential for vengeance. She heard his words again as she shuddered and started looking for what she knew had to be here somewhere, her part of the puzzle that would let them get back to their own world.

Willow did not speak. She was too afraid to speak. She shivered in the heat of the summer night and found a severed, shapely leg in a window display of a shoe store that was more to Cordelia Chase's tastes than her own. It sat with a half dozen others that were just like it, only they were all manufactured and never really meant to be a part of something else. Part of her mind whispered that she, too, was never meant to be a part of something else, but she crushed that thought down and clutched the severed leg in her hands.

It was a lie. She had Tara, the real Tara. As long as she had Tara, she would be all right. She knew that in her heart and in her soul.

And she kept saying it to herself, like a mantra that would take away the murders she'd just caused.

Buffy finally found her way out of the Snake House and moved into the zoo proper. She looked around and frowned, noticing that here, too, all of the cages were open and empty.

"Well, that can't be a good sign." She looked toward the lion's cages and wrapped her arms around herself. "Nice kitties, stay away from little old me." Vampires were a dime a dozen in Sunnydale, but lions? Lions were deadly and fast in ways that vampires only wished they could manage.

There was movement from the darkness on her left. Buffy turned and looked, but whatever had been there was already gone. Not really the sort of place where she wanted to hang out and have a sleepover anytime soon.

There! That movement again. She took a step toward the rustling bushes and saw a penguin waddle out of the darkness. A second later several others followed suit, looking at her with shiny eyes like marbles and making no sounds.

Buffy made a face and stepped back. "Penguins. It had to be penguins." The creatures looked at her for a second longer and then shuffled away, their beaks opening and closing but not making a solitary noise. "I hate the zoo."

In the distance, happily not in the direction of the waddling arctic birds, she saw the glow of flames and smelled a strange mix of herbs. Like as not, it would be a wizard of some kind. Probably she was going to have to slap him around and stop him from turning into a were-jackal or something even weirder. *Why can't people ever be happy just being people? Why do they always feel the need to get nifty new powers or take over the world or call forth demons to make the world a darker place?*

She moved toward the fire and made certain to double check her small array of weapons. *Good thing about Snake Houses: They seem to always have a few knives around.* She thought about that and shrugged. *At least in Sunnydale.*

As she got closer, she heard a deep voice chanting softly. The words meant nothing to her, more gibberish in a dead language most probably.

Buffy?

"Willow? Yeah, it's me."

You okay?

"So far not dead. I call that okay." She paused. "Are *you* okay?"

I got the piece of dead lady. I'm good.

"You don't sound so good. You sound depressed."

Just . . . tired. Listen, I can hear what you hear, and what I'm hearing doesn't sound so hot.

"Why? What do you know that I'm not gonna like?"

I think it's a ritual for raising dead things.

"More zombies?" Buffy slumped her shoulders and looked to the heavens. "I just washed the last batch off a few hours ago."

Well, okay, but at least with zombies you can just go all Terminator mean and not feel bad about it. Willow paused, and even though Buffy knew she was only hearing Willow in her head, she thought her friend sounded almost defensive. Almost guilty about something.

"Willow, what happened. What did you do?"

Don't worry about me. I think the ritual's done. You're gonna have to move fast, get what you want and get the heck out of there, Buffy.

"Will, what are you worried about? It's only zombies. I can outrun most of them if it gets bad."

Buffy. You're at the zoo. *No one said they had to be* human *zombies.*

"Oh?" Buffy thought about the lion's cages she'd passed, and about the empty snake cages. And then there was the bear over on the south side of the park. And the gorillas and monkeys. And the bats. "Oh."

The air vibrated with the roar of something big and Buffy stopped listening to Willow's voice in her head. She was too busy trying not to get torn apart.

First came the gorillas, three of them. They were big, they were fast, they were strong, and they were dead. A huge silverback affectionately called Sunny by the local newspapers came at her, his body knocking aside a pretzel cart and shattering it with casual strength.

Buffy tried to block the swipe he threw at her and gasped as she was thrown against the bars of the gate around the edge of the park. She ducked in time to avoid becoming a casualty and the massive paws slammed into and through the galvanized steel where she'd been trying to recover.

"Unh. Down, big boy. I've sworn off football players." Sunny roared, again his breath cold and rancid. *Snake House. Knives.* Buffy pulled her blades and crouched low. When he charged again she leapt up and over him. His broad hairy back was to her when she landed and she put a back kick into his spine that snapped it with a wet sound. The gorilla grunted and growled, trying to pull itself along with its powerful arms, but the Slayer didn't wait around to check on his progress. She had to get to the fire and whatever had brought the animals back as furry living-dead things.

What had to be Sunny's mate disagreed violently and slapped Buffy with a hand as big as her whole chest. Buffy hit the ground rolling and took advantage of the distance she'd gained to try to get away from the roaring things. Dead or not, they were doing a good clip and didn't look like they were going to get tired any time soon.

Buffy poured on the speed and started making headway. At her current rate she might even be able to avoid the gorillas all together. She looked back over her shoulder and saw that they'd stopped chasing her. "Good. Let that be a lesson to you."

The constrictor didn't feel the need to chase her; it just dropped from the tree and caught her as she was going past. One second she was running and the next the thing was lifting her off the ground, its thick body wrapping around her stomach.

Buffy lifted her arms up above her head, which was great for keeping her hands and weapons free, but not such a nice way to protect herself from being crushed to death. The coiled scaly flesh gripped harder and she felt her eyes bugging out as she struggled to keep her breath. She tensed her stomach muscles and was grateful that she had Slayer strength. The crushing didn't lessen, but it didn't get any worse. Buffy brought the knives down and began the grisly work of hacking through the thick body of the constrictor. She used one hand to block any more coils of muscle wrapping around her and chopped herself free with the other. By the time she was finished, the snake had been cut in half, and both ends thrashed around, spilling more cold, dead blood over her body.

The fire was just there, over the next small hill, and she reached the top with a serious need to put a hurt on the loser who'd called the things out for a good night feeding.

She barely looked at the figure, merely made her way as quickly as she could toward where he sat in a crouch, dressed in the freshly slaughtered hide of a lion. "Bright side, one less lion to worry about. Dark side, ewww."

She moved past several animals, most of which were undead and looking toward her, but she hurtled them like obstacles at a track meet and reached the stage as quickly as she could. She only had to stop once, when what looked like a black panther decided to eat her.

The claws came out of the darkness and slashed

hard, tearing down her right leg and leaving thick scrapes that bled freely from mid thigh down to her calf. Buffy fell down and hit the ground hard, losing her knives in the process. Before she could get up the cat was all over her, the massive front paws pinning her down by the shoulders and digging deep into meat while the back legs clawed frantically, trying to disembowel her. She blocked with her own legs and felt more skin slashed away before she could manage to push her feet against the belly of the cat and push off. The black furred monster fell back and rolled just as quickly as Buffy herself could manage when she was at the top of her game, ready for another round.

Buffy limped over to the bigger of the knives she'd dropped, her eyes on the cat the entire time. "This is so not gonna be fun."

The cat charged and Buffy ducked to the side. Her free hand caught the worst of the impact and her weapon hand slid in fast, driving into the thick meat of the cat's neck, where the blade—meant for skinning, not for combat—broke in half. The cat scrambled, thick claws finding purchase on the rough pebbled surface of the walkway. As it came for her again, Buffy grabbed at the bloodied neck and wrapped herself around the monster's head. Her arms found the heavy jaw and pinned it closed. The panther shook its head violently, trying to dislodge her, and she felt her body slipping. The lips peeled back near her midriff and Buffy felt cold hard teeth pressed to her flesh. If the cat broke free of her grip, she was dead, and she knew it.

Buffy swung her legs around and brought them

together around the cat's neck. The angle was awkward, but it was the best she could manage. She pushed
off of the face she'd been holding onto for dear life,
and felt teeth catch her jeans and tear through her belt
and the thick denim, scraping away a few layers of
flesh at the bikini line before she was out of reach, her
body dropping toward the black back. Buffy twisted
her body and caught her weight against the massive
shoulder blades. Her legs squeezed harder and she felt
claws sinking into her shins as she tried to get enough
force to break the monstrous neck.

She let out a scream and pushed forward again,
riding the cat's neck as it clawed her legs again and
again. The only reason she had any muscle at all left
was because the denim jeans she wore were thick. Her
hand caught on the sides of the monster's face and she
dug in as hard as she could, feeling muscle and flesh
start to part under her fingertips. Then she hauled back
with her arms and pushed with her legs, her whole
body. For five seconds she felt like she was trying to
push a planet or two uphill, and then there was a thick,
meaty snapping noise and the cat stopped.

The man on the stage, his face still hidden by the
lion's mane that he was currently wearing, looked at
her and smiled thinly. She knew the smile. Knew the
shape of that jaw and that chin and all the lines around
that mouth.

"Giles?" Her voice cracked. Earlier in the night
she'd almost had to face the corpse of her mother rising from the grave. It was fair to say that was one
nightmare she never, ever wanted to deal with, and

though she hated to think she might owe the vampire anything, she knew Spike had saved her from that particular fate. *God, I wish Spike was here right now.* This was one of those other things she never wanted to deal with in the world outside of her troubled sleep. In the last few years Rupert Giles had become like a father to her, one of the few things in her world she could depend on. But he'd been a kid once himself, and he'd made a few bad choices of his own when he was her age. One of the worst had been to turn his back on his family's legacy and, in a fit of rebellion, slide toward a lifestyle that would have left him no better than Ethan Rayne. *No, that's a lie. Ethan's a coward. Giles has never been a coward. He's always been stronger, and maybe even meaner when he needed to. And this? This is what he could have been, if he never got over playing with the dark forces.*

The double of her watcher eyed her up and down, looking at her in a way that her Giles never would have considered. His grin was pure poison and his confidence strong enough to almost make her back away. She was right. This was much, much worse than dealing with Ethan Rayne.

"Actually, my friends just call me Ripper." He stood up, a dozen or more medallions around his neck and every finger adorned by rings. Some of the jewelry she'd seen before. None of it was for show. They were objects of power. "But you can call me Mr. Giles."

"What are you *doing* here?"

"I'm having a little party," he explained dryly. "So glad you could make it."

"Willow!"

"No, actually it's a good Burmese hardwood. Never can remember the exact name." Giles grabbed a spear resting against the wall of his makeshift shrine. There were several spears and enough knives to fill her Slayer's bag for a dozen missions. Apparently the new and evil Giles liked pointy things.

Buffy. I'm here. What? Oh. Oh, crap.

"No time for cursing, here, Will. I need help."

Okay, he's probably got some heavy mojo going. Like much worse than the stuff our Giles can do. You need a protection ward.

"I don't have any of those handy right now, Will." Buffy ducked as the spear cut through the air and narrowly missed pinning her to the ground. His throw was deadly accurate and anyone else would have likely been skewered. Buffy felt frost crawl up her spine. This man was not her watcher, she knew that, but the resemblance made it hard to convince her heart.

"I have no idea who you're talking with, girlie, but I think you should pay attention to me. I'm the one who's going to kill you for messing up my new pets."

"God! What is it with every man I ever meet calling me 'girlie'? At least come up with something original." She grabbed the spear from the ground and slid it behind her back with one hand and arm, taking a defensive stance.

Okay, Buffy. Listen. Repeat after me and say it exactly the way I say it. The words can at least shield you from a little of the stuff he throws at you.

Giles started a list of decidedly sexist and

extremely crude comments that made Buffy's ears burn and her blood pressure soar. At the same time, he cast a reddish bolt of energy at her. Buffy ducked and rolled and said the words. The spell hit her and it stung, but she could actually see the magick reflected away from her.

Okay, Buffy. That shield, the one to the right of the little magic setup? That's the shield of R'Morlo the undefeatable. He was an African chieftain a long time ago. I remember him from the books. Get the shield and it can stop the magic completely.

"Hey! You watch your language!" Buffy actually got offended by the comments coming from Evil Giles. "Do you kiss your mother with that mouth?"

Giles looked at Buffy and smiled. "Not since I ate her, actually. But I did once or twice."

Buffy threw the spear, aiming for a spot about two inches to the left of Giles's head. He ducked, which was what she'd hoped for. He also followed her as she started running and caught her with a searing spell that blistered her right leg and burned the shoe completely off her foot. Buffy jumped and landed next to the shield. She grabbed it up fast and panted as she braced it with her arms. The oblong shield was almost four feet tall and two and a half feet wide. It bore a crude representation of a demon that was remarkably unsettling, all things considered. Buffy figured she could cover her entire body with it.

"See here, now!" When he was offended, he sounded exactly like her watcher. "That's my shield and I'd appreciate you playing with your own toys."

He mimicked being almost reasonable, but the bloody war paint he'd put on his face and the wide glaring eyes took away from the illusion.

Buffy shook her head. "Not gonna play that game today, Giles. You have nasty magic stuff and I have a trusty shield. I'm coming over there to kick your butt."

"You little tart." He bared his teeth in a scowl that would have made his panther jealous. "I'll peel the shield from your cold dead hands." He looked at her and leered, winked lewdly. "Then we can have some real fun."

"Oh, that's just nasty!" Buffy charged and Giles touched one of the rings on his left hand. What looked like about a hundred flaming arrows appeared in front of him and sailed straight toward Buffy. She felt them slamming into the shield and ran harder, bracing with her arm. A few arrowheads went thought the protection and one of them sliced into her forearm. She winced and ran faster, looking over the edge of the shield to find her target.

Buffy hit Giles with a full body charge that knocked him off of his little stage for summoning zombie animals and sent him skittering across the ground with a broken nose. "Remind me to never, ever leave you alone with any corpses." The words were bold, but her stomach was doing flip-flops. There was no part of her that enjoyed hurting even this shadow of her watcher.

Giles moaned once and slumped back. She couldn't kill him, so she ignored him instead, throwing down the shield and pulling the arrow out of her arm and looking for whatever part of Cassandra Rayne might be waiting for her. In a steamer trunk adorned with stickers from what had to be every continent and a few small islands, she found a spare pair of Giles's glasses and the mummified, eyeless head and torso of Ethan Rayne's ancestor. Despite her revulsion, Buffy reached toward her prize.

As soon as she touched the mummified remains, she felt the pull of the magic that had brought her here in the first place. She looked on for a moment as the undead penguins waddled over the hill and down toward where Evil and Rude Giles lay slumped. They looked at him and ran faster, their bodies wiggling and wavering as they approached. She vanished just as the first of them looked down at him and started pecking, tearing at his warm juicy flesh and chewing frantically. There had been no fish in two days, and dead or not, they were hungry.

Chapter Ten

They found themselves in the operating room, staring at Sid and Ethan Rayne. Sid had been through the mill. His clothes were shredded and there were several deep cuts in his wooden face and his arms. Every last one of them could sympathize.

"Jeez! Took your sweet time." Sid stepped over what had been a nurse-demon once. Xander looked down and then looked back at the diminutive dummy. David and Goliath had been reenacted while they were gone. "Demons're tryin' to whittle me down to a toothpick and you five are gallivanting around on your nasty little scavenger hunt."

Buffy tilted her head and scowled. "I'm not sure nearly being eaten by zombie penguins counts as 'gallivanting.'"

Willow set her prize down. The leg had withered into so much leg jerky on bone as soon as they'd arrived, and she had a case of the creepy crawlies that did not want to leave her alone. "I don't want to talk about it. Let's just do this and get home."

"I'm with you." Xander nodded emphatically.

Faith shook her damp hair back and smiled warmly at Xander. It was the sort of smile that normally left him flustered, and this was no exception. "Actually, I'm havin' a blast. Beats prison hands down."

Spike shook his head and paced like a caged animal. "Right, look, can we just put the sodding flesh puzzle together and be done with it?" His expression argued against disagreement, microchip leash or no microchip leash.

Spike righted the operating table with a loud crash and threw the leg he'd been stuck holding onto the table. His expression hadn't changed. Buffy set down the withered torso and head and backed away. Xander put his part of the puzzle where it belonged and Faith set the arm she'd captured in the appropriate spot. Willow was last. She moved the leg she carried into position and righted the leg Spike had tossed casually onto the operating table.

"Right." Buffy looked at Sid. "What is supposed to happen now?"

"Beats me, kid. All I know is that Cassandra Rayne was made immortal when she touched the first light. The same power that let her create Hope's Dagger made it so she could never really die. So when the First defeated her, he tore her apart and hid her remains here, in his little home away from Hell."

"So, what?" Xander looked at the dummy, his face incredulous. "You mean we went through all of that and you don't even have a way to bring her back?"

Sid looked at him and shook his head. "I don't think you need to worry too much about that, Xander." He pointed at Ethan Rayne and everyone turned to see what was happening.

Ethan Rayne moaned and stirred, the light finally fading from the eyes he carried in his hand. Before he could do more than blink, the eyes lifted of their own accord and settled into the mummified sockets of the mortal remains of Cassandra Rayne. Everyone watched, even Spike, though he did his best to appear disinterested, as the withered flesh and meat from the different parts stretched and pulled together forming a completed mummy. The eyes sank lower into the sockets, withered skin blossoming open like a dead flower and closing over the vibrant, lively orbs.

Flesh swelled and muscle filled in the ruined gaps. It was like watching a staked vampire become unstaked and reformed in slow motion. Thick, full hair grew from the desiccated scalp, and lips that had withered and been peeled back for years and decades filled out, moistening and parting slightly to reveal teeth that had been blackened with age a moment before. The body and face of a handsome woman were rebuilt in a matter of moments.

Ethan Rayne shook his head in wonder, his face almost boyish. "It's true. I can't believe it . . . my own ancestor, a warrior for the Powers." He stared at the face, studying every detail of the muscular woman's body. Then he shook his head. "I'm so ashamed. I'll never be able to show my face around the Lords of Chaos again."

The opened lips of the corpse parted a little further as if to take a breath, and then the entire body exploded into flames. Thick black smoke reached up to the ceiling, spilled out of the broken windows of the theater, and drifted quickly away, pulled by the change in pressure the sudden heat caused. The body moved slightly, the limbs drawing in toward the torso of the corpse in the intense heat, and Willow stifled a scream.

A moment later the body was little more than a slight pile of ashes.

A moment after that the ashes scattered into the air, where they hung for a second before drifting away. A faint image shimmered into existence, a heat mirage that looked almost solid. Dead and gone, Cassandra Rayne's face looked down at where she had been and then looked at each of the people in the room. Her face was more beautiful when it was in motion, but it was a cold beauty, deadly and almost predatory. The hair that spilled around her head was braided elaborately, and the clothes she wore were leather and well worn, patched countless times.

"Cold." Her face frowned as she spoke and her spectral arms wrapped around her ghostly form seeking warmth. "Why am I so cold?"

She looked at the people in the room, the dead things scattered around, and then at the walls of the operating theater. She closed her eyes, her face strained with concentration, and as she opened them again the room vanished.

Spike cursed and turned his head. "Not again."

They stood on a wide open field, the bodies of the dead around them torn and bloodied and empty. Cassandra Rayne's body was again on the ground, her spectral form floating above it. This body was clothed exactly as the ghostly image that floated and looked down at it.

Not far beyond where Cassandra looked down at her own body, Buffy saw a massive stone keep, a castle that crouched on a hilltop. The trail of bodies led all the way to the opened gates of the hewn stone walls.

Xander shook his head, his voice very small. "Now there's something you don't see every day."

Ethan looked around, his eyes searching everywhere at the same time. "It's here. The First. I can taste its power in the air. It's magnificent." His voice was enthusiastic and Buffy looked at him, her lips sneering slightly.

"Too bad you're never gonna get any of that."

Cassandra looked away from her dead body and moved toward them, her eyes on Ethan Rayne. "You . . ." She stopped in front of him, her eyes narrowed in concentration. Her body, ghostly or not, looked about muscular enough to break him in half. "I sense something about you, some kinship." She leaned in closer still, their faces only inches apart. "Who are you?"

"You're good, lady. Kinship's right on target." Sid looked at her and then at her descendant. "Not that he's anything you'd wanna brag about."

"Ethan Rayne, Madame." His voice was more amused than worried. His smile was pure venom beneath a thin layer of good manners. "Decidedly *not* at your service."

"He's your . . . great-great-something. A descendant." Willow looked at the ghostly image and had an expression on her face that said she was tempted to touch it to see what would happen.

Cassandra Rayne's form stepped back, her brow still knitted, her voice not exactly filled with joy at her reception. "And yet I can feel the dark magick in you, the chaos in your soul." She sneered. Ethan stepped back, either surprised by the sudden venom or afraid for his life. "I was a soldier of light, and this is what my bloodline has come to? You repulse me."

Xander nodded emphatically. His eyes looked to Ethan and promised payback was coming soon. "Join the club." He looked at Ethan and smiled. "Anyone tell you how dead you're going to be when we get out of here?"

Ethan dismissed Xander and looked back toward his ancestor's spirit. "The feeling is entirely mutual." He looked away from her and looked around. "This isn't fair, you know. Technically I've won. The power I bargained for should be mine. But if you destroy The First—"

Cassandra hissed when she spoke, her hatred almost palpable. "Silence, dog. I would silence you myself if I were able."

Spike moved forward eagerly. "Here. Let me get that for you." Spike's fist pumped out from his body and slammed into Ethan's face like a sledgehammer. Ethan let out a startled squawk and staggered back a few paces before landing flat on his back. Spike clutched the sides of his head and closed his eyes tightly. "It was bloody well worth it!"

Cassandra Rayne, looking slightly puzzled, stared at him with gratitude. "My thanks, kind sir. I . . . I know this place. This is where I . . . where I died." Her voice faded for a moment as she considered her last battle with the First Evil. "But who are all of you?"

Buffy fielded that one. "We're trying to finish what you started, Cassandra. Trying to destroy the First. I'm Buffy Summers. The Slayer."

Cassandra's face smiled and was transformed. Xander looked at her with something akin to awe. She was a beautiful woman. "A Slayer. This is good fortune. I am but a lost soul and can no longer wield Hope's Dagger. But you are worthy, Slayer. It shall be you."

"That's . . . that's great and all, so, thanks." Willow looked at Cassandra's spirit and smiled shyly. "But where does Buffy find Hope's Dagger?"

Spike nodded. "No offense, but somethin' tells me you haven't got it hidden under your bloomers."

Cassandra looked from Willow to Spike, puzzled no doubt by the strange language they used. She turned toward Buffy. "Inside the fortress. I cannot remember with perfect clarity, but that is where I stood against the First." She looked back at her body. "That is where I was discarded. Find the place where I died, and there you will find Hope's Dagger. It will still be there. Only one who is worthy may wield it."

Faith shook her head. "You don't gotta be a virgin or anything, right? Cuz *that* could be a problem."

Sid nodded. "Especially in this crowd. Make's a little wooden guy wanna cry."

Willow shook her head. "Hope's Dagger is a piece of the first ray of light to shine down on the Earth. The Powers That Be don't judge someone's worth based on who they love." Then she got that doubtful look on her face and chewed her bottom lip. She looked back at Cassandra. "Right?"

"That is correct."

Faith smiled and rubbed her hands together. "Excellent. All right, B, let's saddle up, kick this guy's ass, and then it's time for cake and ice cream."

Cassandra shook her head and put out a warning arm, almost but not quite brushing her spectral form against Faith. "No. Only one can go, and it should be a Champion of the Powers." Her expression was almost apologetic. "I sense that more than one of you could be a Champion, but I can feel the influence of the Powers That Be most strongly within Buffy. She must go alone. When we find ourselves face-to-face with true evil, we are always alone."

Faith looked at the ghost for a second, her dark brown eyes squinted, and then looked over and Buffy and shrugged. "Sucks to be you."

Buffy nodded. "At times. Now, for instance."

Willow let out a gasp and poked Buffy in the arm. "Ethan! What happened to him? He just went all glowy and then . . . poof."

Cassandra shook her head sadly. "Perhaps the First has plans for my traitorous descendant after all."

Buffy sighed and started toward the castle. She

looked back over her shoulder briefly, once again memorizing faces. She did that a lot, just in case she never saw the people they belonged to again. "Only one way to find out."

Buffy made it to the castle with no encounters, but she almost didn't manage to get inside. She looked back to where her friends were and saw something she had not expected. In the distance, the sound of the horses' hooves muted by range, she saw a small army of mounted soldiers charging across the battlefield and saw her friends react by moving to the bodies around them and grabbing up weapons from where they had fallen.

She wanted to go back to them, to help them, but knew she couldn't. That was what the First wanted her to do. Instead she moved into the building and walked across the open courtyard, beyond the castle's wall. The light of the full moon above let her see the bodies strewn about. She recognized the scarred, eyeless faces of the Bringers, the First's high priests. They too were dressed for war and they too were dead. At least Cassandra Rayne had died defending what she believed in.

Aside from a serious problem with too many suits of armor and a few dozen gargoyles that loomed over the place—and that included two gargoyles Buffy had last seen in the Magic Box, a bit of a shock that left her feeling ooky—the castle was deserted. She found Hope's Dagger with ease. The blade was almost as long as a short sword and glistened with light even where the moon was not reflected. It sat before the mantelpiece of a fireplace meant to heat the entire main hall of the castle. There was no fire burning, merely more darkness.

She reached down to grab the weapon and felt the First looming up behind her. Buffy turned and saw Ethan Rayne, his lips grinning madly, his eyes wide and glowing with the same burning fires she'd seen cast by the First. He was floating in the air, his body surrounded by the heavy dark silhouette of the demonic shape she'd seen twice before.

It was Ethan's mouth that moved and the First's voice that carried through the air, a dark bitter sibilance that chilled her. "Stop now, Slayer, and I will spare you this day. You will live on for a few more precious months, untouched by me or mine."

"Sorry. Got to follow the game plan or I just can't sleep well at night." She grabbed the dagger, and the long thick blade of the otherwise plain weapon flared brightly, like the sun cresting a mountain and beaming down a pure golden light.

Ethan Rayne's body lifted higher into the air and the First's voice roared through the castle. "SO BE IT! LET THIS FINAL FIGHT OF YOUR LIFE BEGIN!"

"Blah, blah, blah. That's almost as washed out as the 'girlie' comments."

The dagger in her hands grew warm, but not hot as she faced the First. He spread Ethan's arms and gestured. The gargoyles around the room moved as one, their heads all turning to look at the Slayer as they rose from their perches.

"Oh that's just perfect. No one said anything about having to deal with your servants too."

"They will have their way with you and then I will finish what they have begun."

She made a face and slashed at the first of the stone demons that dropped down and spread massive stone wings, sailing toward her with talons at the ready. Hope's Dagger cut through the stone as if it were little more than air. The blade grew in her hands, lengthening into a sword-length weapon that was perfectly balanced and weighed almost nothing. *Luke Skywalker, eat your heart out.* "Are you making a pass at me? 'Cause I gotta tell you, I'm just not at all interested." The gargoyle shattered as it struck the wall, and a piece of stone the size of her head bounced off Buffy's backside. She staggered but kept her feet. "Right, less talking more slaying."

Her body ached, her legs were torn and bloodied, but she was still the Slayer and she still moved like a Slayer. The gargoyles came, whipping through the air and trying their best to tear her apart. One of them actually caught her by her shoulders, stone claws clutching and bruising, and lifted her off the ground, sailing up toward the ceiling with great slashing swipes of its wings.

Buffy took it the easy way and cut the ankles that held the thick claws to her shoulders. The move hurt and broke skin on her left shoulder, but she was free and the gargoyle was in worse shape.

Once again she had that special advantage that sometimes was all the difference between winning and losing. She didn't have to sweat hurting her friends or having them used as hostages. They were already in enough trouble on their own.

She didn't know how the fight was going, but guessed it probably wasn't going very well. There had been a lot of soldier-types that had charged their way on horses. On the other hand, Willow was a powerful witch and apparently even more powerful over here. She was pretty sure that they were still in the First's pocket dimension, because from everything she'd learned about the First after her previous encounter with the evil behind her current situation, it could not affect the material world, but could only influence the minds of those it chose as tools. Faith and Spike could hold their own, and Xander? Xander had a penchant for surviving, and she had to hope Faith would watch out for him as much as Willow did.

She lost herself in the dance for a while, cutting and hacking at the gargoyles. A lucky strike almost broke her collarbone, and another left four deep trenches in her back that ran with blood.

If this isn't finished soon, it's gonna be finished soon. She was beyond tired, and the gargoyles were hitting more and more often. The good news was that the weapon in her hands was really great for hitting their off switches. One cut and the stone demons fell inactive, and sometimes just plain fell.

There were pieces of gargoyle all over the place by the time she was done.

And through it all, the First merely watched, using Ethan Rayne's body as a corporeal form and looking down from his place near the high, vaulted ceiling of the main hall.

He only came down to play at the end, when two

unsettlingly familiar gargoyles caught her from behind while she was cleaving another in half. They pulled her hands away from her body and held her, their muscular arms undaunted by her efforts to pull free.

"Now, at last, Slayer. You will be mine."

Buffy panted and shook loose hair from her eyes. She stared at Ethan Rayne's face and at the darkness that surrounded him.

"Want to at least pretend you were tough enough to take me on your own? Or are these two losers going to hold me still while you cut me in half?"

It was almost Ethan's voice that answered. The First was still there but seemed weaker, and she understood immediately why that was. She still held Hope's Dagger in her hand. "Let her go. I will finish this."

The gargoyles let her go and stepped back to their original places near the fireplace. Once there, they settled down into crouches and froze. Buffy was aware of that but didn't take the time to actually notice.

The First looked at her with Ethan's eyes and gloated. "You are mine. I will ruin your soul and shape you, make you my personal servant when I am finished. Like the little puppet man, you will try to escape and find that there is nothing you can do to avoid being mine for eternity."

That was when Buffy swung her new toy and Ethan's body jerked backward, howling as Hope's Dagger scratched his chest and drew first blood.

"You talk too much. And that's really saying a lot when it comes from me."

The First reared up behind Ethan and the sorcerer's

body went along for the ride, his hands clenching together as a dark shape formed between his doubled fists. In an instant there was a sword in the sorcerer's hands. "I have a weapon too, Slayer. And this one has existed even longer than the trinket you bear." The blade didn't just look black. It was darkness, pure and untouched, unstained by the light of anything good. It did not glisten or gleam but seemed to actually suck in the light of the room.

All of the light save that which spilled forth from Hope's Dagger.

Buffy nodded and then the fight was on. They both swung and thrust and parried, blades clashing with sounds that were as primal as the forces trapped within them. The weapons screamed and roared and wailed into the air around the two combatants, and whenever Buffy received the slightest kiss from the darkness of her enemy's blade, she felt the cold of the grave try to creep into her body. But she knew it was just as bad for the First, who was no longer gloating or posturing. He grunted and cursed and breathed hard as he fought back.

On three separate occasions Buffy tried to strike with her flesh instead of merely with the sword, and by the third time she acknowledged that her assumptions about the First were not necessarily true. Ethan Rayne's body was struck and reacted when she made contact, but the form of the First, the darkness that surrounded him, was unfazed. Only the blade made any difference.

Buffy parried a blow that send shivers through her arms and back and kicked out with her right foot, striking Ethan Rayne's body in the ribs with enough force to break at least three of them. The First roared and swung the sword again, and as she blocked his fist, hit her in the face, sending her staggering back. *Okay, that's cheating. Unfair advantage. I call foul!* He swung again and again, at speeds she could never hope to keep up with, even if she was fresh and rested. A cut formed on her left hand and then her right. A slash crossed over her shoulder and then down to strike deep in her thigh. Buffy backed away as quickly as she could and felt the wall press to her back.

The First moved forward, sword lifted above his head, and prepared to chop her body clean in half. Buffy flipped Hope's Dagger in her hand and was not surprised to find the blade was short once again. It was a powerful tool and the dagger almost seemed to read her mind. Her fingers caught the very edge of the weapon, and Buffy jumped to the right and threw the dagger at the First even as he began what was meant to be the deathblow for the Slayer.

For one second, for one eternity, Buffy Summers held her breath, watched the blade leave her fingers and slide through the air, glistening like a comet as it cut through the darkness and arrowed toward Ethan Rayne's chest. The sword in Ethan's hands came down, slashing through her hair and nothing else. As the arms of her enemy fell, the dagger slid into the opening between them.

Buffy exhaled.

The light of Hope's Dagger sheathed itself deep in the breast of Ethan Rayne and in the spirit of the First Evil.

Ethan Rayne fell backward, his body dropping like a felled tree, and where he had stood, the First looked at Buffy with shock on the dark, vile features she would never get out of her head.

The eyes of the First closed for an instant and flashed back open, looking at the Slayer with nothing but hatred. Buffy covered her face and the light of Hope's Dagger exploded deep in the center of the First's body.

There was nothing, no sound, no motion, just light, bright and brilliant that shattered the darkness, drove it back and away. And then Buffy heard the First's scream of fury in her head. She clutched her hands to her skull and cried out in agony all her own as the roar went on and on spilling forth like a wave of violence and hatred and vomit and disease, washing over her and through her as it dispersed.

A few moments passed in silence, and she finally let herself look down at Ethan's body. He wasn't dead, but he was dying. She'd never taken a human life.

Not until now.

A small time passed.

And then there were noises, comforting sounds. Someone calling her name, the voice sweet and worried.

"Willow?" Buffy looked up from Ethan's still form.

She did not see her best friend. Cassandra Rayne was there, her body looking fainter than before. "It is over, Slayer. Well done. You have accomplished what I could not."

Buffy blinked uncertainly and looked at the woman. "Is it dead?"

Cassandra's head shook sadly. "I do not think the First Evil can die. It is an integral part of the universe. But you have dispersed its evil across all realities and dimensions. If fortune is with us, it will be centuries before it can coalesce again."

Buffy looked down at Ethan again and heard the tremble in her own voice. She didn't want to cry. She *refused* to cry for the likes of Ethan Rayne. "What about Ethan? I . . . it was the only way. But I can't just let him die."

Cassandra looked at Buffy and her face seemed to understand exactly what the Slayer was feeling. She had sympathy in her eyes and empathy. "Nor can I. Despite my revulsion at his cruel nature, I know that he was but a pawn here. Weakness of spirit is a poor reason to die." She knelt beside her descendant, her spectral fingers caressing the air above his pale, sweating brow. "I will share my essence with his, my spirit with his. I have touched the purest light in creation. Perhaps *my* touch will illuminate some shred of decency in him."

The ghostly woman looked at Buffy and spoke without words. She spoke of being proud to have met a warrior as strong and brave as the Slayer. Then she fell forward, dispersing into little more than a mist that settled over Ethan's body.

A moment later Ethan groaned and his eyes fluttered.

"Buffy!" Willow ran up to her and touched her arm, the other girl's soft open and friendly eyes delighted to find her alive.

Faith moved up, only a few paces behind Willow.

Her body looked as bruised and battered as Buffy's felt. She smiled anyway and put her hand on Buffy's uncut shoulder. "You did it, B. Thanks for the ringside seat."

Xander looked around and smiled. Then he looked down at Ethan and scowled. "So what now? How do we get back?"

Willow smiled. "It will happen on its own. I can . . . I can feel this place unraveling."

Spike shrugged and lit another cigarette. His body was looking less beaten but more bloodied. "None too soon. I think I left a pot of tea on the stove."

"What about you, Sid? What happens now?" Buffy looked at the dummy, who was now missing an arm completely.

"Now?" He shrugged his one remaining shoulder. "What I've been praying for all along, honey. Now I get to rest, at last. I've heard it said Heaven's different for everyone. For me it's gonna involve cards, babes, and whiskey." He waggled his eyebrows lewdly. "Maybe I'll try to look up that doll Cassandra when I get there. Fella like me could show a girl like that a real good time." He faded as he spoke and Buffy started to feel that pulling sensation again, like she was being drawn through a pocket of pressure that was dozens of times denser than the rest of the air around her. A moment later she was in the hospital again. Giles's room. Giles looked at her and did a double take, taken off guard.

Buffy spoke the words on her mind and smiled softly before she looked at Giles.

"I'll bet you could, Sid. I'll bet you could."

She reached out and touched Giles's hand, gripping

it softly. She was back and they were safe. Ethan Rayne was alive, and that too felt good.

Ethan was just stirring, and when he looked up and saw the faces around him, he groaned in deep disappointment.

That felt even better.

ABOUT THE AUTHOR

James Moore has been writing professionally for the last thirteen years. He has written eight novels, including *Under The Overtree* and *Serenity Falls,* as well as several comics for Marvel Comics and multiple role-playing game supplements, mostly for White Wolf Games. During that time he also served as an officer in the Horror Writers Association for three terms. He lives in the suburbs of Atlanta, Georgia. His Web site address is http://www.jimshorror.com.

As many as one in three
Americans with HIV...
DO NOT KNOW IT.

More than half of those
who will get HIV this year...
ARE UNDER 25.

HIV is preventable.
You can help fight AIDS.
Get informed. Get the facts.

www.knowhivaids.org
1-866-344-KNOW

"Well, we could grind our
enemies into powder with a
sledgehammer, but gosh,
we did that last night."

—Xander

As long as there have been vampires,
there has been the Slayer. One girl
in all the world, to find them where
they gather and to stop the spread of
their evil and the swell of their numbers.

LOOK FOR A NEW TITLE
EVERY MONTH!

Based on the hit TV series created by
Joss Whedon

2400-01

E eryone's got is demons....

ANGEL™

**If it takes an eternity,
he will make amends.**

❖

**Original stories based
on the TV show
Created by Joss Whedon
& David Greenwalt**

**Available from Simon Pulse
Published by Simon & Schuster**